LIFE ON THE EDGE

THAT SEVENTIES SERIES - BOOK 4

ANDRENE LOW

Squabbling Sparrows Press

Squabbling Sparrows Press

Have you ever wondered what happened to those characters that appear briefly in a series, only to then be left alone to get on with their lives?

HEELS AND A TIARA : Ever wondered what Brenda was up to before she joined forces with Sam and Jennie? She was busy working as a bikini-clad Gold Coast Meter Maid. It's only a stepping stone, but a big one.

OUT OF BOUNDS : We revisit Janey and Maria, those good Italian girls who helped Sam deal to 'Salami Boy' in Friday Night Fever. And with major consequences if their mama finds out the cops are after them.

MAID IN CHELSEA : Get to know Vivienne and find out why an intelligent woman is stuck working as a general dogsbody and nanny to a spoiled purple poodle. She'd have to be on the run from something truly terrible, wouldn't she?

GOLD DIGGER : Join Stef as she puts all that training from Eadie to good use. Lucky for this strapping Cockney girl, she strikes it rich in more ways than one. And of course she takes care of her old mentor in the process.

It'll take more than
spare change
to escape this mess.

Andrene Low

Gold Coast - Australia

*B*renda can't work out which hurts more: her feet or her pride. She's tottered back and forth out front of the Gold Coast's newest hotel for hours for nothing. All she's got to show for her efforts are blisters and fewer coins than she had at the start of her shift. She looks down at her gold platform shoes in disgust. The bloody things were never designed to cover this many miles.

On the upside, being a Surfers Paradise Meter Maid is better than being stuck in some cruddy office job. She's over being at the beck and call of some middle manager with an ego bigger than his dick.

Sneaking behind one of the pillars that props up the hotel's front veranda, Brenda rearranges the bottom half of her gold lamé bikini. This, along with a tiara, blue sash and a coin purse make up her *uniform*. Unfortunately, the synthetic nature of the cossie in concert with the summer temperatures has sweat trickling between her butt cheeks. It's not a pleasant sensation and certainly not one she can attend to in public.

The 'Surfers Paradise Progress Association' had certainly known what they were about back in 1965. They'd come up with the genius idea of bikini-clad women topping up expired parking meters. The plan to encourage shoppers to stay longer had worked. To ensure they get the credit, after she's topped up the meter, Brenda pops a small card under the windscreen wiper.

YOU HAVE JUST BEEN SAVED FROM A PARKING FINE BY THE SURFERS PARADISE METER MAIDS.

Thirteen years on and all Brenda wants is for someone to save her from being a meter maid. It's a pity she needs to cover her rent on the glorified beach shack she calls home.

She took this over from Chloe, another meter maid who'd hit the big time by snagging herself a local car dealer. Something that involved hundreds of return trips in front of his high-end dealership. It got to the point Chloe worried the number of Ks on her body clock would affect her resale value. But the way she told it, the risk had been worth it. And, if the car she's currently driving is any indicator, she'd been on the money. Brenda suspects, more than once.

Brenda's home is rough around the edges, rather like herself. The place was only ever meant to be a weekend getaway, not a permanent home. That was until the Gold Coast took off and rental properties became scarce. Then the owners decided there was a tidy profit to be made and they'd rented it out.

Nothing in the place matches, everything scabbed from buildings either being ripped down or close to collapse. It's a roughly assembled pile of cast-offs that still somehow manages to be charming.

And the view isn't half bad, either.

Miles of white-sand beach are swept clean with every surfer-laden wave coming in to land from far out in the Pacific Ocean. This 20-mile asset turned the Gold Coast from a chain-store necklace of small, sleepy towns into the 18-carat piece of jewellery it is today.

While marriage or modelling are the main aims of most of the meter maids, Brenda's angling for something far more lucrative. And a lot less permanent.

She's already selected the car; it's just a matter of getting her timing right.

A couple of hours later Brenda staggers into the shack, briefly stopping to wipe her feet free of sand on the mat at the back door.

The second best thing about the place is its proximity to the main drag, a short walk along the beach. Not a bad way to finish a shift, with the massaging qualities of the wet sand equal to the pain inflicted by those gold platforms. The salt water has dealt with more than a few infected blisters, too.

Her shoes are dropped just inside the door along with her regulation-issue purse of loose change. By rights, she should have returned this to the office at the end of her shift. Hah, fat chance. The idea of walking a couple of blocks in the opposite direction to home didn't bear thinking about.

On her way to the shower, she peels off her sash and hangs it over the door of her minuscule bedroom. Her tiara is placed carefully on the bedside table. Not because it's the real deal is she so careful, but more that it isn't. Easier to treat it gently than to constantly glue the bloody rhinestones back on.

The gold lamé bikini stays on for her shower, because if she doesn't wash the sweat out, it'll be crusty by the end of the week. Brenda's in the shower until the hot water runs out, and even stays after this, chilling her body to avoid sweating by the time she's dried herself.

Cooled, free of crud and any remaining sand, she settles into the couch with a bottle of beer, not even minding the condensation dripping onto her bare stomach. Following her shower she changed into her white crochet bikini. Its softness and familiarity make her feel positively off-duty after the scratchy, sweaty work one. She might go for a swim before dinner. If she can even be bothered with dinner.

Damn it, she's still pissed off about being dumped by Dennis, her last meal ticket. It wasn't that she did anything wrong, but more he couldn't cope with the humiliation of his poor performance. Perhaps if he hadn't drunk so much beer, it wouldn't have been a problem and her sighing at his flaccid state hadn't helped. But for that, she'd be having dinner at one of the nice restaurants dotted around the area. Instead, she's facing toast and peanut butter.

Again.

She'd tried to mend the rift but the conditions Dennis had put on them resuming their relationship placed too much power in his hands. Now the main barrier to again living in the lap of luxury is that damned Mercedes. So close she can touch it and yet she can't seal the deal.

Only when it's fully dark does she turn on the squat lamp sitting on the upturned beer crate next to the couch. It takes a moment for her eyes to adjust to the relative brightness of the room. And when they do, she spots something on the floor next to the unused front door.

That's weird; she doesn't remember seeing that before.

Putting her empty beer bottle down, she hauls herself out of the couch. She waits for the head spins to stop and walks over to check out what it is. Probably another reminder about the overdue phone bill.

Examining the envelope on her way back to the couch doesn't throw any light on the sender. It's not a window envelope, which is a good thing. That it's addressed to the tenant is not. Throwing herself back onto the couch, she flips the envelope over in her hand. There's no return address.

Five minutes of looking at the scuffed and dirty envelope and she's no closer to a decision. Maybe it's the single beer or lack of food, but it takes longer than it should for her to see what's missing.

There aren't any stamps or Post Office marks.

Loath as she is to do so, Brenda turns it over one last time and wiggles her finger under the flap. Even a quick glance is enough to show the letter is typewritten. Not good. Not good at all.

A skim is all it takes for the beer to bubble up into her throat, scalding it with stomach acid. Not bothering to read further, she drops the letter and staggers to her feet. She just makes it through to the toilet before beer hits porcelain.

Brenda takes in her reflection in the bathroom mirror. Her eyes are bloodshot thanks to her violent regurgitation, while her throat burns. After splashing her face with cold water, she brushes her teeth. Damn it all, why should she be surprised that life has kicked her while she's down? She should be used to it by now.

One thing's for sure, with the rent going up as much as it is, she'll have to work double shifts. At least until she can suss out how to get her hands on that Mercedes.

Her feet covered in plasters, Brenda trawls back and forth in front of the Iluka Motor Inn. It's not the flashiest place in Surfer's Paradise, but it's the one favoured by the owner of the gleaming silver sedan sitting out front.

To hell with anyone stupid enough to overstay their welcome in any of the streets she's supposed to be patrolling when she's on duty. She's lost count of how many shortened circuits she's completed before she spots her opportunity.

The footpath is deserted.

Except for her quarry, presently opening the driver's door of the Mercedes.

Damn, she would have to be at the turning point of her lap and as far from him as possible. Defying the ankle-breaking physics of her shoes, she moves quickly in his direction, coming close to jogging in her desperation to get there in time.

Her boobs fight to escape her lamé bikini top, but she doesn't care. In two weeks of patrolling this section of footpath, this is the first time she's spotted the bloke. There's no way she's not nabbing him while she has the chance.

Her timing is spot on, the conditions perfect.

She falls against the parking meter beside the car, fumbles a coin into the slot and turns the handle. Placing the small card under the Mercedes' windscreen wiper is a piece of pure theatre. She's squashed so hard against the windscreen that if he starts the wipers, she'll lose a nipple.

Peering at him through the glass lets her know that one of her puppies must be loose. He's the possum to her headlights and even more so when she straightens and makes a show of tucking everything away.

Very slowly.

And that, folks, is how we seal the deal.

The guy is out of his car and next to her on the footpath faster than should be possible for someone sporting such a large beer gut. Damn it, she was so busy racing for the car she hadn't had a chance to check him out properly. Now, she's not sure what to do.

Dating older guys is her preference because they're easier to keep in line, but that's not to say she doesn't like them to be attractive, too.

However, if his triplet-sized gut is all that sits between her, a decent meal and a room upgrade, she has to re-evaluate her standards.

He stands close enough that his stomach touches

hers, meaning he's either a pushy sod or spatially unaware of his size.

"So, you're the sweetheart who's been topping me up."

It takes a conscious effort to pull her gaze away from his belly and look him in the eye. If she can ignore his double chin, the bloke isn't too bad looking. But handsome enough that she won't need to get hammered to bed him?

She'll find out soon enough.

2

he Sun Court Motor Lodge is nowhere near as ritzy as the name would imply. The sun, sea and sand have been cruel in their treatment of the old girl since her birth in the sixties. This tatty, faded exterior informs Brenda what Hilton, the owner of the Mercedes, has planned for the afternoon.

The pool is a token gesture; the concrete in bad enough shape they must have to top the damned thing up daily, if not hourly. A quick scan of the large paved slab next to this glorified bathtub and Brenda spots a couple of sun loungers going spare. She doubts they'll stay that way for long. Especially not if the family of inbreeds spilling out of a nearby unit have anything to do with it.

When not hampered by sky-high footwear, Brenda can put on quite the turn of speed, even in her thongs. She swiftly slip-slaps her way to the loungers and throws herself down on one, then drops her handbag onto the other. A filthy look from the mother of the ferals confirms she was right to hurry.

A lift of her shoulders and she both dismisses them and rids herself of her white muslin shirt. She's settled in before the mother gives up on the evil glaring and shepherds her brood towards the beach.

"Are you really going to sit there?"

This primly voiced question comes from the other direction to that of the beach, and it takes Brenda a moment to realise it's directed at her.

The question too asinine to waste breath on, she tips her head to the side, slides her sunglasses down and simply looks at the women. Her expression designed to make her sod off and mind her own bloody business.

Why the woman is huffy is soon apparent. Her other half rocks up with cocktails sporting enough fruit salad and twizzle sticks to take your eye out. Seeing Brenda, the drinks in his hands are forgotten and only quick action by his missus stops them from falling. Unencumbered, he takes the opportunity to thrust his hand in Brenda's direction. "Barry Evans, from Tassie. Call me Bazzer."

Ignoring Bazzer's outstretched paw, Brenda slides her sunnies back into place, hoping Hilton isn't too far off.

"We're here on holiday," says Barry, stating the bleeding obvious and blithely ignoring her pointed lack of response.

Even without looking in their direction, Brenda has no doubt the bloke's missus isn't happy he's chatting with the bird in the tiny white bikini. That much air sucked in through flared nostrils is a sound she's all too familiar with. She suppresses a snigger when he's dragged away complaining as loudly as any three-year-old who hasn't had their fill of the playground.

Sleep is claiming Brenda when she experiences a total eclipse. The complete lack of sun chills her immediately. My god, she'd thought Hilton's stomach looked big behind a straining business shirt. Au naturel, it's something else altogether.

The one thing not large about the bloke is his swimming trunks. But what they lack in size, they make up for in volume, their decibel rating attributable to a bright orange and yellow tropical print more suited to curtains.

What is it about fat blokes that they have no shame? If she were carrying even half that much excess weight, the only thing she'd be seen dead in outside the house would be an effing iron lung.

"You're looking bloody ripper," says Hilton, his gaze all over her body. "And almost as hot as I am."

For a moment Brenda thinks he's saying he's 'hot' as in attractive. His cannonball into the swimming pool puts paid to this. It also puts paid to her looking glamourous as Hilton's bulk displaces a good third of the pool water. A large percentage hits her with as much oomph as if someone had upended a bucket over her. She's left spluttering and muttering.

While he swims a couple of lazy lengths, Brenda dries herself as best she can. She didn't even bring a towel with her and neither did Hilton for that matter. In the end she resorts to using her muslin shirt to avoid sitting with water dripping off her. Damn it, even the insides of her sunglasses are wet. Thank god her waist-length dark hair is up in a high ponytail or else it'd be hanging in rats' tails.

Swiping under her lower lashes, she inspects her finger. Damn it all to hell, she shouldn't have needed waterproof mascara for their date. Thank god her bikini is transparent when wet. Hilton will be looking everywhere but at her panda eyes. A couple more gentle swipes and her finger comes away reasonably clean. It's not great, but it's the best she can do for now.

She's just resumed a striking pose when Hilton clambers out of the pool, with about as much finesse as a large bull seal mounting an ice floe. He then stands right next to her and proceeds to flip his head about wildly, deliberately showering her with more water.

What the hell? Does he think he's five or something?

Apart from having him looking like a juvenile, no one sporting a comb-over as cantilevered as his should shake-dry their hair like that. She's seen less action on ceiling fans.

It transpires when Brenda's halfway through the beer Hilton's bought, that he owns this homage to a bygone era of holidays.

"Worth a bloody fortune for the land alone," he assures her after a healthy swig. He drops his head to close the distance between them before adding, "Gonna be bowling the old bird in a coupla months. Just gotta sort out the cash for the new place. It's gonna be bea-u-tee-ful."

He emphasises how beautiful by arching his arm in

a manner commonly used by game-show hostesses. All this does is emphasise what a dump the Sun Court is. But, it's clear to Brenda he can already see the new hotel that'll be taking its place.

Their date goes to a whole new level when another round of beers arrives. Brenda didn't even see Hilton order them and as before, the waiter puts the tray on the small table between their loungers. This time as well as the beers, there's a key on the tray. It's a large, dark green, plastic tag with peeling gold room number that is hard to ignore.

Hilton doesn't; instead, he picks it up, dangling it for Brenda to see. "May as well make use of the old girl while she's still around."

He closes his meaty fist around the key and makes a show of sliding it down the front of his swimming trunks. He leaves Brenda in no doubt she'll be expected to retrieve it later. He chugs his second beer in a brick-through-a-plate-glass-window display of his eagerness to get on with it.

Brenda will not be rushed. What was that saying about buying a book when you can use the library? She wants way more than a few drinks and average sex in a less than average motel. She intends to proceed with care.

Shame she can't plan for these situations. She's still mulling over her options when she latches onto something Hilton mutters.

"I don't dare use the facilities at any of my other properties."

She braces her feet against the end bar of the lounger and slides herself into a more upright position. "Other properties?"

He hesitates for a moment, obviously torn between

keeping his true worth on the QT and boasting to a chick in a bikini about how much money he's got. As always, the little head wins out over the big head.

His portfolio is extensive enough that Hilton would be better suited as his surname. Brenda's unsure whether to be impressed or pissed off. Impressed at the number of hotels and commercial properties he claims to owns, supremely peeved he's chosen the skussiest, low-rent one of the lot for their tryst.

The cheap bastard.

"You're obviously huge …" Brenda drops her gaze to his tackle, squashed beneath the overhang of his stomach. "… in property. I'm actually on the lookout for a new place myself."

She paints a tale of woe about her bastard landlords from Brisbane fleecing her by doubling the rent. She lays the paint on thick and in a nice pink hue she hopes will remind him of other things. Okay, so they haven't doubled it, but the price hike is enough that it's unattainable without a lot of help.

The more she thinks about it, the more she's better off staying where she is. Sure, it's a little grungy, but it's close to the beach and the main drag.

There's also the fact Hilton's name wouldn't be on the rental contract, meaning he can't evict her if things go tits-up. This isn't to say it's her name on the contract, either. Her preference is to travel under the radar, if only to avoid old speeding fines or jealous wives.

"What are they putting the rent up to?"

This has Brenda's internal calculator whirring full steam to work out what she'll need on top of the increased rent to cover her day-to-day expenses. She spits out the amount as though it's poison.

He looks confused, his brow knotted, leading Brenda to believe she might have stuffed up her calculations. She runs through the figures again. She confirms the total is correct before he speaks again.

"But that's nothing. I can cover that for you."

Wait … for … it …

"So long as I'm allowed to visit every now and then." His eyebrows wiggle like caterpillars on a hot footpath, indicating the visits will be anything but platonic.

And, *bam*, just like that her latest benefactor has been hooked and damn near landed. Hopefully, he'll last longer than his predecessor, and for that to happen there's no way she's putting out today. He can rearrange that bloody room key in his trunks as much as he likes, she's not biting. Or sucking. Or anythinging.

Scrabbling around in her handbag, Brenda finds the battered Rolex that had belonged to Brian. He'd been the first guy she'd been able to convince should pay all her bills. It hadn't been easy perhaps because she'd made as many mistakes as she did? Lessons learned, and then some.

"Wow, is that the time?"

She looks at it purely for show. The blasted thing has never managed to keep time. She hangs onto as a reminder to never lose sight of the end goal. She'd failed spectacularly with Brian.

"But, I thought …" Hilton shoves his hand down the front of his trunks in a desperate attempt to retrieve the well-hidden room key. It's as if finding it will make her decide to stay.

Tossing the useless watch back into the depths of her bag, she gains her feet. She makes a show of tucking various body parts back into her bikini. This is guaranteed to have his old fella upping the ante, making it even less likely he'll get to the key in time.

"Oh, I want to, believe me. But I can't tonight."

She hands him a crumpled piece of paper with her address on it to lessen the blow of abandonment. "I'll be home tomorrow night, though."

3

*N*ext evening, Brenda makes a point of being out. Not that she's out on the town, just out of the house. Hunkered down in the dunes, she makes sure of a clear view of her back door. Hilton won't think of looking for her here thanks to the note she's left for him.

If he follows her instructions, this will leave her with a rent advance and a certain degree of power. She needs control over when and where they catch up: she doesn't want him turning up unannounced, as though he owns the place.

The rent's not due for another week, giving her time to hook him good and proper before she'll require more rent money off him. She sure as hell can't have him paying it direct. Even she doesn't do that.

It's dark before she sees him in the weak light of the bare bulb dangling over the door. She knew he'd come around the back because of an army of terracotta pots guards the front door, rendering it useless.

As far away as she is, she still hears him swear when he clocks the envelope stuck to the middle glass panel of the door. Not that audio is necessary, given how savagely he rips the envelope free. He makes short work of opening it and, as she'd hoped, his body language changes. Slumping against the door frame, he stares slack-jawed at the contents.

His free hand drops to his crotch to jiggle his bits into a more comfortable arrangement. Brenda has to smirk; the photo of her wearing nothing more than a smile always gets them. And sure enough, Hilton's hand moves from his crotch to the side pocket of his pants.

Brenda's shoulders drop and her lips curve into a smile. At least she hopes he's going for his wallet and not better access to the family jewels.

Nope, she's good.

She gives it five minutes then stands, shakes her clothes free of sand and tiptoes back to the shack. Paranoid? Hell, yes. She's learned the hard way never to read a situation at face value. It's saved her arse on several occasions. When it comes to getting their end away, guys can be downright sneaky. She's learned to be sneaky in turn. Fortunately she'd ever been the innocent, thanks to the unorthodox upbringing her parents had subjected her to.

Her folks were criminals and spectacularly unsuccessful ones at that, leaving Brenda to fend for herself for as long as she can remember. That sort of training never deserts you, and the only person she fully trusts these days is herself, and even that can be touch and go.

Dammit, why aren't meter maids allowed to wear flip flops? Brenda stares at her gold platforms, her heart brimful with loathing. Or maybe it's anger that she has to earn a living traipsing the streets. She's like a poor man's hooker.

She shoves a coin into the next expired meter she comes to and another shopper too stupid to work out how long since they parked. It's either that or they're from out-of-state, so the chances of them being tracked down to pay their fine are next to zip. Why bother paying in the first place?

She's destined for better than this, even if she has to lie, cheat and extort to get there!

Despite Hilton leaving her a good few notes the other night, she's not confident enough to chuck in her only other means of income. On the upside, all this walking has her more toned than she's ever been. She could bounce coins off her arse if she wanted to.

It's her third circuit in front of the Iluka and she hasn't seen any sign of Hilton, or his car. He left his phone number along with the money, but the problem with phoning a guy is you never knew who'll answer. She can fake it being a wrong number, but after the third or fourth time, the missus is usually on high alert. After that, you might as well cross the guy off your list.

Brenda's days of dealing with women who are so complacent they've lost track of their bloke are over. Much easier to stick to a few ground rules and keep everyone happy. That it leads to her patrons being a lot more generous is simply a bonus.

She spins on her heel and heads back towards the Iluka, with each footfall akin to stomping barefoot on broken glass. Overwhelmed by the pain, it takes a second to see what looks to be a brand new Mercedes pulling to a stop in front of the hotel. Nice car but black is a bloody stupid colour in this climate. The damned thing would have the heating properties of a stove.

Keeping an eye on it, Brenda pauses at every meter, topping them up if necessary. She's a couple of cars away from the black Merc when she sees Hilton drag himself out of the car, bringing her up short. Sheesh, what was wrong with his old car? At most, it had only been the previous year's model.

Despite sore feet, there's no way she's passing up this opportunity. Rent day is coming up and with this being the first at the new rate; she needs his help more than ever.

A quick hobble is all she can manage. It's enough for her to intercept him in the middle of the footpath, her hand on his back to stop him. How come he hasn't noticed her? It's not as though her uniform is subtle.

"Can I help you, miss?" His voice is loud, its syntax unnatural enough to have alarm bells ringing.

"Oh, I'm sorry. I thought you were someone else."

Brenda's volume is equal to his, her words as feigned. Hoping to get away with the screw-up, she swings away from him and looks at the meter by the front of his car. A sideways glance leaves her in no doubt as to the reason for his hasty retreat into the hotel.

Torn between getting away from potential trouble and maintaining her supposed innocence by topping up the meter, it takes all Brenda's nerve to keep to her role. For the first time ever she tops up a meter with someone in the car, albeit in the passenger's seat. She isn't sure of the correct protocol around handing over the small card.

Should she put it under the windscreen as usual, or wait for the window to be wound down and pass it over personally? Does she even need to bother with the card given it's obvious who has completed the good deed?

The last option has the most appeal. After a weak smile at the hard-nosed blonde glaring at her through the windscreen, she spins on her heel. Brenda makes her way along to the next car, all the while trying to look as though she hasn't got a care in the world.

"Oi, you. Stop right where you are!" It doesn't take a science degree or a rear-view mirror to know this command is for her. But screw taking any notice of it.

Keeping up her pace and even quickening it slightly, Brenda abandons topping up meters.

A quick shufti in a side mirror lets her know she's gotten away. For now. Even encumbered with impractical footwear, Brenda's niftier on her feet than the fifty-something woman behind her. She's currently tottering along in heels that should never be worn by someone that age. Brenda makes the most of it and turns into the next walkway she comes across and cuts through the block as though the cops are on her tail.

She doesn't slow her pace until she's out the other side and on one of the streets she's meant to be patrolling on this shift. Even then it takes a while for her heart to settle, as much from the exertion as adrenalin. She hopes she hasn't blown it with Hilton, because she doubts her feet are up to double shifts.

A hand slams down on her shoulder and her heart rate soars back up to triple digits.

"Where the blimmin' heck have you been?"

Facing Sonia, the chick she's sharing the beat with, Brenda's unable to stop her hand straying to sit flat on her chest.

"Ah, sorry, I ah, got caught. Up."

Her excuse is weak and there's no way Sonia swallows it. The woman can't complain, she's been scoping out a few prospects herself. Nothing temporary for her though, hers are of the matrimonial variety.

Sonia jerks her head back the way she'd come and Brenda spots the uniform of a council parking warden, not far back. "Come on, we still need to do the other side of this street and there's a parking warden hot on our heels."

"Hah, not on our watch." Despite her feet hurting and a feeling of being hunted hanging about her, Brenda concentrates on doing the warden in the ugly uniform out of a job.

Sonia and Brenda are halfway down the other side of the road and well ahead of the parking warden when a black Mercedes drives slowly past. If Brenda hadn't been looking up, she might have missed the look Hilton's wife gives her. Brenda also doubts the woman is rearranging her pearls when she slides her finger across her throat. Of greatest concern, the woman looks bat-crazy enough to follow through on it.

And just like that, double shifts to make rent aren't looking so bad. Perhaps even working in another state.

"Jeez! What was that about?" Sonia's eyes are wide. Not only has her fellow maid seen the gesture made by the older woman, she's spotted Brenda's reaction.

"It's nothing, just a misunderstanding."

"Best you sort that out. You know who she is, don't you?"

Opening her mouth to answer, Brenda can neither confirm nor deny. She wouldn't have a clue what Hilton's surname is or if the blonde is even his wife. Although odds are she is. All Brenda knows about him is what he'd boasted pool-side at the Sun Court. It's not as if he has his name plastered over every building or company he's dabbling in like the real Hiltons.

"That is Marcia Taylor. Word is she not only likes wearing stilettos, she carries them, too."

"Italian?"

"Sicilian! Apparently she's nuts enough to be on horse-strength medication."

"Jeez."

"Yeah, and rumour has it she washes the pills down with the hard stuff."

Yikes. Brenda isn't sure what the weather is like in New South Wales is at this time of the year, but it might be worth the risk. Brenda does a quick tally of readies she can lay her hands on.

There's the advance Hilton left for her the other night. She's also collected a large jar of coins during her stint as a meter maid. If she sells off everything not nailed down at the shack, she should have enough to hit the road.

The problem would be where to hightail it to? It wasn't as if she had any contacts outside the state of Queensland. Not that her contacts inside the state are anything to rave about either. The one member of her family she stays in touch with is her Auntie Pat. Although even that relationship is strained because of Brenda's habit of leaving in the middle of the night.

"Just keep your head down for a week or two and

you should be golden. At least, I hear that's worked for others."

"Hmmm, if you say so." Brenda has to accept Sonia's assertion that lying low will have the target on her back faded enough for her to feel safe.

One thing's for damned sure; she'll be bloody careful how she proceeds with Hilton.

It's for this reason she ducks behind the nearest car when she sees the black Mercedes coming back down the street. Mrs Taylor sits forward in her seat, she scans the footpath with all the concentration of someone pig hunting without dogs.

4

The booming "Knock, knock!" thrown through the back door snaps Brenda from half-asleep to wired in seconds. She rushes to tweak her crop top and denim cut-offs the better to reveal what's on offer, and then flops back on the couch.

"Come on in."

Hilton doesn't need asking twice and Brenda gets the impression if she'd taken much longer, he wouldn't have waited at all. She doesn't like his sense of ownership about her or the place she's living in.

"Have you been avoiding me?" His frown does nothing for his looks.

"Hardly. More like I've been keeping out your wife's way."

"My wife?"

"Yeah, you know the blonde with murderous tendencies. That old bird."

Without waiting to be asked, Hilton lifts her legs in the air, sits and plops them on his lap. But with his gut filling most of the available space he has to hold them in place, taking the opportunity to rub his hands up and down her legs. Thank god she'd shaved them that morning.

"You're fine. I told her you'd mistaken me for someone else because of the new car."

"And she believed you?" Brenda's unable to temper her disbelief and Hilton's hackles raise in short order.

She wracks her brain for something more complimentary than, "and I'm sure you got away with lying through your teeth like that." Instead, she settles on, "That is, why wouldn't she? I'm sure you were… ah… very convincing."

"Convincing enough I've wrangled tonight out. I thought we could spend it together."

While Brenda is carrying out internal fist pumps, she doesn't show any response outwardly. Her reserve is deliberate. Experience lets her know if a protector has to work for her favours the results are better all round.

"Oh, yes?" She throws doubt into these two small words and leaves them hanging, interested to see what response she'll get from him.

It's not what she's expected, but she'll run with it.

After digging around in his back pocket, he rains a handful of money down on her. Even unable to count it, she gets that there's enough to cover her rent for the next few weeks. On seeing a one-hundred-dollar bill settle in her cleavage, she revises that estimate to at least a month's rent. And expenses.

"As enticing as you look lying there, do you have anywhere with a little room for us to spread out?" Looking into the bedroom while he says this is hardly necessary. This isn't her first go around.

"Well, we could move into the bedroom, but to be

honest, the bed's a single. If we try half the positions I've got in mind, we might break it."

Her words, while sounding flippant, have been carefully chosen. She's promised him the earth, but discounted them getting it on right now. Sure, there's the floor, but she doubts he'll be keen on that. If he's like most guys over fifty, he won't be able to get down there, let alone get it up while down there. At least not without anti-inflammatories being involved, which rather defeated the purpose.

The cogs whirring behind Hilton's eyes threaten to wobble off their axles before he breaks the silence that has settled on the room.

"We could adjourn to the Sun Court."

He runs his hand up her leg and dangerously close to her crotch. She'll need to be smashed before she can do the deed with this guy. Not a happy thought.

He stops stroking her legs. "The place isn't that bad?"

Hah, he's taken her moue of disgust as being for his choice of venue. It's just typical of his sort.

"What about the Iluka? I hear the views from the top floors are spectacular." Brenda knows any distraction from the task at hand will be welcome.

His expression is now that of someone desperately in need of laxatives.

"Unless, of course," she pauses, "you can't get us in there."

He picks up the gauntlet as she expected. It's the speed with which he acts on the challenge that comes as a surprise. Boy, she's got him good.

Her feet hit the deck with a thump, thrown from his lap when he jumped up, ready to leave. He drags her to her feet, managing to run his hands all over her in the process. Grope completed, he's out of the door and heading towards the beach and the shortest route to the Iluka.

However, he's not gone far when he stops. "I'll be back in half an hour. Make sure you're appropriately dressed."

Brenda walks over to the door and watches him as he stumbles through the sand dunes, his haste making his careless. If he's not careful he'll over-balance and be pinned to the beach by that gut of his. Unable to rid her mind of the images that ensue, she slaps her hand over her mouth keeping her laughter where it is.

Half an hour? That doesn't give her much time to get the necessary drinks under her belt, let alone get dressed. In the end, she saves time for drinking by simply ditching the crop top and shorts and throwing a crocheted dress over the top of her skimpy underwear. It doesn't leave anything to the imagination, but that's the point, isn't it?

She's chugging through her third chardonnay when he returns about twenty-five minutes later. It's not her favourite drink, but it was in the fridge and the alcohol content is greater than that of the bottles of beer stacked on the bottom shelf.

They're halfway through the dunes when Brenda comes to her senses. "What about your car? You can't leave that parked outside my place."

There's no way Brenda wants it sitting there like a beacon where someone like his wife might clock it.

He tugs on her arm to get her moving again. "I parked a couple of streets up and cut along the beach." His voice is tinged with indignation as though she's labelled him a rookie.

That worry removed, Brenda allows herself to be

hauled along the beach in the direction of the Iluka. Damn shame the place isn't absolute beach-front as they'll still have to run the gauntlet of the Esplanade before they make cover.

They're on the beach across the road from the hotel and below the high-tide mark before Hilton speaks to her again. "Okay, I'm going in through the front doors, but you'll need to nip around the back. Once you're through the double doors marked 'staff only', go to the service elevator, and head straight up to the twenty-first floor. I'll be in room 214."

"Room?" Brenda's unable to hide her reaction to them not being in the penthouse and at having to sneak in the back way. Deep down she'd like, just once, to be escorted in through the front doors. To be escorted to the top floor as someone to be proud of, and not the opposite.

"Sorry beautiful, the penthouse is booked and even with the place practically dead at this time of night, I can't risk taking you in the front way. It'll be worth it, I promise."

His expression is that of a small boy who's just been let loose in the confectionery aisle at the supermarket with twenty bucks. His face also covered with a fine sheen of sweat, the result of their dash along the sand.

That bloody mini bar better be chock-a-block to overflowing for this to work.

Despite his assurances that the back areas of the hotel would be as good as deserted, this doesn't prove to be the case. She walks through the double 'staff only' doors as if she owns the place. So far, so good. She's traversing the wide-open area inside when she spots a suave-looking bloke leaning against the far wall having a cigarette. He's a little over six foot and dressed from head to toe in black, but it works. A tousle of dark hair shot with silver and olive skin pegs him as Mediterranean in origin. That he looks to be closer to fifty than thirty is the icing on the cake for Brenda.

Her steps falter momentarily when he raises an eyebrow, obviously questioning her presence. She's not thrown for too long, answering his query with a wide smile. Reaching the service elevator, she presses the 'up' button, watching the display above the doors to avoid looking at him again. Tempting, so very, very tempting, but if he's working here, he's not worth her time.

After what feels like an eternity, the lift dings its arrival and she squeezes through the doors before they're fully open. She presses the button for the second floor and a few others repeatedly. The doors won't be hurried.

They haven't budged from their widest point when the dark-haired smoker drops his cigarette to the ground. Pushing himself away from the wall, he steps on the butt on his way over to her.

Finally, the doors hiss as they close, causing him to speed up. Thankfully, his outstretched arm is a good few feet away when they clatter shut. Brenda has enough time to wink at him before he's blocked from view. Perhaps she shouldn't have been that cheeky, but damn if he isn't cuter than the lard arse she's here to see. Life can be cruel at times.

Ignoring Hilton's instructions, she gets off at the second floor. She sends the service elevator on alone, having pressed at least half a dozen buttons. It won't make it back to the lower level any time soon.

The second-floor corridor is empty, meaning she encounters no one on her trip from the back of the building around to the front where the main elevators are. Once again she summons an elevator.

One arrives, and she gaily sends it on its way having pushed enough buttons for it to visit almost every floor between here and heaven. The second elevator arrives not long after its companion is on its way.

Her finger hovers over the little-used '22' button. She knows pushing it would be a waste of time with the keyhole next to it clearly telling her she's not good enough. She pushes the button below it and again as the doors close, she sees the cute guy from downstairs. Again he's a second too late and Brenda's unable to stop herself from laughing delightedly. Not to his face, instead waiting until the elevator is moving and the chances of him hearing her are zilch.

The elevator takes forever to climb its way to the twenty-first floor, and Brenda hopes her handsome pursuer has the lungs of your average smoker. Even if he takes the stairs, he won't be able to catch her.

Stepping out of the elevator, she knows she's gotten away with it.

So far.

Room 214 is off to her right and visible from the elevators. As much as she'd like to, she doesn't have time to muck about pretending she's meant to be here. She walks briskly to the door with its large gold number and knocks loudly and rapidly.

The door is answered immediately, swinging open while she's still knocking. She stumbles forward and comes close to smacking Hilton's chest instead of the door.

Whoa. Now this is a surprise.

If nothing else, underpants would have been nice.

Not that there's anything to see with that belly flap of his adequately hiding his manhood.

He steps to the side, and she zooms past him; something he takes as a sign of her eagerness rather than her desire not be caught in the hallway.

Slamming the door closed, Hilton is airborne a second later, severely challenging at least two of Newton's laws of motion. The third thing that's challenged is the bed, when he lands spread-eagled in the middle of it.

Bloody hell, three chardonnays are not nearly enough. "I'd love a drink."

Any luck and she'll be able to get enough down him that he passes out before she does.

To avoid eye contact with her now furious paramour, Brenda wanders over to the large sliding door that gives access to the balcony. She makes a show of looking through it as though able to see the view beyond. The truth is she can't see a damned thing with the window acting like a huge mirror.

This allows her to see a naked Hilton bouncing himself off the bed. She's close to exploding with a horrified guffaw when he bends over to check out the contents of the small mini fridge. It's only slapping her hand over her mouth that stops it.

For each drink he offers, she comes up with an excuse. Too strong, too weak, too sickly.

"Can't you get something from room service? Bubbles would be nice."

Clambering up from his hands and knees, Hilton

stalks over to the phone beside the bed. He picks it up and dials a single number, scowling. A testament to how annoyed he is.

The order placed, he spins in her direction, and the centrifugal force lifts his stomach sufficiently that she gets an eyeful of his jewels. No challenge there.

"How about you slip into something more comfortable? Like your birthday suit." He wiggles those damned eyebrows of his again.

And right there, in that moment, Brenda has to decide.

It's a decision she doesn't dwell on for long.

5

*B*renda learned long ago life isn't easy and that it was necessary to do bad things to achieve your overall goals. When it came to a life of ease, there wasn't much Brenda wouldn't do in its pursuit. And so, with the merest of hesitations, she walks over to the end of the bed, drags her lacy dress over her head and drops it. All that's standing between her and being in the altogether is sheer lingerie.

Even though he's already seen her in her bikini, she slowly turns, giving Hilton plenty of time to inspect her like a side of beef. She'll pass with flying colours, she always does. She's grade-A arse, and she knows it.

Her hands, snaking around to undo the clasp of her bra, halt when there's a discreet knock. Wow, room service in this place is fast. She drops her hands to the side to wait until Hilton answers the door. No point in a floor show if no one is watching.

Again, he swings the door wide with little regard for whoever is on the other side getting an eyeful of his bits. But this macho display doesn't hold up. His hands drop to his crotch in an effort to hide anything not covered by his gut. He staggers away from the door until he backs into the bed, dropping to its bronze satin coverlet with a high-pitched squeak.

Brenda waits for whoever is out there to walk in, but no one does. Hilton stares at the open doorway, seemingly stuck in place. It's something that fills her chest with dread. There's one person who could instil this much fear in her erstwhile suitor.

Marcia!

Well, screw facing the crazy bitch wearing nothing but her undies. Brenda grabs her dress from the floor and yanks it on not caring if it's the right way around or not. Hilton is also in motion, making short work of racing into the bathroom. There he grabs a bathrobe off the back of the door and scrambles into it. He scoops his clothes up off the floor and walks out of the room without a word, throwing her for a loop.

But the door doesn't close and so she waits, expecting Hilton's missus to storm in and drive a stiletto into her foot, or her chest. Brenda gets her handbag off the sideboard, ready to go down fighting if needs be, but no one enters.

Eventually, curiosity gets the better of her or maybe it's the suspense of waiting to see who's out there that's killing her slowly. Either way, there's no way she's staying trapped. Given the weight of her handbag with all those coins in the side pockets, heaven help anyone who gets in her way.

If she's lucky, there won't be anyone there at all.

A quick peek around the edge of the door puts paid to this hope.

· · ·

Well, this isn't who she'd expected and given he isn't out of breath; Brenda assumes he didn't use the stairs.

But why would Hilton be scared of him?

He's simply an employee.

Isn't he?

"May I come in?"

"Ah, yeah. Sure, why not?"

Throwing her handbag behind the door where it lands with a resounding thump, Brenda stands back so he can enter. Maybe tonight isn't a complete wash after all. She's about to close the door when room service arrives in the form of a pimply youth pushing a small trolley. This boasts an ice bucket, a bottle of yet-to-be opened bubbles and glasses.

"Put it there." Mr Sauvé indicates a spot over by the window with an assured air, labelling him as anything but hired help.

The youth is subservient which is also interesting, and when he leaves without getting either of them to sign for the bubbles, Brenda knows for sure.

Interesting turn of events and one that could well work in her favour.

"So," he says, moving towards her, "bed or balcony?"

The fizz of excitement that explodes in places that had earlier been quivering in dread is spectacular. Brenda smiles broadly before making a real production out of pretending to ponder the choices he's given her.

"Hmmm, the bed does look comfortable." She waits until he moves towards it before adding, "But I do love a view."

"Oh, we use both, but the choice of first is yours."

God, even his broken English is sexy.

If, as she suspects, he also has shares in this place, she might get her room upgrade after all. She wouldn't mind sharing with him one bit. Once again Brenda lifts her dress over her head and drops it, but this time she has help with her bra.

On leading her out onto the balcony, he's as naked as she is.

She cries her release to the view twice before they move back inside.

It takes Brenda a minute to work out where she is, although she has no difficulty working out what it is that's woken her. That man's head is beautiful in a lot more ways than one. Easy on the eye and easy on the lips, who'd have thought it?

Before room service arrives with their breakfast, she returns the favour, for once not finding it a chore. She isn't even halfway through her first croissant when he ruins her appetite.

"Why ees beautiful woman like you, with the brutto husband of my sister?"

Because of the accent, it takes Brenda a second to untangle the relationship. Oh, bugger. No wonder Hilton had been quaking in his boots.

"It'll be our secret, right?" Brenda crosses her fingers under the table, but she's not holding out much hope. Things had been going far too well for it to last.

His negligent shrug lets her know she's screwed.

"Marcia ees family."

"Do I at least get a head start?"

"There ees no rush to leave."

It's an offer she's happy to accept. Especially not when her next action will be to race home along the beach, throw everything into her car and move. Anywhere, it doesn't matter. Somewhere that crazy tart won't track her down. Or worse, run her down. Brenda's not keen on either option.

It's a couple more hours before she's hurrying along the beach on legs so wobbly, they're as good as useless. In between bouts of great sex, she'd found out it's not Hilton's money in all the hotels and commercial buildings. It's family money that Marcia's relatives will never hand over to him in a million years. They consider their daughter and sister to have married beneath herself. Despite her dislike of the woman, Brenda has to agree. Without money, Hilton is nothing but a fat slob. In truth he'd still be one of those, even if he was loaded.

She's cutting up through the dunes to the shack when she looks back at the Iluka. There's no missing last night's lover standing naked on the balcony of their room. He gives her a lazy wave. Damn it, she hopes he keeps his promise to do nothing more than tell his sister what Hilton has been up to. And, that he'll do this without bringing up her name. Not that he knows what it is.

Opening the door to the shack, she staggers to a halt. Hilton is out cold on her couch, snoring like a cane toad with a head cold. Dammit, she doesn't have time to deal with him now. Scooting through to her bedroom, she's pissed off to see his distinctive black Merc parked in her driveway, effectively blocking her Toyota Celica in. That fool. He may as well have written her address down and handed it to his deranged wife.

· · ·

Without bothering to wake him, she crams her belongings into the two battered suitcases that have been her travelling companions for the past couple of years. Damn it, she'd wanted to have time to strip the place of any valuables and flog them. Not happening with that chump Hilton passed out in the lounge and his brother-in-law no doubt having already dobbed them it. It's just a matter of time before Marcia is out and about looking for blood, hers.

She's sneaking past Hilton with a suitcase in each hand when there's a break in his snoring. She doesn't want to find out if this is simply an adjustment in his breathing or a sign he's waking. She scarpers.

Suitcases safely stowed in the boot, Brenda tiptoes back into the shack. She needs to find the keys to the Merc, move the damned thing and get out of there. It's not a choice she can take. The keys are nowhere to be seen, but then she spots a bulge in the front pocket of Hilton's shorts. Even without a medical degree, she can tell it isn't one designed by nature.

Damn it; it'll be impossible to get them out of there without waking him. If his shorts weren't so tight, she'd give it a whirl. As it is, there's no way she's going near his goolies unless there's no other option.

Her foot is poised above his gut ready to put the boot in when she remembers the beer in the fridge. She'll be stuffed if she's leaving that behind. There's another delay while she transfers this to a beaten-up Esky and shoves it in the boot next to her suitcases.

Hilton is still unconscious when she walks back into the lounge. She has no remorse about filling a pot of water and tipping it over him.

"What the hell?" Hilton splutters and curses, pulling himself into a seated position.

Leaving him to his couch yoga session, Brenda tosses the pot into the sink.

"Keys!" She holds her hand out, beckoning with her fingers to hurry him along.

"What?"

"I need to move your car so I can get the hell out of here. Your nutty wife is probably already cruising the streets looking for the Merc."

"No, she won't." Hilton settles back into the couch, looking supremely confident.

"She will! Her brother was leaving to tell her about us after I left him just now."

6

*H*ilton puts the pieces together faster than a group jigsaw puzzle at a retirement home. He knows he's been replaced and before he's seen any action, too. Brenda has no regrets. This is one bridge she's happy to incinerate, never having been keen on crossing it in the first place.

Her failed protector's face turns a dangerous mix of purple and red. This hints at a killer combination of dodgy ticker and high blood pressure. If anything, his colour deepens when he jumps to his feet and stalks across the room in her direction.

"You slept with that bastard, Stefano?"

Brenda neither confirms nor denies this. She does, however, take note of the gorgeous Sicilian's name, all while bouncing to distribute the adrenalin evenly around her body. She's mid-bounce when his meaty paws grab her upper arms in a cruel grip. She doesn't hesitate. She jams her right knee hard in the direction of his nuts in a move she's perfected over the years.

Here's hoping she's given it enough of a boost to get past his stomach.

His kneecaps come in for some rough justice when he drops to the wooden floor with a lung-emptying *"Oomph"*. Brenda shoves him fully to the ground with her foot, leans over and takes possession of his keys.

Sprinting back outside, she makes short work of unlocking the Merc, starting it and throwing it into reverse. Screaming out of her driveway, she continues down the short lane leading to the main drag. There, she keeps reversing until she's backed the car out and onto the Main Beach Parade. She doesn't so much park it, as abandon it. She even leaves the keys in the ignition in hopes someone will nick it for a joy ride.

As tempting as it is to keep it–because even in reverse the car handles better than her own–she doesn't want to add a stolen car to the mix. A second after jumping into her piece of Japanese junk, she screams like a banshee.

"Screw it all to hell!"

Her crocheted dress and sheer undies were never up to the challenge of saving her arse from the heat currently generated by the black vinyl upholstery. She doesn't waste time getting a towel, instead wiggling her bum around until the worst of the burn dissipates.

She's glad of this when on turning out of the lane and onto the main road; she sees a light blue Mercedes pull up behind the black one. The car is exactly as Sonia has described and so Brenda doesn't dare floor it for fear of drawing attention. Instead she putters along all while simultaneously keeping an eye on the road and the action in her rear-view mirror.

She's close to being able to turn right and escape properly when she takes one last peek at the scene behind her. Marcia's looking in her direction, her hand up to shield her eyes from the sun.

"Crap!"

Brenda's expletive is two-fold. Firstly, she doesn't like the way the woman has continued to stare in her direction. Secondly, on turning back to face the road, she has to jam her brakes on for fear of taking out an old lady shuffling across the road. She's pushing a walking frame the insurance company should have written off after the first accident it'd caused.

What is it about the elderly that they're under the mistaken impression they have as many lives as cats they own? Just because you feed nine or more of the little suckers, doesn't mean you're bullet-proof.

Giving up on the old girl getting out of the way, Brenda pulls out onto the wrong side of the road and slowly inches past. Turning the corner, she's glad she's done so when she sees Marcia weaving her way back to her car.

Brenda doesn't wait around to check whether she's just being paranoid. She floors it, taking as many corners as she can in as short a space of time as possible. Finally, she pulls into the driveway of the motel where Sonia lives rent-free in exchange for cleaning the units.

Brenda doesn't slow until she's at the end of the driveway and has turned into the parking space behind the last unit. She'll be okay leaving the Celica here because the space is Sonia's, and the girl doesn't own a car.

There's nothing polite about Brenda's request to stay. She knocks on the door with both bags sitting at her feet like patient hounds. The door is barely open before she picks one of them up and barges inside, pushing Sonia out of the way in the process. The woman is still stuttering for an appropriate response when Brenda grabs the second bag.

"I take it you'd like to stay?" The unnecessary question out of the way, Sonia shoves one of Brenda's bags to the side so she can close the door. "Hope you're happy with the couch."

Sonia slides the net curtains to one side and checks the end of the driveway as though expecting Marcia to swing in there any second. "I'm not sure I want you here if that crazy cow is after you."

"I'm telling you. I got away without her seeing me or where I went. I'll need to crash here for a couple of nights." Surely it won't take long for the drugs and alcohol to kill off enough of Marcia's brain cells? At least enough that she can't remember Brenda or where she lives.

"Hmmm, okay." Sonia doesn't sound convinced, but Brenda grabs this half-arse offer like it's a lifeline. Anything is better than crashing on the beach or in her car. She knows from experience how dangerous that can be.

Sonia looks at Brenda from the meter she's currently topping up. "I did warn you she was trouble."

"Nothing I can't handle." Brenda slides the small card under the wiper, straightens and readjusts her tiara.

Despite this show of bravado, she feels vulnerable. None of the other wives she's ever run into have been as tenacious as Marcia. She'd even had to crawl on her belly up through the dunes to the shack to retrieve some stuff she'd missed. There was no way she could arrive out front with Marcia parked at the end of the lane as if on permanent patrol. The bloody woman needed to get herself a life.

Sonia tops up another meter, before turning to Brenda. "I need to, ah, go check something out. You okay on your own?"

Knowing exactly what, or rather who, it is Sonia needs to check out makes her smile. "I'm good."

"I'll be back soon."

Being left on her own is a relief. Without Sonia there to set the pace, she can slow down. It was like the girl thought they got paid by the kilometre and not the sodding hour.

Brenda tries her best to look relaxed as she strolls along topping up expired meters. With a wary eye out for a certain light blue Mercedes, she's anything but. She'd have hoped Marcia would have given up by now, knowing Brenda is no longer interested in Hilton. But on the other hand, she shouldn't be surprised. Vendetta is an Italian word and not to be ignored even if it does sound more like a moped than a blood feud.

Sensing movement out the corner of her eye, Brenda turns with dread. Fortunately, the car crawling in tandem with her is red and of a design that lets everyone know the driver is loaded, if not necessarily hung. Checking him out, Brenda's smile is tentative. While she knows what's on offer is a match for the flamboyance of the vehicle, she still isn't sure where Stefano's loyalties lie.

Maybe having ratted Hilton and her out to his sister as he said he would, he feels he's done his part?

Brenda's still hacked off that her liaison has put her on the run. In her eyes, she's not the guilty party here; Hilton's the one who's married.

The red sports car remains in Brenda's peripheral vision and she's unable to stop herself from speeding up. Much as she'd like a repeat performance, if he's going back on his promise, the more distance she can put between them the better. Thanks to all the hours spent traipsing around, she knows every alleyway and arcade on offer, where the back entrances lead to and those leading to dead ends.

She turns off the footpath as soon as possible, speeding down the arcade as fast as she's able. She turns when she's at the back door that leads to a car park and thereafter to another arcade. On seeing Stefano has abandoned his car in traffic to follow her she quite rightly freaks out. His having stopped in the middle of the road, insistent beeping soon has him climbing back into the sports car and roaring off.

Now she's faced with a decision. Does keep walking through the car park and out the other side? Or does she complete a U-turn and head back the way she's come? What would Stefano expect her to do? She's still dithering when the door next to her is wrenched open. If she wasn't as badly dehydrated as she is, she'd have had an accident.

"Come, you need to go. My sister she know what you look like."

Damn it! "And why is that?"

Brenda has a good idea and Stefano's air of mild guilt confirms it. She smacks him hard on the shoulder in retaliation. "Bastard!"

He looks at her, his face a picture of stunned surprise. "My sister, she ask me."

"And what if your wife asked you something? Would you spill your guts then, too?"

Brenda waits. The last thing she needs is to have two Italian women gunning for her.

Stefan's smile is broad, his eyes twinkle. "Ah, no. But she ees not blood."

"Thank the lord for small mercies."

"She ees not even Italian," says Stefano, further adding to her sense of relief.

On hearing his sharp intake of breath, Brenda looks up to find his gaze locked on the street at the end of the arcade.

"Sod it!" The bloody woman is sticking to her like poo on a blanket.

"You go. I meet you again soon."

Not wanting to risk him changing his mind, Brenda slides through the gap between him and the door jamb. She then speed walks across the car park and into the arcade opposite. Instead of rushing through to the next street, she slides into a shop near the back. She's fairly sure Marcia won't see her hiding among the racks of dry cleaning waiting for collection.

Putting a finger to her lips in a plea for silence from the old bloke behind the counter is as much life insurance as she has time for.

7

*B*renda counts one-one-thousand to ten, really slowly to allow for Marcia's odd, weaving gait. She then slides a couple of plastic dry-cleaning bags to the side and peeking out. Her view of the arcade is the merest slit, but it's Marcia-free and that's good enough for her. Counting off her heartbeats, she waits until she deems it safe to pop her head out of the doorway, looking in the direction of the street.

Seeing Marcia turn onto the footpath, Brenda is off, stumbling back into the car park at speed. She's not more than a couple of feet into the space when she stumbles to a halt. She can decide what's more surprising, Stefano still being parked there or him beckoning for her to join him.

She's torn. On the one hand, the reason Marcia is on her tail is that he's ratted her out. On the other hand, he didn't hold on to her earlier, making it a piece of cake for his sister to nobble her.

The tan leather seat is nowhere near as hot as she's

expecting. It's certainly a lot cooler than the vinyl seats of the Celica would be if they were open to the elements like this. She's doing her seatbelt up when he fishtails out of the car park and off down the Esplanade.

"Where to?"

Brenda rattles off the directions to Sonia's place and is pleased when Stefano follows them, at speed, pressing her back into her seat. She loves the power of the car and wishes there was more time to enjoy it, but it's about as subtle as her work uniform. Couple that with it being a convertible and she's easy prey for Marcia, even at a distance.

She doesn't know if he's showing off but is alarmed when he manages to get the car into second gear in the short driveway at the motel. Fortunately, the brake pedal is as effective as the accelerator, which stops them ploughing through the rickety wooden fence at the end of the drive.

"You need leave town."

"You think?" Brenda's unable to hold back her sarcasm. If he'd kept his trap shut, she wouldn't be on the run at all. She hasn't finished with Surfer's Paradise by any stretch, preferring to leave a city on her terms. Being run out by a Mafia wife with a drinking problem and mental health issues doesn't sit well.

Climbing out of the car isn't as easy as getting in had been. Complicating her exit is Stefano grabbing her when she's nearly free of the seat and planting a toe-curling kiss.

Damn it, he's some of her unfinished business.

"Until next time."

Without an address, phone number or even a blood

type, Brenda's not sure how there's supposed to be a next time. It's not as if he'll be able to pop around here and see her. In another ten minutes she'll be on her way out of town.

Scratch that. Out of state.

The plus on packing now is that she hasn't had the time or space to unpack since arriving at Sonia's a mere two days earlier. No time to pick up her pay packet, no time to hand in her notice, no time to return the uniform. Brenda doesn't even give herself the luxury of changing. Instead, she throws a towel over the molten lead driver's seat and buckles herself into the Celica. She anticipates driving like a maniac in the near future.

She pulls out of her parking space at the same time there's a bang on the roof of the car. She's close to using the towel to absorb something other than heat.

"And where are you off to?"

"Jeez, Sonia, you scared the crap outta me."

Brenda's unable to keep the edge off her voice; the girl had given her a hell of a fright.

"Is this anything to do with that crazy Italian bitch ripping me a new one down on the Esplanade?"

"Huh?"

"Yeah, I just had a run-in with the lovely Marcia. Took me a while to convince her I hadn't been banging her husband."

"So why the hell are you here? She coulda followed you."

"She pulled an effing knife on me. I need a drink and a change of underpants."

"Bleedin' hell."

While the two of them might have joked about Hilton's wife being a sandwich short of a picnic, this is way more serious than Brenda had considered. Stefano hadn't been kidding about her getting out of town, and soon. "Gotta go!"

Shooting backwards into the drive proper, she nearly takes Sonia out in the process. "Sorry!" she yells through the open sunroof before putting the car into first and accelerating down the driveway to the road. Rather than pull out blindly, she checks carefully in case the crazy tart is in the neighbourhood, but the way is clear in both directions. She turns away from where she'd last seen the light blue Mercedes thinking it better to get away cleanly than quickly. She's relieved her trip to the main road out of town is without incident.

The last thing she needs is to run into that headcase, or vice versa.

Not that the drive to the Pacific Highway is without risk. There are a limited number of ways out of Surfers Paradise because of the waterways that surround the area. Brenda heads for Southport then shoots across to the Pacific Highway and heads south from there. With any luck, Marcia will be driving around the city streets and not venturing farther afield.

Safely reaching the highway, Brenda relaxes enough to take her eyes off the rear-view mirror. She even shoves a mix tape into the stereo, because long drives are always better with music.

She's cruising along, inside the limit, and singing with gay abandon when a sixth sense nudges her to look in the rear-view mirror.

The chorus sticks in her throat.

There's no mistaking the make of car and the colour is easy to spot, too. Even if it's a reasonable distance behind her.

Dammit, you'd think with her leaving town, the bloody woman would give up, but no. Just her luck to strike a tenacious one. Usually, once Brenda was actively on her way, wives left her to it.

Without conscious effort, Brenda puts her foot down; pressing the accelerator as far as it will go. Better to face a cop than Marcia. Not that putting her foot down makes much difference to the Celica's progress. It's nowhere near the same league as the vehicle rapidly closing in.

One thing's for sure, Brenda can't stay on the highway. She's dead meat out here. But where to go? And won't her turning off mean slowing down?

Nevanwood? She's never heard of it, but she's just passed a sign saying the turnoff is coming up on her right. But soon enough to help her?

A quick peek in the rear-view mirror and Brenda's surprised to see the Mercedes is no longer as visible as it had been earlier. Her view of it is blocked by Sefano's familiar red sports car weaving left and right, stopping the Mercedes from passing. And for once, the sports car isn't going flat out. If anything, it's slowing down and forcing the Mercedes to do the same.

Ripping her gaze away from the action behind her and back to the front, Brenda almost misses the turnoff to Nevanwood. She has to take the corner faster than she'd like, or is recommended. Lucky for her there's no traffic coming from the other direction, but keeping her car on the road is still touch and go. She doesn't let up on the accelerator, passing cars in riskier spots than she normally would.

Only when she can no longer see Stefano's car does she throw hers down a side-road. The tar seal doesn't last long, soon replaced by gravel. It's not what she needs, with a huge plume of dust hanging in the air behind the Toyota.

The other thing not in her favour is the road she's now on running straight for ages, with plenty of opportunity for Marcia to catch up. Decision made for her, Brenda swings onto a side track that's really a glorified fire break. The grass running down the middle swishes the underside of the car and there's an occasional thump. Brenda hopes her dust trail will now be hidden, but to be sure, she keeps flooring it until she's around a couple more bends. On spotting a short drive leading to a shed that's seen better days, she slides off the track and around the back of the building. She jams on her brakes and slides dangerously close to the trunk of a large gum tree.

Clambering out of the car, she scans in all directions.

Thank god, if she can't see the track because of the shed and all the foliage that surrounds it, by rights she should be hidden from anyone passing by. At least she would be if it weren't for the blasted dust hanging stubbornly in the air.

For once Brenda feels vulnerable being half-naked. Dragging what she hopes is the right suitcase out of the boot, she dumps it on the ground. She then has a good rummage, pleased to find what she's after a moment later.

There's nothing flattering about the poo-coloured shorts, or the t-shirt that's faded to a dull olive green. Regrettably they're as camo as anything she has on hand. She doesn't bother removing the gold bikini, instead pulling the shorts and t-shirt on over it. The addition of sneakers and a cap, and she's ready to go down fighting.

Suitcase safely stowed back in the car, she has a quick look inside the shed. This is made easy by the back door having long been taken out by rot and termites. She's relieved to see a rake leaning against the wall just inside the door where she can reach it. There isn't a chance she's going inside. Apart from the crap that fills the place, it's no doubt heaving with snakes or worse. She hefts the rake getting a feel for it and is glad it's a heavy-duty, old-school variety. It's more than a match for a medicated Sicilian with a knife.

Taking the towel off the front seat, Brenda spreads it on the ground under the tree. Despite being shaded as it is, there's no way she's waiting in the car. As well as being too hot, it'll be too easy to get trapped if Marcia sneaks up on her.

She sits there for a quarter of an hour on high alert before allowing herself to relax marginally. The adrenalin eventually abates leaving her hungry and thirsty. There's nothing she can do about her hunger, but a lukewarm beer from the Esky in the boot will be better than dying of thirst.

Leaning the rake against the front of the car, she staggers to her feet and back around to the boot. It's while she's retrieving a beer that she hears a car and it's closer than she'd like.

She can tell by the engine sound that it's not Stefano.

"Crap!"

Beer shoved back in the cooler, Brenda lowers the boot lid and quietly clicks it into place. Only when she's back beside the tree with the rake hoisted in front of her does she have any sense of comfort. Yet again her heart is hammering in her chest and her body is awash with adrenalin.

The car gets nearer ever so slowly, with the driver taking their time either because of the state of the track, or because they're looking for something.

Or someone.

Brenda's torn between staying hidden and moving enough that she can check out the track. In the end, the anticipation builds to the point it's impossible to keep still.

She takes a couple of steps to her left, but it's enough.

More than enough.

*D*amn it. The woman has the homing instincts of an effing bloodhound, but where is Stefano? Brenda shoots back to the base of the tree, hoping to hell the woman doesn't think to look behind the shed. The car pulls to a stop and the sound of the handbrake being yanked on gives her the answer, even if it's not the one she was after.

Screw staying here and facing the crazy bitch. While not being dense, the bush behind her does offer some cover. Brenda flees, as quickly and quietly as she can. Only when she can no longer see the red of her car through the greenery does she stop. She takes refuge behind a large clump of ferns, the rake firmly under her control.

Even unable to see the action from this distance, she has no trouble working out what's going on. The scream from Marcia says all too clearly that the woman is pissed off at not being able to find her prey. There follows the sounds of someone wearing stilettos kicking the hell out of a car.

Damn it. Brenda hasn't got money for a panel-beater.

A couple more loud dings and she's had enough.

She's nowhere near as quiet on her return trip to the car. She thunders through the bush, using the rake like a battering ram and yelling. She was never going to be able to sneak up on Marcia, so to hell with being quiet.

She bursts into the opening, rake raised above her head and ready to do the woman an injury for damaging her car. Marcia looks to be as angry as Brenda, albeit for an entirely different reason.

"I'm leaving, what is wrong with you?"

"I share nothing!"

"Jeez, you're welcome to the fat bastard. Just leave my car alone."

Brenda reinforces this request by brandishing the rake like a medieval weapon. She may as well be flinging a feather duster about for all the difference it makes. Marcia appears so blinded by anger that rational thought is lying in a heap somewhere back on the Pacific Highway.

"I share nothing!"

"Yeah. I heard you the first bloody time." Brenda jabs the woman in the stomach with the flat end of the rake. It's not hard, but it's enough to topple the barmy blonde off those stilettos of hers. She lands on the ground and bumps a couple of times before settling. Brenda isn't able to stifle a giggle.

Big mistake.

If she thought Marcia was pissed off before, it's nothing compared to now. By the time she's managed to stand again, the woman has steam coming out her nostrils.

In Brenda's favour, the older woman isn't steady on her feet, despite having kicked her heels off when sprawled on the ground. Brenda suspects if she could get closer to Marica, she'd be able to smell the alcohol she'd used to swallow her medication.

Half an hour later and they're still at an impasse. Brenda has stopped the woman smacking the Celica with her stilettos by threatening her with the rake. How is she supposed to get out of here without having to inflict a prison-worthy injury — or worse — suffer it? Much as she'd like to deck the stupid tart, she can well do without a GBH charge hanging over her head.

Unfortunately, all the running around is taking a physical toll on Brenda, her tongue now firmly stuck to the roof of her mouth. "Bloody hell, I need a drink."

For the first time since she arrived, Brenda notices something approaching sanity in Marcia's gaze.

Surely it couldn't be that simple?

"Stay there!" Reinforcing this instruction, Brenda jabs the rake so close to Marcia that the woman flinches and again lands on her bum with a bounce.

Not sure she'll stay like that, Brenda races to the boot and grabs two bottles of beer. Surely with the woman already half, if not fully smashed, it won't take much to have her out cold? Even drunk enough to shove her in the Mercedes and tie her up would suit Brenda.

Without an opener handy, Brenda uses the rake to pop the cap off the first bottle of beer. She puts this on the roof of the car before repeating the process with the second. Screw handing the woman a full bottle of beer while her own hands were busy. Brenda has been in enough public bars to know how that ends.

Only once Marcia is drinking her beer, does Brenda guzzle her own. Gross. Warm beer sucked, but it was better than suffering a dehydration headache.

It takes half a dozen more beers for Brenda to get Marcia to a point it's safe to go near the woman without being armed with the rake. Jeez, the old bird is a booze hound. If Brenda hadn't deliberately paced herself, she'd be out cold by now.

The woman lying on the ground at her feet might well be a blubbering wreck but she's nowhere near unconscious. But she is quiet enough that Brenda will be able to tie her hands behind her back. It won't matter how angry she gets then, it's bloody hard to drive a car without your hands. The belt from Brenda's black sundress will be perfect for hog-tying Marcia and thanks to her earlier rummage, she knows exactly where it is.

She's putting her suitcase back in the boot when she hears the Merc's engine roar into life.

"What the hell!"

How the hell did Marcia go from wallowing around on the ground and into her car so quickly? Obviously, she's not as under the influence of the beers as she'd made out. Bitch.

Marcia is now armed with something a lot more dangerous than a stiletto or an old-school rake. She's in possession of enough alcohol to preserve a dead wallaby and sixteen hundred kilos of German engineering.

It's not a good combo in anyone's books.

Running out from behind the shed, Brenda's in time to see her nemesis reversing up the track at speed. Brenda doubt's she's leaving. The car skids to a stop and half the gear box is removed in the change from reverse to first. Marcia floors it and while the wheels initially spin, they soon gain traction and the large car lurches forward. Its speed is impressive for such a huge hunk of metal.

Without time to think, Brenda reacts, throwing the rake javelin-style at the Mercedes. It hits glass and keeps going, shattering the windscreen into a million pieces. A large step back into the ferns that feather the track is all that saves Brenda from being totalled. Well that, and the smashed windscreen.

Marcia swerves wildly to one side.

This also puts the Mercedes on a collision course with the old shed. But with no let up on the accelerator, the car hits the glorified pile of firewood with a horrendous splintering crash. The old building proves no match for the large car and it groans in protest before collapsing around the vehicle like a deck of cards, imprisoning Marcia in the process.

Without waiting to be asked, Brenda crawls out of the undergrowth, belts over to her car and is hooning her way down the dusty track a short time later. She doesn't know if Marcia is alive, and quite frankly she's not waiting to find out. She'll ring someone later and let them know where they can find the poor cow.

Not even when she's safely back on the Pacific Highway and heading south again does she ease off on the gas. She's pushing it for getting a speeding ticket, but for all she knows Marcia is on her tail again, complete with the bloody shed. She's like the baddie from a Bond movie. Unstoppable.

The needle on the gas tank slips into red territory and Brenda has to stop sooner than she'd like. After a nervous glance in the rear-view mirror, she turns into the next servo on her side of the road. She's relieved she can pull in on the station side of the fuel pumps. She's doubly pleased when a large off-road vehicle pulls in on the other side of the pumps, concealing the Celica even further.

Gas tank filled to over-flowing Brenda's fumbling to screw the cap back on when she hears something that doesn't immediately make sense. What starts out like a mosquito fuelled by alcohol, soon morphs into the distinctive scream of a high-performance engine pushed to the max. Stefano flies by a second later.

Thankfully there's no sign of the Mercedes.

For now.

Her gas paid for in coins, Brenda is back on the road with her foot now more lead-like than ever. She doesn't know if she's got a hope of catching Stefano, but there's a slim chance the blue Mercedes is behind her somewhere. Slowing down is not a risk she's prepared to take.

The highway is hugging the coastline before Brenda spots Stefano. If he hadn't stopped for gas, she doubts she'd have caught up with him at all. While both cars are red, there any similarities die. Constant checking of her rear-view mirror reassures her that, for now, Marcia is nowhere near. Brenda worries that in another half hour she won't even have that luxury, with the sun in the tropics going down like a lead balloon. One minute you can see, the next it's lights out.

Pulling into the petrol station, she parks well away from the pumps and as far back on the property as she can without being in the service bay.

Having earned her trust when he'd run interference earlier, she leans casually against the pump next to his car waiting for him to return from paying for the gas. Walking through the doors of the petrol station, which doubles as a local store, he looks at her, but doesn't react.

"What the hell?"

Dammit, she'd forgotten she was still in her Camo Barbie outfit. She whips off the cap and shakes her hair free. A quick flip of the front of her t-shirt flashes him her bikini top and resulting in his smile being as bright as the gold lamé.

Rather than walking around to where she is, he opens the passenger door gesturing for her to get in.

Tempting though it is, there is no way she's abandoning her car, and more importantly, all her stuff. "I'll follow you."

He shrugs, closes the passenger door and makes short work of walking around the back. He pulls her into a crushing embrace involving more tongue than is common in a petrol station.

Reluctantly pulling her lips free, she whispers, "I hope we're going somewhere close."

"Melbourne close enough for you?"

"Melbourne? But that's not close at all."

"Ees where I live. I visit family een Gold Coast. For holiday."

Now this is something Brenda can cope with. The idea of moving to a city two States away from Mad Marcia appeals. And now she's got a solid gold, or at least gold-plated contact, it's even better. Issue is, will she be able to keep Stefano on as short a leash as she'd like, although tied to her bed would be preferable?

EPILOGUE

The trip down from the Gold Coast takes a lot longer than it should. It's also a hell of a lot more fun with Stefano forking out for their accommodation. Brenda had been expecting to sleep in the back of her car, so a king-size bed is a pleasant surprise.

Shame the five-star accommodations don't last once they're inside the Melbourne city limits. After this Stefano is cagey about her camping out at any of the hotels his family owns, preferring to put her up in one of his rental properties. Brenda thinks this is mostly to do with him not wanting his Mrs to stumble upon them.

Still, after being chased all over the Gold Coast by the crazy Marcia, Brenda's a little gun-shy on running into wives. Maybe Stefano's approach might be better in the long run.

Meantime, she's stuck in a scuzzy hostel for young ladies in South Melbourne. While she might be young, she's no lady and the old bird who owns the hostel keeps a beady eye out for any shenanigans. As if you'd bring a bloke back to rooms as grotty as these. Candlewick bedspreads are the greatest passion killer known to a man as far as Brenda is concerned.

She looks around the room that's been her home for the past month. Everything is faded and worn. Make that threadbare and even plain old dirty in places. Stefano had better sort his shit out and get rid of the current tenants at a three-bedroom property he owns on Punt Road in South Yarra.

"Brenda! Phone!" is shouted up the stairs. As an intercom system it's crude, but effective. And, with the only person knowing where she lives being Stefano, Brenda crosses her fingers this is the call she's been waiting for.

She's out of bed in a flash, drags on her dressing gown and thunders down the stairs. She grabs the receiver before anyone walking past has a chance to hang the phone up because they're expecting a call themselves.

"Stefano?"

"Eet ees I. My tenants, they have gone!" His voice is chock-full of anticipation as to what this will mean for him.

Her response to this amazing bit of news is a deliberately tepid. "And?" While she might be as happy as he is about this development, her motto is treat 'em mean, keep 'em keen. It works a treat, especially on men like Stefano.

"And I was thinking you'd like to move in. It would mean I could see you more *often*."

"Fine, although I don't appreciate having had to wait this long. When can I look at the place?"

It's arranged she can call around to see it that very

morning. Boy, he's really keen. While she's playing it cool with him, she can't move in soon enough. Shelling out money for rent when she could be getting her accommodation in return for favours is not ideal in her world.

After scrawling the address on a page she's ripped out of the telephone directory, Brenda saunters into the kitchen hoping she can nab a piece of toast off someone. Luckily for her, there are two New Zealand girls who have bread to spare. Brenda nods towards the loaf sitting on a less-than-clean cutting board. "Don't suppose I can help myself to a slice of bread? I haven't had a chance to go shopping this week."

"Sure help yourself. I'm Samantha, by the way. Call me Sam," says the blonde girl. "This is Jennie."

Brenda looks at the second girl who's a lot taller with short, brown curly hair, receiving a tentative smile in return. That the girl slides a block of butter and a jar of Vegemite in Brenda's direction has her warming towards her.

"Grab yourself a coffee if you want," says Sam, shaking a jar of instant like it's a maraca.

Brenda makes the most of their generosity and while she's slicing herself a second doorstop she overhears something that has the blade stopping mid-loaf. Surely it can't be this easy?

She looks up at them. "You're looking for somewhere to live?"

Both girls nod in response.

"How much do you want to spend?"

They answer in perfect unison leaving Brenda unsure if they mean each, or for both of them. A moment later it's confirmed they're talking each. With them both paying that sort of rent, and the flat actually costing Brenda nothing, she won't need to work unless she wants to. And she doubts that's happening soon.

She'd feel bad about it, but at the end of the day, they're still getting a cheap place to stay.

"Just so happens I know of a place going, I'm checking it out in a couple of hours. You can meet me there if you're keen."

Later that morning and Brenda pulls her car into a side-road up from the address Stefano has given her. Because the flat is on a main thoroughfare, there's no parking right out front. Striding down the footpath, she swings in through the open gate to where Stefano is sitting on a bench in the garden. He's smoking a cigar and checking out a track guide.

If he hadn't been there, Brenda would've thought she was at the wrong address. The place looks stunning and more than she could have hoped for. His face lights up when he sees her; he pats the seat next to him in invitation.

Brenda smiles in return before sauntering over and giving her walk every ounce of seduction she can throw at it. Watching his eyes widen, she knows she's got the mix spot on.

Sitting next to him, she doesn't give him a chance to speak before taking hold of his chin and kissing him deeply. He's responding when she pulls away. "My friends, are they here?"

"They are inside, but you, you do not need to hurry."

Brenda pulls out of his embrace and looks at him as if he's slipped a cog. "I do if I want the best bedroom."

She leaves him where he is and walks into the flat; the two Kiwi girls are in one of the bedrooms.

"Sorry I'm late traffic was a complete bitch for a Saturday morning so what do you think of our new landlord?" she says, in one breath.

"Very cute and married by the looks of things. Mind you, we might be able to come to an arrangement on how we pay the rent," jokes Sam.

"Too late, why do you think the place is so sodding cheap!" Not that Brenda's letting on it's as cheap as it is. No point in that.

"What! You didn't?" says Sam.

"Multiple times," says Brenda.

"How can you do that?" says Jennie, aghast.

"I can give you a book, if you like." Brenda's unable to believe the tall girl is as prudish as she is. It's 1979 for goodness' sake.

"Not that! I know how to do it. But sex should be special. It should be with the right guy."

Brenda rolls her eyes. "Screw me, that's 'virgin' on the ridiculous."

"You mean verging," says Jennie, a little primly.

"Yeah, whatever." Brenda leaves them, wandering off to check out the other rooms.

By the end of the visit, they confirm they'll move in that very afternoon. It will piss off the landlady at the hostel no end, but it's something they can all live with. Brenda's even looking forward to living in a flat with two other girls. Who knows what sort of fun they can get up to? She just needs to work on loosening up that Jennie chick. Couple of casks of wine should do it. Actually, make that three.

THE END

I hope you enjoyed the start to my 'That Seventies Series'. If you want to find out what trouble Brenda, Sam and Jennie get into, check out Friday Night Fever. While this is Sam's story, Brenda's in there boots and all. Actually she's usually the one who gets them into, and even sometimes out of, the trouble.

Out of Bounds

She's out to escape
a gene pool that's
only ankle-deep.

Andrene Low

1

Melbourne - Australia

*J*aney stares unseeing at the familiar landmarks as her tram rattles along Victoria Ave in Melbourne. When she'd taken the job in the cosmetics department at David Jones, she hadn't anticipated how exhausting it would be. Standing around proving the efficacy of the products she's flogging–thanks to her already flawless skin–is harder than she'd have thought possible.

Deep in the vagaries of cleansing, toning and moisturising, it takes a while for her addled brain to register the tram has sailed past her stop.

"Bugger!"

She slaps her hand over her mouth. If her mother were here, she'd have received an even harder slap to the back of her head. Chewing on her lip, Janey adds it to the ever-growing list of things to confess next time she attends Mass; whenever that will be.

Yanking hard on the leather cord above her head,

she hears the bell ding faintly in the driver's cab, signalling him to brake at the next stop. He doesn't so much stop as slow ever so slightly. Janey jumps off the ancient vehicle and comes close to landing in a heap in the gutter.

So. Very. Tired.

Tired enough her eyes water, and the shimmering heat on the footpath gives the impression it's coming up to meet her. She closes her eyes for a moment to clear them, swaying slightly in the process, before trudging her way home.

Home for her and younger sister, Maria, is an outwardly genteel hostel for young ladies in South Melbourne. Inwardly it's a bit of a dive, but this is better than being socially buried back in the country with their parents.

No contest, really.

Especially not with her mother dropping hints Perry Comb-Over–and her second cousin for goodness' sake–is a good catch. Even though she's not long turned twenty-four, her Italian-born mother, considers her well settled on the shelf, and Janey is in agreement. However, she doesn't want to settle for any guy. To her, the Italian heritage is a starting point, not the be-all and end-all it is to her mother.

It had taken full-on hysterics, nagging, and pleading to convince her parents her idea of six months in Melbourne was a good one. The way Janey had put it, the visit would give her some much-needed town polish, and the opportunity to look farther afield for a potential husband. Someone who isn't related *before* the ceremony would be good.

There was no way her parents would let her travel to Melbourne on her own and so Maria had been enlisted as a chaperone of sorts. Both Janey and Maria knew they'd dodged bullets on this front. Their standard chaperone is Aunt Fina, a woman guaranteed to kill any sexual energy on a date. If the guy so much as lifted a finger, their aunt was capable of killing him instead.

Entering the boarding house through the back door next to the kitchen, Janey is revived by a cool breeze. This is the result of both this and the front door being thrown wide. She briefly greets the girls getting their evening meals ready, before trailing along the hallway. The sisterhood in the household is an unexpected but welcome bonus to living here, with Janey feeling as though she has twenty sisters, rather than one.

Her foot is raised, ready to climb the stairs to her and Maria's first-floor bedroom but she isn't given the chance.

"Janey, a word if you will?"

What on earth does the landlady want with her now? *Surely she isn't putting the rent up, again?* The woman runs the hostel with a firm hand, its heavy nature due to her overall weight. Saying she's let herself go is an understatement.

While Janey's mother might be carrying a few extra pounds thanks to all that delicious Italian cuisine, she hasn't given up. She never leaves the house without makeup, her hair is always immaculate, and her dresses firmly starched and in pristine condition.

By comparison, the landlady, sloths around in housecoats ugly in both design and shape, reminding Janey of Demis Roussos, except *he* sports less chest hair. The overall look is awful, like the woman herself.

Turning away from the stairs, she plasters on what

she hopes is her professional 'I'm going to sell you makeup' face. "Yes, Mrs Wallace, how can I help you?"

"Do you happen to know anything about the black BMW parked out front?"

So random is this question, it takes a moment for Janey's muddled brain to process it. "Ah, black BMW?"

"Yes, it's been parked out there for the past two hours. I asked the gentleman behind the wheel what he was doing, but he was vague in his responses."

Janey gives up trying to make sense of this, ambles along the hallway to the front door, looks outside and chokes. She hopes Mrs Williams hasn't heard.

Her shock under control, she turns, unable to stop herself from rushing her reply. "No! No, I can't say I *know* him." Technically this is true. She doesn't *know* him, she only *knows of him*. Her assertion is correct enough that she won't need to mention it in the confessional.

Mrs Williams saying, "Can you send Maria down, please?" signifies the woman has swallowed her half-truth.

"I can answer for Maria. We both know the same people and so if I don't know him, neither will she."

Again, she trips over her words in an effort to propel them free of her mouth as rapidly as possible. She answers for her sister, because of the girl's propensity to admit to any bad deed at the slightest provocation. Even their priest back home had become bored with the 'sins' she trolleyed out every Sunday.

It isn't that the girl is the saint she professes to be. It's more her top ten sins get aired only after the priest has fallen into a catatonic state courtesy of a litany of mundane transgressions.

Mrs Williams isn't happy about being fobbed off.

But short of accusing Janey of lying, there's not much she can do about it. And her bulk decrees the first floor is out of bounds. Her scowl is dark as she lumbers back into her office at the rear of the property and shuts the door firmly,

The main reason for closing the door being that her office is the sole room on the premises to benefit from air conditioning. None of the girls in the hostel complain. Anything that puts a hold on the woman's sweat glands is a plus in their books.

It takes all Janey's effort to make her way up the stairs and along the hall to the large corner room she shares with her sister. Maria is sprawled across her bed, chin propped on the window sill that overlooks the front of the hostel. She's peering through the lace curtains so intently that they're stretched tight over her face, her yellow sundress is hiked enough to reveal her white lacy knickers.

"We've got a problem!" They both say simultaneously.

Janey drops her handbag on the end of her bed before absently rearranging her sister's sundress. "You've seen him?"

"I had to walk around the block and come in the back way to avoid him. I'm lucky I spotted him before he clocked me." Maria's response is muffled because her head is now hanging out the window.

"For goodness' sake, get back inside. If he looks up, he'll see you." Janey tugs on the girl's shoulder until she's back behind the lace curtains.

Removing her shoes, Janey places them in the bottom of their shared wardrobe. Next she shrugs out of the regulation-issue baby-pink smock and black pencil skirt that are the uniform of all the girls in the cosmetics department. A quick sniff of the underarms indicates she's got at least one more day out of the top. Better this than having to visit the grimy laundry, bolted onto the back of the boarding house as an afterthought.

Not bothering to dress, she sits in her underwear on a small stool at the dressing table that's jammed in the corner of the room. At least here it won't collapse if asked to support anything heavier than a hanky. Janey expertly twists her hair into a messy knot on top of her head before slathering her face in baby oil. It takes this and dirtying half a dozen makeup remover pads, before she's looking like herself again.

It's crazy she's pedalling the stuff, when she hates wearing it. Thanks to her Italian heritage, her skin-tone is perfect without coating it in the latest from *Shiseido* or *Elizabeth Arden*. Likewise, her lashes do not need mascara and her lips are defined without the heavy application of lipstick.

Free of gunk, she gives in to the temptation to lie back on her bed; her body flopping back into the mattress like an under-filled hot water bottle. In reality this has more to do with the mattress being knackered than true relaxation on her part. Even faked relaxation is out of reach these days, their time in Melbourne fast running out and nothing to show for it, yet.

Maria turns away from the window. "What are going to do about him?"

"I'm not sure. After what we did to him, I'm surprised he'd show his face here again."

"Maybe he's as stupid as Sam and Brenda say?"

"Must be. Give me a moment, will you? I'm so tired I can't think straight. Just five minutes."

. . .

"Crap!"

This gets Janey's attention like nothing else. Sure enough, when she opens her eyes, Maria is counting her rosary beads in a futile attempt at damage control.

"What?" Janey drags herself into a sitting position, aware that for her sister to swear, things are dire.

"Cops!"

Janey's up, across the gap and onto her sister's bed in seconds, collapsing in a heap before her head has stopped spinning.

Looking at the scene below, her heart hammers. This is not good. Not good at all. The landlady must have called them because as far as Janey knows, there's nothing illegal about sitting in a parked car for hours on end.

Weird, but not illegal.

Leaning over the car by the driver's window, the two cops are menacing in their stance. The effect on the Greek guy behind the wheel is negligible. Throwing his door wide–and clipping one of the cops in the process–he drags himself out of the car. Standing next to them, everything about his body language speaks of anger. If she were closer, Janey suspects she'd be able to see spittle at the corners of his mouth. Swinging his arm wide, he gestures wildly toward the boarding house, accidentally smacking one of the cops on the shoulder hard enough to make the officer take a step back.

Any hopes Janey has that this distraction will work in her and Maria's favour, are dashed. Instead of reprimanding the guy for striking an officer, both cops look up.

Jerking away from the window, she worries she's been spotted. "Bloody hell!" Ripping the rosary beads out of Maria's hands, she kisses them, mutters a plea for forgiveness, and hands them straight back.

Common sense tells her the cops won't have seen through the thick lace curtains. However, thoughts of being sent home with a police escort have rational notions flying out the window, a lot like the curtains are now. Risking another peek, she sucks in hard, while Maria hyperventilates next to her. Seeing the cops disappear under the front portico beneath them, they spring into action.

Abandoning her usual careful consideration about her outfit, Janey grabs whatever is to hand and throws it on. She's knotting the laces on her sneakers when they hear Mrs Williams yelling for all the girls to assemble downstairs in the side lounge that overlooks the courtyard. This is one roll call Janey and Maria will go AWOL for.

Hearing the rooms around them emptying, they risk opening their door a crack, enough to see the last stragglers. Inching their door further open, they crawl on hands and knees along the landing to the fire escape at the back of the building.

It's not the first time they've exited the property this way, but if they get caught, it might well be the last. The rusty ladder squeaks as it takes their combined weight, forcing them to move with care. They keep their feet on the sides, where the corroded rungs are less likely to collapse.

Unfortunately, they can't take their time either, with the ladder ending a good few feet off the ground and visible through the window at the back of the hallway.

While dropping to the ground, Janey gets a quick snapshot of all the girls milling around by the bottom of the stairs. It's this human blockade that hides her and Maria from the cops standing next to Mrs Williams.

Of more concern is Salami Boy, the moniker given to the creepy guy by Samantha and Brenda who'd thought he was Italian, standing right behind the officers. He's bouncing on his feet in an effort to see over their shoulders. *Fancy thinking that piece of human garbage could pass as Italian.* It's something that still annoys Janey.

The jolt from landing on the concrete pad under the ladder slams up through Janey's body, proving beyond a doubt five minutes' rest was not enough. Maybe if she'd managed to sleep last night, she'd be okay. Her insomnia is rampant as she worries about being forced into a loveless marriage with Perry Comb-Over.

Maria lands next to her with a grunt. "Now what?" the girl whispers, her lips close to Janey's ear.

"We need to get as far away from here as possible. Mrs Wallace knows we're home and so if we don't show up, she's gonna be looking for us."

Maria chews on her lip. "She can't manage the stairs."

"No, but she'll send someone up to get us."

"Well, holy Mother of God!" explodes Maria, the words bouncing off the concrete surrounding them. A quick search of the pockets of her dress and then her purse and she comes up empty-handed. Without rosary beads, Maria might even insist they go to church this Sunday. Fortunately, Janey locates her own in time to avoid the possibility.

In an effort to speed things up, Maria manages to get "I believe in God…" out, before she's even in possession of the rosary.

She's not fast enough for Janey who's been expecting a short prayer and not the full-on-real-deal. "We don't have time for all of that. Do it later."

"Yes, yes, yes, you're right," says Maria, shoving the beads back into Janey's hands before racing off, leaving her to follow as best she can.

On reaching the footpath, Janey's alarmed to see her sister sneaking around the front of the hostel. She waits to see what her hare-brained sibling is doing this time, with there being no point in both of them being arrested. It's no wonder she spends as long as she does in the confessional. If she weren't Catholic, the girl would be going straight to hell.

With Janey hard on her heels.

A moment later, the black BMW crawls around the corner. Janey's system has over-dosed with adrenaline before she sees Maria at the wheel—not Salami Boy.

They'll need more rosary beads.

No other option open to her, Janey shoots around to the passenger side of the car, throws open the door, and climbs in. Before she can close it, Maria stomps on the accelerator and the car jumps forward. Seat belt buckled, Janey pulls her visor down and uses the mirror to see what's happening behind them.

Nothing so far.

Maria throws the car around the first available corner, allowing Janey to look back. It's to see the police car shoot out of the side road in pursuit.

"We need to get away from here as fast and as far as possible." Janey knows she's stating the obvious, but this doesn't stop her from saying it.

"You think?"

Maria's face is grim with determination as she concentrates on driving. She needs to; their route is so convoluted, Janey's on the edge of throwing up from a stomach-churning blend of worry and motion sickness.

Her hand over her mouth to keep things where they are, she's shocked when her sister stomps hard on the brakes. If Janey hadn't thought to do her seat belt up earlier, she'd now be doubling as a hood ornament.

"What are you doing?" Janey yells at Maria, who's already opened her door and is standing next to the car.

Maria leans forward and smiles at Janey. "Follow me!"

Again, Janey's left to tag along in Maria's wake. *As the elder, shouldn't it be me leading the way?* Maybe if she weren't so tired, things would be clearer. Staggering out of the car, she also leaves her door hanging wide. She stumbles to catch up with her sister, who's racing down an alley that cuts through the block in the direction of the beach.

Catching her toe on the edge of the footpath, Janey comes close to tripping and a few large, ungainly steps are all that save her from smashing onto her knees. Shaky on her feet, she's grateful when Maria retraces her steps to help her along. They're not even halfway through the block when a squeal of tires comes from somewhere behind them.

"Brilliant! I was hoping that'd happen." The smile on Maria's face speaks of amusement and relief, and she slows the pace.

"What?" Janey has no idea what's just happened.

"Didn't you see the deadbeats hanging around the front of the house where I stopped?"

Janey shakes her head.

"That's why I stopped there."

Words fail Janey; her sister coming through for them, again. She's not relaxing though, as her sister's plans have also been known to fail, spectacularly at times. "Let's go to the beach. I need to lie down before I fall down."

Breaking out onto the footpath on the other side of the block, they're in time to see the BMW race past. It's followed by a cop car with lights flashing and siren blaring. Lucky for them Salami Boy, sitting in the middle of the back seat, is too intent on keeping an eye on his precious car to take any notice of them.

Another block of walking resolutely with heads bowed, they reach the relative safety of the beach. They drop to the sand in silent agreement, pretending like they've been there for hours. Even though still clothed, they look a lot less guilty this way than storming along the beach as though the hounds of hell are after them.

Using her handbag as a headrest, Janey lies back and closes her eyes against the sunlight. Lucky for her, it's late enough in the day she won't risk sunburn and, if she's extra lucky, she can catch up on some missing sleep.

But her body is so full to the brim with adrenaline, this is impossible. Jeepers, any stiffer and someone could take her surfing.

The sun is low in the sky before it dawns on them they've gotten away with it. It's almost a let-down after being so hyped. Walking up the beach to the street, they risk a quick peek over the seawall. They're in luck: the coast is clear for them to head for the nearest tram stop. There'll be a bit of a wait now rush hour is over, but it'll still be faster than walking home.

A scan of the timetable posted in the rickety wooden shed that serves as a waiting room shows they've got an hour before the next tram. If it turns up on time.

"We may as well get something to eat." Janey's suggestion is punctuated by her stomach growling, reminding her she hasn't eaten since her lunch break at midday.

"Good idea, there's that Italian place around the corner that Simone was telling us about."

Knowing there'll be no resistance to this suggestion, Maria is already on her way.

Janey hurries to catch up, rounds the corner a second after her sister and slams straight into the back of her, sending both of them flying.

Janey steadies herself against the front of a butcher's shop, its window empty but for a slew of pristine white tiles interspersed with the occasional piece of plastic parsley. "What are you doing?"

Maria doesn't answer; instead, she steps backwards, something not possible with Janey where she is. Her sister twirls on the spot, bringing their faces within millimetres of each other.

"The cops are here!"

Pulling herself to her full height, Janey peeks over her sister's shoulder and sure enough, there's a black-and-white police car parked right outside the restaurant. Following a moment's panic and some rational thought, Janey slows her response and examines the two cops. They're not the same two who'd visited the hostel earlier. They're also missing the optional Greek in the back seat.

"Act natural." Janey controls the movement of her lips enough that she's sure they're moving about as much as a Broadway ventriloquist's. "We can do this."

Stepping to the side, she walks around her sister and along the footpath to the door of the Italian pizzeria, hoping Maria is following. It's only when she steps inside the air-conditioned coolness of the restaurant that she's sure Maria is still with her. One thing in their favour is there aren't any cops in here. In fact, there's no one else in the place. It's so deserted, Janey wonders if it's even open for the evening.

That is until a small man pops up from behind the chest-high counter right beside the door.

"Ah, table for two," says Janey.

"*Si si*, you sit anywhere you like."

Janey's usual practice would be to sit near the window and watch the world go by.

It's not a choice she'll make today. Instead she opts for a table at the back where they can watch the front door and the street beyond.

They're still settling in when glasses of water and menus are plonked down by a girl whose expression says she'd prefer to be anywhere but here. Reading the menu makes Janey's mouth water. The immediate panic over, she's hungry, perhaps even borderline ravenous.

Maria taps the menu deep in thought.

"I wonder if the lasagne is any good?"

"Not as good as Mama's, that's for sure."

They decide on dishes their mother doesn't make to avoid comparisons. One thing in the restaurant's favour is the food arrives promptly. It's also surprisingly good for such a small, local place. Janey's *Veal Parmigiana* is possibly even better than her *nonna's*, while Maria's unwilling to share her *Spiedini Siciliani*.

They're halfway through their meals when the door to the restaurant opens and two men walk in. A forkful of food held forgotten in mid-air, Janey swallows. Maria looks at her with knitted brows;

getting nothing in response, she looks over her shoulder before turning back, her face split with a huge grin.

These two are the best-looking men they've seen since arriving in Melbourne. Add to this they're chatting to the man at the front counter in Italian and–if Janey listens hard enough–she can hear her mother whistling the wedding march.

The men move with confidence. They're tall, but not freakishly so. After a quick check of ring fingers, Janey gives into the temptation to drool. While both of them are handsome, her gaze is drawn to the one with a buzz-cut vicious enough she can see his scalp. The day-old growth covering the bottom half of his face has a piratical air to it. But his eyes are his most arresting feature.

These dark brown orbs spell out B-A-D B-O-Y in letters so big the message is clear. And with 'lettering' this attractive, she'd happily read it twice or even three times.

What on earth are they supposed to do now? Picking up guys in restaurants isn't something they're practiced at, having always been introduced by a family friend or relation to potential suitors in the past.

Even seeing these two at The Veneto Club would have made a proper introduction possible. The Italian social club has been given their mother's stamp of approval, something that took place during their leave-taking at the train station. Up until then, Janey hadn't known her parents were members. Certainly they'd never mentioned it prior to that.

As it is, the most Janey can hope for is the guys look in their direction. She yanks the hair clip out of her hair, allowing it fall in waves around her shoulders, before pasting on a smile. Meanwhile, Maria nibbles at her lips to increase their colour and give them the appearance of fullness. Not that they need it.

It's pointless.

The two gorgeous guys have just been seated at a table within spitting distance of theirs, when a uniformed cop puts his head in the door and coughs discreetly. There's no doubt the two men know the cop by their reaction to his summons. With no discernible hesitation or regret, the men pull the napkins off their laps and toss them on the table. They walk out, taking Maria and Janey's dreams with them. It's not that the men have left the restaurant; it's that the chances of them being cops are super high.

The girls take their time finishing their meals, wanting the cops to be well on their way before they themselves leave with a promise to the old guy to return.

Hopefully not in five to ten years.

They're in luck when it comes to catching a tram home. There's no wait at all, the irony being the tram is running super late rather than on time.

Janey examines her reflection in the tram window, made into a mirror by the gathering darkness beyond. "You realise we'll have to move."

"I guess so. But I'm not going back home until we don't have a choice."

"I'm with you on that front. Would Brian and Gary mind if we stayed with them above the pub in St Kilda? It wouldn't be for long." It wouldn't be their mother's first choice of accommodation for them either, but what she doesn't know about won't hurt her.

The pub in question is where Maria had worked when they'd first arrived in Melbourne. The girl knew her wine, and spirits, and beer–anything alcoholic really–and so the job had been perfect for her. The hardest part had been Maria not confessing to their mother where she was working during their hour-long weekly phone call.

It was, therefore, something of a relief for Janey when Maria's shifts changed to evenings, putting the kibosh on what was a cruisy job. Without a car and the hostel being two suburbs away, her sister needed a taxi home, guaranteed to chew through most of her wages and tips.

Leaving on good terms, the younger girl registered with a temp agency and hadn't been out of work since. This is for the best. Their mother would have had a fit if she'd known her youngest daughter was working at the most notorious gay bar in Melbourne. And statistically one the safest places in the city for the girl to work.

All's quiet but for the simple clacking of the tram on its tracks, both girls lost in thought. Janey stews on whether they'll be moving that very night or if they can hold out until the weekend, two days away. She hasn't decided when Maria leans in front of her to pull the stop cord. They sneak in the back door of the hostel and have even made it halfway up the stairs, when they're collared.

On the plus side is that it's by Mrs Williams, and not the police.

"I requested everyone come downstairs earlier this evening. Where were you?"

Janey thought this might happen. Looking over her shoulder and keeping her tone as casual as she can, she says, "We went straight out for dinner as soon as I got home. We must've missed it."

It's a brazen lie, and a hopeless one. The evil–and lazy–eye the woman keeps on the place, the chances of them leaving without her knowledge are slim. Regrettably there isn't another option. Better to question the woman's sanity and hearing than admit to ignoring roll call.

The landlady's expression is dark–darker than usual. "You will join me, now!"

Instead of disappearing back into her lair, she lurches along the hallway and in through the door of the side lounge. Much as she wants to run to their room, pack and get away, Janey's years of being a good daughter compel her to turn and retrace her steps. Maria is right behind her. Entering the lounge, they wait for strips to be ripped off them.

They're therefore surprised when, rather than harangue them, the landlady throws herself into the nearest chair capable of coping with her bulk. The resulting fart is the icing on the cake of what is proving to be a stressful evening.

"Guillerlmina Russo? Maria Russo?"

This question comes from behind them and they spin on a cent.

Sure Janey wanted to know more about the gorgeous guys from the restaurant. However, she didn't want this to include their rank and force ID numbers as printed on the credentials they open to show the girls.

It's also not a good sign they know her birth name. It was something she'd changed on the second day of their time in Melbourne; it is easier to answer to Janey than have her name constantly mangled.

What is the sentence for joy-riding these days?

Janey suspects it will be trifling compared with the penalty for drugging, kidnapping and torturing someone.

3

The B-A-D B-O-Y takes Janey into the front room, calling in one of the other girls from the hostel as a witness. He's also careful to leave the door open. His partner grills Maria in the side lounge with Mrs Williams as chaperone, but who in reality is simply being a nosy cow.

Janey can't decide whether she's pleased or not to be with Anthony Bertolino. Sorry, make that Detective Inspector Bertolino. He's the better looking of the two officers, at least in her opinion. Even his brutal haircut doesn't detract from his movie-star good looks coupled with the physique of an Aussie Rules player. It's a deadly combination, and she suspects her heart would be beating faster even if he wasn't grilling her. Natalie, the girl roped in as witness, has a glazed expression as she hangs on his every word.

"So, let me see if I've got this straight," he looks at his pad of scribbled notes. "You're saying you don't know a gentleman by the name of Ricardo Manos?"

Again, Janey gets off on a technicality. Until the

Detective Inspector had said the Greek guy's name, she'd had no idea what it was. Now, if he'd asked her if she knew someone called 'Salami Boy', she'd have been duty-bound to admit to it.

There's also the fact Ricardo Manos is no gentleman.

"No, I can't say I do." Janey struggles to keep her response succinct and slow.

His frown says he isn't buying it. "That's interesting, because you and your sister fit the description he's given us. His allegations are serious."

Janey's wondering where Salami Boy is in all of this, when the Detective Inspector speaks. "As soon as we can get back in touch with him, we'll get you in for a formal identification."

Formal identification? Black spots flutter across Janey's vision. She must look lousy too, because the Detective Inspector is on his feet in a flash, forcing her head between her knees.

"Breathe deeply and slowly." His hand rests gently on the back of her neck. Janey wishes she could have met him in any other way than this.

"I've never even had a parking ticket," she mumbles into her knees. "This can't be happening."

She's not aware Natalie's left the room until a glass of water is thrust under her nose. "Lift your head slowly and sip this."

Janey does as instructed by the girl, although she's not sure it makes much difference. A glass of water won't take away the fact she's about to be arrested. Heaven knows what Maria is admitting to next door. The haziness surrounding her doesn't clear, and she watches the Detective Inspector, as though through a frosted window. He grabs his notepad off the table and slides it and his pen into the front pocket of his dark brown suit jacket.

"We'll be in touch."

Neither Janey nor Maria utter a word until they're in their room. The fact they're here and not in a holding cell tells Janey her sister must've been able to hold in every confession she's ever wanted to make.

It's a miracle worthy of Lourdes or Fatima.

The door to the bedroom shut, the floodgates open, even if at whisper level and in Italian.

"I was hoping we'd have until the weekend, but we need to be out of here tonight." Janey is already on her hands and knees, retrieving her suitcase from under the bed.

Maria, on the other hand, is slumped on her bed, her face made ugly by a deep scowl.

"What if they're watching the place?"

"It's a risk we'll have to take."

Her suitcase open in the middle of her bed, Janey stalks over to the windows and yanks the curtains closed. Hidden from view, she makes short work of emptying her side of the closet and the two bottom drawers of the dresser. She dumps everything in a heap on the bed next to her bag. Rummaging through it all, she selects clothing in dark colours. She doesn't have anything in black; Italian tradition reserving this colour for widows. Still, even chocolate brown will blend better with the night than the all-white outfit she's wearing.

Changed out of the Capri pants and T-shirt and into her escape outfit, she stuffs everything into her suitcase. She forces the lid down to lock it.

Resigned to moving this very night, Maria is likewise packing. Following visits to the bathroom by both of them, they're as ready to go on the run as they'll ever be.

Janey flicks off the lights and, after a quarter of an hour, risks peeking through a small gap in the curtains. It's enough to see a black-and-white police car parked down the road a short way. "Seriously!?"

She walks across the room, making sure to avoid both suitcases, and eases their door open. She's relieved to see there isn't a guy tipped back on a kitchen chair out there. Instead, the hallway's dark. Darker than it usually is, and it takes her a moment to see why. Some clever spark — or, in this case, daughter of a sparky, and the witness to Janey's interrogation — has removed all the lightbulbs.

Thank you, Natalie.

Tiptoeing along the hallway to the back of the hostel she's thrilled to see the window is wide open. The blasted thing always makes a hell of a racket no matter how carefully you ease it up. In the quiet of the night it would be deafening. Janey will miss the comradery of the girls in the hostel.

A quick look through the window shows the backyard is deserted, unless someone is hiding in the laundry.

At movement in the shadows, Janey jumps away from the window, but not so far that she doesn't hear an urgent *"Pssst!"* from below. Doubting the Detective Inspector is responsible, she shoves her head out the window, the weak moonlight enough to show Gaylene smiling and waving below.

Surely it can't be this easy?

Unfortunately, out of options, they have to take

this lucky break at face value. They're sneaking down the hall with bags in tow when a doorway on their right opens.

The occupant of the room slouches against the door frame, belying the fact she's naked. Simone is from Queensland, her parents are hippies, and from the sounds of things, aren't too concerned about clothing around the house. It's something Simone embraces wholeheartedly. "You'd better give those to me, in case you have to make a run for it. We can get them to you tomorrow."

"Thanks, you're a star." Janey's careful to keep her gaze firmly locked on Simone's face.

Their suitcases stowed under the resident nudist's bed, Janey scribbles the address of where they'll be staying, goes to hug Simone but changes her mind. There's nothing for it now but to leave. The squeaking fire escape as they clamber down shatters the night, Janey expecting arrest at any moment.

She isn't aware of holding her breath until she and Maria are hidden under an old army blanket on the back seat of Gaylene's bile-coloured Corolla. Even when they're on their way, Janey's in constant dread of flashing lights and sirens.

There's no conversation on the drive to St Kilda. This has nothing to do with Janey and Maria being stuffed under a mountain of slightly mouldy wool. It's more to do with the volume of the music, with the stereo having been cranked up as soon as they were away from the hostel.

Peeking out from under the blankets, Janey knows the minute they arrive at their destination. The hot pink neon sign on the corner of the pub is distinctive. Gaylene hasn't had time to pull on the handbrake when Maria and Janey inch their way out their respective doors. They push them quietly shut, before scurrying across the road to the side door leading to Brian and Gary's flat. Gaylene is well on her way back to the hostel before someone responds to the sisters' frantic knocking.

The door swings wide, spilling light out onto the footpath and exposing Janey enough that she forgets her manners. She pushes past first Gary and then Brian to get inside. Maria isn't far behind, even going so far as to prise Gary's hand off the knob and shut the door, double locking it for good measure.

"Well, good evening to you, too." Gary's eyebrows are raised and his manner imperious.

Janey glances between Brian and Gary, knowing she must look as desperate as her sister. Maria even wrings her hands together in supplication.

"We're so sorry to barge in like this, but we had nowhere else to go."

Brian is the first to relent, enveloping Janey and Maria in a crushing hug. "You come tell your Auntie Brian all about it." He ushers the girls upstairs and through into the large living room-cum-kitchen that spans the back of the property.

Cups of tea are being drunk all round when Janey and Maria get 'the look'.

This won't go down as well as the English Breakfast.

Janey focuses on Brian, the more accepting of the two. "Do you remember the guy we got drunk?"

Brian's laughter is uproarious. "Which one?"

"We'd need specifics." Gary scoots to the edge of his seat.

"You know the one. That, ah, *friend* of Sam's, if you

can call him that." Maria sits back as though this scant information should be enough for them to understand who she's talking about.

At the blank looks they're getting, Janey spells it out, even though she's loath to do so. "He was stalking Sam. We got him hammered on Uncle Luca's special brew. You guys covered him in whipped cream. We took photos."

"So?" Gary shrugs. "What of it? A bit of harmless fun, nothing else."

"He's been talking to the cops. He may have embellished things a bit and we can't say he's lying without admitting our guilt."

Janey waits for all hell to break loose and Brian and Gary don't disappoint with their theatrics, worthy of the trouble they're all in.

"And you came here?" Gary's tone is as incredulous as his expression. Even Brian is now looking shocked at their presence.

"We weren't followed," says Maria.

Gary jumps to his feet, spilling his tea in the process. He slams his cup on a side table and minces over to the window that overlooks the side street. There's no subterfuge about his next actions. He yanks the curtains wide, slams open the sash window, pokes his head out, and proceeds to look up and down the road.

Brian is now hanging over his shoulder. "Can you see anything? Is there anyone there?"

"I can't see anyone, but it doesn't mean to say they don't know the girls are in here."

Maria jumps to her feet. "Maybe we should look out the front windows?"

She's at the door to the hallway when the other three yell, "No!"

Gary steers her back to her seat, forcing her to sit. "You stay here. I'll check."

"I'll help." Brian's already on his way.

While the two men check the front of the property, there's nothing for Janey and Maria to do other than finish their tea. It's something Janey finds difficult, busy as she is choking on her fear. Even the biscuits Brian has arranged on a small Queen Anne bread-and-butter plate taste like sawdust to her.

The blend of wood shavings and her heart being stuck in her throat has Janey close to passing out by the time the men explode back into the room. Their expressions give nothing away, but surely the speed with which they've entered the room doesn't bode well?

"Oooh, you girls are soooo lucky," says Brian. "This calls for a tipple." He rummages around in the glass liquor cabinet until, a moment later, his cry of "Aha!" bounces round the room, much like the man himself.

Seeing what it is he's holding up in triumph, Janey isn't surprised. They'd brought two bottles of Uncle Luca's homemade grappa the day they set about getting Salami Boy as naked as the day he was born. Decorating him like a Christmas Pavlova had been all down to Brian and Gary.

4

*J*aney is up and dressed before anyone else in the building the following morning, early enough the cleaners haven't even arrived. Considering the trouble they're in, she can't believe how well she slept. Maybe it's sleeping in a bed with a decent mattress? Or maybe it's that she allowed Brian to talk her into having three, or was it four, shots of Uncle Luca's brew as a nightcap.

Either way, she's energised.

That is until she faces the realities of the day, the biggest being that she needs to go into work. Her reasons for this are two-fold. Firstly, her work ethic means she can't leave without notice. Secondly, and more importantly, there's the fact today is payday, and she needs the money. *Just how much does it cost to go on the run, anyway?* Even discounting fake IDs, she and Maria need to pay for the small bedrooms they're now occupying.

Janey knocks on the door of Maria's room at the front of the property, and not waiting for an answer, walks straight in, opening the curtains a moment later. She doesn't dwell near the window, staggering backwards into the room as quickly as her numb limbs will allow.

But they'd got away! How can this be?

"Maria! You need to get up now!" Janey reinforces this request by shaking her sister, hard.

"Just five more minutes." The response is muffled by the pillow Maria holds over her face as a means of protection from the harsh light streaming into the room.

"The cops are here!"

This comment sends the pillow flying across the room, followed by a few choice words. That her sister doesn't search for her missing rosary beads is a barometer of how upset she must be.

"Look, we might be okay. Any luck, they might be here because Salami Boy might somehow have sussed out where we took him that day."

There are a lot of 'mights' in this statement. Janey knows she's grasping at straws and other fragile items, given Salami Boy was blindfolded for the trips to and from the pub. *But it might be the reason the cops have found the place? Mightn't it?* No matter why it is, they need to get away, and soon.

Maybe hiding out at work for the day is the perfect solution? Their landlady doesn't care where they work, just so long as they pay their rent on time. Janey removes her badge at the end of each day to avoid people she doesn't know calling her by name. There's nothing about her uniform to show who her employer is. The girls in the hostel will never let on, proving last night where their loyalties lie.

Problem is their bags with all their clothes are still back at the hostel.

"If the cops are here, will they still be watching the old place?"

This question from Maria, points out the obvious. They're up early enough they've got time to get over to the hostel, dress for work, and even clock in on time. *What was it the hot cop had said to her at the end of their meeting yesterday?* "We'll be in touch.".

He didn't say when. Surely he won't be there before eight o'clock? Not if he was on duty at nine last night. It's not like the investigation is life or death in nature.

Shoulder bags slung cross-wise, they descend the rickety wooden stairs at the back of the pub, stepping into an alleyway not visible from the street. The narrow space backs a row of shops, forcing them to race along it for a good distance before they find a gap.

It's only just wide enough for them to squeeze through sideways. Sadly the space is perfectly suited to its role as a late-night urinal and receptacle for half-digested fast food. Gross.

Janey's glad she's wearing sneakers, but Maria isn't so lucky, shod as she is in delicate sandals. The girl's lip curling speaks volumes on how disgusting the sensation of slime oozing between her toes must be.

Stumbling out onto the footpath, Maria takes her sandals off, holding them by the straps to keep her fingers well clear of God-knows-what. Luckily for them, they've exited close to a tram stop, and it's but a short scuttle across the footpath to the bench there.

Dropping her sandals on the ground, Maria rummages through her large shoulder bag. "Blast!"

"This help?" Janey holds a pristine white handkerchief she's retrieved from the depths of her own bag.

"Thank goodness. I didn't fancy going without shoes and I sure as heck can't put them back on like they are." Maria makes short work of cleaning as much of the gunge off as possible. Finished, she holds the dark brown handkerchief up for inspection, an eyebrow raised in question.

"Ick no, get rid of it!" Janey doesn't want a bar of the thing now. Even letting their mother loose on it wouldn't see it clean again.

They choose to approach the hostel from the sea rather than from the city, allowing them to enter the back gate without being seen.

It's not yet eight o'clock, so their sedentary landlady will still be tucked up in bed. Even knowing this, the girls don't race in without a care. A quiet tap on the kitchen window grabs the attention of one of the girls preparing their breakfast. Just as quietly, the window slides up a fraction and Janey stretches on tiptoe to get as close as she can to the small gap.

"Is it safe to come in?"

"Yes, but you'll need to be quick about it. I can hear the 'lardlady' already crashing around in her room," says Natalie.

The girls don't need any more encouragement than this, sliding in through the back door, tiptoeing along the hallway, and nipping up the stairs. They don't bother going near their old room, instead tapping on Simone's door. They're peering over the banister when she opens the door behind them, beckoning wildly for them to get into her room.

"What on earth are you doing back here?" She leans against the closed door, as though to stop anyone else from entering.

Janey, who's already on her hands and knees and rummaging through her suitcase for her uniform, stops what she's doing. "We went to the pub in St Kilda, but the cops were outside there this morning. We weren't sure when Gaylene would turn up with our bags but we sure didn't want the police seeing her arriving with them. We need to hide out at work."

Maria is mid-scramble through her bag for something to wear, when she stops. "We don't have time to get our bags to the pub this morning. Can you hang onto them for us?"

She opens her mouth to say more but before she can, Janey slides her hand over her mouth, stopping her sister's words where they are. On getting a small nod, Janey removes her hand. "Do you hear that?" Her voice is low, while her ears are set on high, listening for something in the hallway that's out of place.

Simone turns her head until her ear is pressed hard against the door. Her eyebrows shoot into her hairline: she too has heard something she shouldn't have.

Wasting no time, Janey stuffs everything back into her suitcase, jams the lid shut and slides it underneath the bed. Maria catches on and her suitcase joins her sister's.

But where on earth are they supposed to hide?

There's not enough room under the bed and the curtains are too miserable to hide behind. That leaves the wardrobe. It's small, but not so small two desperate girls can't cram themselves in there, sitting sideways across the bottom. It's a tight fit, but they make it.

They get themselves arranged as best they can, while Simone yanks the curtains closed. She then strips to her underwear and flies over and closes the door on them. Mere seconds after it clicks shut, they hear thumping on the bedroom door.

Simone hasn't even had time to get back into bed and pretend she's been asleep.

The wood veneer on the 1920s oak wardrobe is thin enough Janey can hear clearly the conversation in the room. It's as though she and Maria are sitting on the end of the bed and not hiding out amongst enough crushed velvet to keep a hippy delirious.

Janey would know that voice anywhere. If she closes her eyes, she can see his face. Question is, what on earth is Mrs Williams doing allowing a man onto the second floor? This breaks rules number one, three, five and seven, maybe more. The cops must have a search warrant? And if so, they're screwed.

"My, oh, my. Suddenly I'm not so sleepy after all," says Simone.

Even through ancient wood, the sultry tone of Simone's voice is discernible. Janey can well imagine the girl standing there brazenly in her underwear. Here's hoping it's enough to make Detective Inspector Bertolino back off.

Then they hear something even more out of place on the second floor than a guy's voice.

"Mrs Williams? What are you doing here?" Simone sounds as shocked as Janey is feeling. Pity the poor fireman who's been roped in to help the woman achieve this level of altitude. Unless, of course, she convinced the cops to help. Janey covers her mouth to stop any wayward giggles. She's not amused for long.

"I… promised… these… fine… police officers… I'd help search… the rooms." The woman doesn't so much sound winded as dead on her feet. *Maybe they didn't help much after all?*

Janey thanks her lucky stars for a decent night's sleep. Her brain working overtime, she goes through scenarios, deciding on the most likely. Even in the relative dark of the wardrobe, she's able to locate her wallet, tucked as it is in the side pocket of her shoulder bag. She always puts it in the same place, too hard to find it otherwise. She empties it in readiness.

The wardrobe door doesn't open. Instead, she hears what sounds like a couple of bags of potatoes being dumped on the floor right in front of it. *My goodness, has the woman keeled over?* She hadn't sounded healthy.

A moment's silence is followed by a high-decibel fart and a lot of choked coughing.

By now Janey has tears streaking down her face, and the wardrobe vibrates to her suppressed laughter. *Take that, Bertolino.*

"They're not under here." This comment from Mrs Williams is muffled, as though her head is still shoved under the bed.

There follows a lot of scuffling, banging, crashing and grunting. Some of this is courtesy of the woman herself, the rest belongs to Simone who, it would appear, has been called on to help the landlady regain her feet. If this proves to be the case, Janey and Maria will be covering Simone's visit to a chiropractor.

Things have just settled again, when a deep baritone asks, "What about the wardrobe?"

5

That Bertolino has asked Mrs Williams to look inside the wardrobe doesn't surprise Janey. It's what she'd have done in his boots.

She's ready when her landlady opens the wardrobe door. Without a peep, she holds the crisp notes out. Thank God the three-foot-wide barrier of house-coat and human lard in front of them is enough to block them from the cops' sight.

Mrs Williams makes quite the show of flicking through the clothes hanging in the wardrobe. She snatches the notes out of Janey's hand, shoving them in her greasy cleavage, and closing the door on them.

They're stuck inside the wardrobe until the cops, with Mrs Williams as their sniffer dog, have searched every bedroom on the floor. One thing's for sure, Janey's now late for work. It's a first for her. Not until all is quiet do they open the wardrobe door. Well, they would, if it wasn't locked from the outside.

"No, no, this can't be happening!" The panic in

Maria's whispered voice has an acrid quality to it, something Janey finds contagious.

"Breathe through your nose." It takes all of Janey's resolve to keep her voice calm, when in reality all she wants to do is scream "Help!" at the top of her lungs.

Her legs hooked around her sister's waist, she's able to tell when the younger girl calms, helping her to achieve her own Zen-like state. It must be her turn to save them, surely?

Her grandmother had a wardrobe like this. If she remembers right, they should be able to turn the metal piece holding the door shut from inside.

Both she and Maria break fingernails in the process, but they're free. Never has fart-tinged air smelled so sweet! A quick look at her watch and Janey is on edge. She's due at work in about the same amount of time as the tram journey takes on a good day. Wrenching her suitcase out from under the bed, she's dressed in her uniform a matter of minutes later. Maria, likewise, is dressed for the day, even if her outfit isn't to the usual high standard.

All they need to do is get out of the hostel without the cops seeing them, or Mrs Williams, for that matter. Janey is fresh out of cash and the odious woman doesn't take cheques. Getting into work and collecting her pay packet is now more important than ever.

They're inching their way down the stairs when Mrs Williams lumbers out into the hallway, blocking their escape. Much as they'd like to stay frozen, they walk in dread to the bottom of the steps, expecting the woman to kick them out. They're plumb out of luck on that front.

"As of today your rent will be fifty dollars a week,"

Mrs Williams announces. They're still reeling from the unfairness when she adds, "Each." She doesn't wait for an argument, instead turning and huffing and puffing her way back to her office.

"Fifty dollars?" In lieu of rosary beads, Janey wrings her hands together. "That's about what I make in a week!"

"You and me both, sister."

Deep in thought, they walk to the front door. A quick peek through the side windows next to it confirms they'll be going out the back way again. You'd think, given the place has been searched from top to bottom; the cops would have left for greener pastures, like the pub in St Kilda.

After checking the coast is clear, they're easing the back door open when a voice behind them says, "You two are running late. Want a ride?"

Yet again, Janey and Maria find themselves hidden under a blanket on the back seat of Gaylene's car.

Keeping a close eye on where she is, Janey counts off the tram stops in readiness to pull the leather cord to stop the tram. It's the first time she's visited North Melbourne where her sister is currently working.

What a horrible day she's had.

It had started with her being fifteen minutes late–a miracle considering how behind schedule they'd been running. While this earned her a stern lecture from her supervisor, Mrs Patterson, it was the sin of turning up with a fresh face that earned the biggest rebuke. She'd had to sit still while Mrs P trowelled on enough makeup for Janey to fight for supremacy with the store mannequins. Adding insult to injury, her pay was docked a full hour to cover the time this had taken.

Janey pulls the cord signalling the tram to stop with plenty of time to spare. The coffee bar is exactly where Maria said it would be, its glass windows sparkling, the dark wood surrounding them glowing with fresh polish. The inside is cool and welcoming after the stickiness outside.

A quick scan of the interior and Janey sees Maria, near the back at a small, marble-topped table, her sister hunched, contemplating the dregs of her drink. Janey hadn't realised she was running so late. Instead of joining her sister, she heads for the counter and orders herself a Coca-Cola. She's handed the shapely bottle and a glass half-full of ice, topped off with a pink-striped straw.

Sitting opposite her sister, she doesn't have a chance to pour her drink or even speak before Maria wails, "They gave me the sack!"

"They what?" Suddenly, having her face caked in makeup isn't so bad.

"They said they needed reliable people. It's the first time in three months I've been late by even a minute!"

"How much have you got saved up?"

Maria stares into space, her forehead scrunched in concentration. "With my final pay packet today, it will be somewhere around one hundred and forty-seven dollars and fifty-three cents." Maria has always been good with numbers. Maybe it was all those hours spent on Catholicism's answer to the abacus?

"Up until today, I could have got you a job with me, but I'm no longer in Mrs Patterson's good books." And this on a day when she'd sold more makeup than ever before.

Maria takes a proper look at her sister. "Oh, my goodness. She did a number on you, didn't she?" Her sister tentatively touches Janey's cheek, snatching her hand away and wiping it on the napkin her glass is sitting on to protect the table from condensation. The dark brown smear this leaves is in stark contrast to the pristine whiteness of the fabric.

"One thing's for sure, we definitely can't keep living at the hostel." Janey takes a couple of sips of her Coke, before continuing. "Even though the cops have searched the place, there's the not so small issue of the rent hike."

"Greedy old cow."

"I'm wondering if Brian and Gary will let us stay on with them. They've got space." It's something Janey's been stewing on all day, looking at their predicament from every angle without coming up with a solution. The hostel is now too expensive, and even though the cops are watching the pub, there aren't any other options open to them. Well, nothing that isn't miles from town or will leave them severely out-of-pocket. The budget doesn't run to staying in a hotel.

"We could use the back entrance to the pub until things die down." Maria shudders. "We'll need to buy gumboots, though."

"True. Any luck and the cops will get sick of waiting if they don't see us around."

The more they discuss it, the more this solution appeals: they'll visit the boys at the pub to see if staying with them is even possible.

Janey snaps the last rubber band into place on her makeshift plastic bag gumboots. Until such time as they know they'll be living above the pub for the rest of their time in Melbourne, they don't want to invest in new footwear. "Are you ready?"

Sitting next to her on the seat at the tram stop, Maria too is jerry-rigging makeshift gumboots in readiness to sidle through the melange in the breezeway. So what if there have been a few raised eyebrows from the people passing by?

They're therefore pleasantly surprised when they step into the skinny gap between the buildings. Instead of wading through a nausea-inducing mix of beer-based urine and day-old vomit like last time, it's firm underfoot. Shame they didn't check it out first.

They don't waste time removing their makeshift plastic footwear, hurrying along the alley behind the shops and climbing the wooden staircase to the living room window of the apartment.

If they're lucky, Brian or Gary or both will still be home and not already working in the bar downstairs for the evening. They've been knocking a good five minutes before Brian walks into the living room, wearing a towel, a very small towel. It's something that would usually send Janey and Maria running for the hills. But with Brian's heart belonging to Gary, they're safe to stay where they are.

"Where on earth did you girls get to?" Brian drags them into an awkward embrace, bringing them far closer to bits of his anatomy than they're comfortable with. To add to the discomfort, his towel slips dangerously before he grabs the corner and re-tucks it. "We were so worried! We got up this morning, and you were gone. No note, no nothing!"

This is weird. Janey thought she'd left this sort of

chastisement at home with their mother. They've both been reprimanded before she manages to find the right words amongst the clutter in her head. "But, but… There was a cop car out front."

"Yes! It wasn't there when you checked last night," adds Maria.

Brian looks at each of them in turn, confused. "Yes, it was. There's one parked there all the time. We feed the officers and they keep an eye on things. That's why I didn't bother mentioning it."

What?! They could have waited here for Gaylene to bring their bags over this morning. She could have gone to work as usual and not had her pay docked. Maria would still have a job. And all because Brian failed to mention the makeshift outdoor security system. Janey doesn't know whether to laugh or cry.

Maria opts for throwing a fit. So loud are the histrionics, Janey almost misses the knock at the door downstairs. Brian doesn't though, bounding off to answer it, still wearing nothing but a towel.

"Shhhh, shhhh. You need to be quiet. We don't want anyone knowing we're here."

No sign of the rant abating and her sister beyond caring, Janey firmly puts her hand on the back of Maria's head. She yanks the girl's face hard against her shoulder to muffle the worst of the noise.

Banging, crashing and the occasional oath carry up from the stairwell before Brian and Gaylene stumble into the living room, lugging a bag a piece. Only then does Janey release her stranglehold on Maria.

"What a palaver!" says Gaylene, dumping Janey's bag unceremoniously at the end of the couch. "We had to manhandle your bags out the back way and lug them for bloody miles to avoid the cops seeing us."

"What about Mrs Williams?"

"You owe me twenty bucks." Gaylene's expression is grim.

6

The following morning, Janey drops into the couch next to Maria. "Are you sure you'll be okay at home on your own today?"

Maria scrunches the newspaper she's reading into a heap in her lap. "Of course I will. Stop worrying. After breakfast, I'll go and register with this temp agency." She flattens the newspaper and taps an ad in the middle of the page before continuing. "All going well, I'll get work for the next week."

Janey is pleased to see Maria getting over the disgrace of being sacked the day prior. Both of them have a strong work ethic and so to be pulled up about their behaviour, and worse, let go for it, cuts deep. There's also the fact they need the money coming in to cover rent, allowing them to stay on for the full six months negotiated with their parents.

The plan for the evening is to visit The Veneto Club in hopes of being introduced to some eligible guys. They hope that introductions made under the watchful eye of the senior ladies at the club will be agreeable to both sisters *and* parents.

They haven't had much luck on this front to date, their only introductions to blokes their mother would wholeheartedly approve of. Given the selections to date, they could end up lumbered with a Melbourne version of Perry Comb-Over.

Janey grimaces at herself in the mirror that sits over the dresser in her room. She leans forward for a closer look and is horrified to see there are cracks in her foundation. All down to her letting Mrs Patterson apply 'evening makeup' at the end of her shift. The woman's fondness for Shiseido products has Janey looking like a Geisha with a tan.

It's not all bad though; as well as stroking Mrs Patterson's ego, Janey looks a lot more glamorous than if left to her own devices. She had also paid close attention and replicated the look for Maria, to a lesser degree.

When Janey enters the lounge, Gary's wolf-whistle is piercing. "Wow! Who's hoping to get lucky tonight?"

Taking her hand, Brian twirls her around the room. "Those boys at the club won't know what's hit them."

Janey's not used to this much attention and isn't sure she likes it. She's in dread of what sort of reception they'll receive at The Veneto. There's a fine line between attracting a guy your mother approves of and earning the censure of the crones on the sidelines. It's the middle ground she and Maria are aiming for.

"Can you keep it down when Maria is finished getting ready? She's a bit of a tomboy and if you make her too nervous about her outfit, she'll bail on me. I don't want to give up this close to the end."

The boys both pantomime locking their lips and throwing away the key, without a peep. It looks to be a struggle, but they both manage to keep their faces blank when Maria scuttles into the room. She's done up to the nines and wearing more makeup than she has in the entirety of her life. She's a knockout; one who's oblivious of the fact. She won't blend into the woodwork tonight and will be like catnip to the Italian boys at The Veneto.

Maybe this isn't such a good idea after all?

"Taxi's here!" Gary's voice is faint, half hanging out of the side window of the living room. "Move it or lose it, ladies."

For once, Janey throws caution to the wind. If this is what it takes to avoid a loveless marriage to Perry Comb-Over, she's all in, low-cut top and all.

Twenty minutes later and their taxi sweeps under the concrete entrance arch above The Veneto Club's front gates. It swings around the fountain with its column and winged lion, and up to the main building. This large concrete edifice is a mere seven years old and has a crispness the original clubhouse lacked.

Janey's pulse speeds up. Her usual style is a lot more subtle. Even alone at home she'd have more buttons done up than she has tonight. Seeing Maria trying to sneak another button closed on her shirt, she smacks the girl's hand. For them to be successful, subtlety is the last thing they need.

The taxi disappears down the drive and they pause to ready themselves, before making their way up the steps to the front doors. They're not even halfway there when Maria stumbles to a stop.

"What?"

"It's… it's… it's…" She stutters to a halt.

Following the direction of her sister's stunned gaze, Janey does some stuttering of her own. In all the times they've visited the club, they've never seen him here before. She'd have remembered; Bertolino's partner is easily as good looking as the Detective Inspector himself. She swivels every which way, checking to see if he's about, too.

Talk about being careful what you pray for!

Both girls wanted there to be some good-looking men on the premises tonight. Not like this, though. Janey swings away from the entrance and, seeing Maria is still frozen, manhandles her sister around to face the fountain.

"We need to go." She forces Maria down the front steps, adding an urgent, "Now!" when the girl doesn't move fast enough. In the forecourt, she steers them off to the left and onto the grass before hiding behind one of the small trees dotted around the border of the soccer pitch. They stand side-on, in an attempt to make themselves as inconspicuous as possible. One day in the future the trees will provide shade, but for now they're a hopeless hiding spot. The one thing in the favour is that thanks to a long, hot summer, the ground is concrete in all but colour. This stops their heels from sinking in and saves them from flailing their arms around to remain upright.

Five minutes waiting gives the impression of being a lot longer, to the point Janey is thinking they may need to sneak inside and phone for a taxi. She's close to despair when they're blinded by the headlights of a car swinging in through the gates of the club. It zips up the driveway and swings around the forecourt, narrowly missing the fountain.

On seeing who gets out of the taxi, Janey sucks in enough air that it brings on a coughing fit. She stuffs her face into the crook of her arm and pulls air in through her nose, stopping this. Maria's so freaked out she doesn't appear to be breathing at all.

This is gonna be tight.

It will be a toss-up between flagging the taxi down in the brief space between Detective Inspector Bertolino entering the club and the taxi driving past where they are. Kicking her shoes off, Janey scoops them off the ground and takes off, sprinting towards the front gate, keeping behind the trees as best she can. Thank goodness her outfit tonight is of subdued tones, perhaps to compensate for the fact it's exposing more than she'd like.

So fast is the taxi going when it travels under the archway at the entrance, its driver comes close to ploughing into Janey. Her heart threatening to claw its way out of her chest, she staggers around to the side, wrenches open the back door and climbs in. Maria isn't with her.

"Ah, can you swing back around to the entrance so we can collect my sister?"

The driver gives her the eye in his rear-view mirror, because let's face it, her request is weird. There isn't room to turn around in the driveway. Something Janey appreciates when the driver throws the car into reverse and screams back to the bottom of the front steps.

Oh hell! She didn't want him backing up this far! After a nervous peek at the large glass doors of the club, she's horrified to see Bertolino, still standing in the foyer, examining the contents of the visitor book. Janey slides over to the driver's side until she's as far away from the front doors as possible, but she can still see the Detective Inspector. Meaning he can still see her.

"Not here," she squeaks.

"Then where, love?"

Janey leans over the front seat, her head jammed in the small gap between the driver and the side of the car. Anything to hide from the gorgeous Italian in the club. "Down the driveway a bit, on the left."

"Fine!"

Breathing down his neck in relief, she's thrown back when he puts the car into first and stomps on the gas. Goodness, does he drive nowhere slowly? Lying in a heap on the back seat and struggling to get herself upright, she howls, "Stop!" Even as quickly as she's yelled this, she knows he'll have overshot Maria's hiding spot.

Rather than her sister climbing in, as expected, nothing happens. The driver twists around in his seat and looks at her with narrowed eyes.

"Hang on a second. Don't leave." Janey pulls a fiver out of her wallet and hands it to him, hoping he won't take it as the world's largest tip and scarper.

As a sort of insurance, she leaves the passenger door wide open before scooting across the open ground to the trees. She finds her sister thanks to the headlights of a newly arrived vehicle. She's annoyed to find her sister dragging on a cigarette like her life depends on it.

"What on earth?" Janey rips the glowing cigarette from her sister's mouth, throws it to the ground and stomps on it. "If Mama gets so much as a whiff of smoke on your clothes, you'll be checked into a convent faster than you can say Pall Mall Menthol!"

Taking her sister by the hand, she drags her in the direction of the taxi, bundles her inside and climbs in after her. She's closing the door when the driver plants his boot hard enough to do a Fred Flintstone. To compensate for this, he slams on the anchors when they reach the street.

"Where to?"

Janey rattles off the address and is thrown back into her seat a heartbeat later, their vehicle narrowly missing that of yet another new arrival. Maria sits mutinously on her side of the car playing with her pack of cigarettes and refusing to make eye contact with Janey. To say the journey is a quick one is an understatement, it's faster than any trip to or from The Veneto Club in the past. If she didn't know better, she'd think the driver was being pursued.

Handing over the rest of the fare, Janey is conscious of her hand trembling. "Keep the change," she stutters. It's not that he deserves a tip for his driving, rather she worries she'll drop any coins he hands back to her.

She's hurrying Maria out of the taxi when they're illuminated by a car pulling to a stop farther up the road. Nervous about being out on the street, Janey slams the taxi door shut and hustles her sister across the footpath to the door at the side of the pub. While she locates the key Gary gave her earlier in the day, Maria dares to put another cigarette between her lips in a taunt. She doesn't go so far as to light it.

It takes a moment to get the door unlocked, during which time the lights on the car up the road remain stubbornly on. They ruin her night vision and make it all the harder to get the key in the lock. Even then, the lock is of the old variety and it takes a deal of perseverance and bloody-mindedness on her part to get the tumblers to move.

Annoyed at the sight of the cigarette hanging from Maria's bottom lip like she's Rizzo from Grease, she snatches it from her sister's mouth. She steers her sister through the open door and the headlights are switched off.

Maria isn't interested in tea or talking about their debacle of an evening. She's cut her losses, shoved in earplugs and gone to bed. Janey, too, knows she'll need to resort to earplugs again tonight, something the boys supplied them with early on.

At first, Janey didn't know what it was she was being handed, contained as they were in a small box. Now she wouldn't be without them. The music isn't loud enough you can hear the lyrics, but the bass beat and the general hubbub of conversation is hard to ignore. Add to this the occasional squeal of laughter and sleep isn't made easy.

Her sister tucked up in bed, makeup probably still on, Janey wonders what she'll do with the rest of her evening. It isn't late, just after nine o'clock. Still hyped up about the evening, and the adrenaline of the taxi ride home, sleep is the last thing on her mind. One thing she's doing is take all the damned makeup off. Here's hoping her half-full bottle of baby oil will be up to the task and she won't need to resort to using a butter knife.

· · ·

Her face scrubbed clean and look-at-me-boys clothes hanging in the wardrobe, Janey is dressed in loose cotton pants and a T-shirt that double as sleepwear. She settles into the large couch in the living room, picking up the newspaper to see what's on telly. Reruns and documentaries? Do they want to force people out of the house? She tosses the paper on the coffee table in disgust before looking idly around the room. Her gaze lands on the bottle of Uncle Luca's rocket fuel sitting on the sideboard; she knows exactly how she'll get to sleep.

Cosying back into the pillows propped against her headboard, she holds her small glass out and toasts her bedroom. "Here's to the future Mrs Perry Comb-Over!"

She gulps the entire glass in one go. It burns her throat before landing in an explosive heap in the bottom of her stomach.

The second doesn't hurt so much.

The third doesn't hurt at all.

She turns the bedside lamp off and waits for sleep to claim her, then remembers her earplugs. She's doing her best to scrunch them up enough to stay in her ears when she hears noises from downstairs. Bumps in the night in this building aren't unusual although they tend to be of the bump-and-grind variety, except these noises aren't from the bar. They're from the door at the bottom of the stairs and they stand out amongst the laughing, squealing and bed-rattling base notes.

It's too early for it to be either Gary or Brian.

Holy heck, did I lock the door?

7

Janey mentally retraces her steps from when they'd jumped out of the taxi, to propelling Maria through the door and up the stairs. There's a blank when it comes to taking the key out of the lock. It's a sobering thought. She throws the blankets to one side, the amount of swaying when she gains her feet suggests she's sober in thought only.

Zig-zagging to the bedroom door, she pauses long enough to take an antique bed-warmer off the wall. The thing is original to the building and already battered enough, she's sure Gary and Brian won't mind her adding a few more dings.

Holding it in her right hand, she presses her ear against the solid wood door that's all that separates her from the landing at the top of the stairs. The problem is, with her ear so firmly jammed against the wood, she can't hear much at all.

Janey's never thought of herself as brave, but it won't stop her from opening the door enough to see what's going on. Leaning the bed-warmer against the dresser next to her, she uses both hands to open the door as slowly and quietly as she can.

On her side in this endeavour is Gary's obsessiveness when it comes to the maintenance of the old property. The hinges have been well cared for and oiled over the years. The door opens soundlessly.

Opening it a sliver, Janey peers through the gap and over the balustrade into the darkness below. Leaning to the side, she fumbles around until she grips the handle of the bed-warmer. Her ears straining, she listens for anything out of place and is rewarded with the unmistakable sound of the stairs creaking.

Janey has never understood the weird saying about your heart being in your mouth. Now, she's close to choking on hers. Risking a peek through the gap by the hinges, she makes out an intruder in the gloom, the height and wide shoulders pointing to it being a male.

He stops on the landing, as though to get his bearings, before disappearing into the living room without so much as a squeaky board giving away his location. Him sneaking back out onto the landing without the TV or stereo, tells Janey this isn't a burglary. He's now gliding along the dark landing in her direction.

She suspects when he sees her bed is empty, he'll move on. She stops, dead. *Maria's in the next bedroom!*

Her heart goes into overdrive when he sneaks into her room, a slab of wood all that separates them. Maria's virtue might be at stake if she doesn't intervene: a primordial part of Janey yammers to come out and play.

After counting off what she hopes are the correct

number of footsteps, she eases the door shut. She then introduces the bed-warmer to the back of the intruder's head with a satisfying and very loud *boing*!

This melodious note is followed by him groaning and collapsing in a heap half on the bed. Dropping the bed-warmer on the floor with a clatter, she puts her shoulder against his bulk, and shoves hard enough to have him rolling onto his back.

Flicking on the lamp so she can tie him up before getting help, she's horrified. He's the last person in the world who should be sneaking in here. But is she wracked with guilt at knocking him out?

No, she's not!

She's experiencing something else altogether.

On top of her worry about clobbering a police officer with an antique is the errant thought that Bertolino is even better looking when he's not grilling her. His breaking-in like this, means she's about to undertake some interrogation of her own. She's watched the cop shows with her dad. She knows he's supposed to knock and show a warrant.

He groans again, and worrying he's about to come to, she hurries over to the dresser to grab makeshift bindings. It's while tying his feet to the railing at the bottom of the cast-iron bed with pantyhose, she notices the handcuffs clipped to his belt.

How handy.

Both feet securely, she moves onto his hands, pausing. What on earth is she meant to do now? There's only one set of handcuffs, the aim of them being to lock up bad guys, not naughty ones. In the end, she handcuffs his right hand to the head of the bed, hoping he's not left-handed.

He's trussed up like a Sunday roast before reality kicks in. She hasn't thought this through. He didn't give her the opportunity. And his being here on his own doesn't make sense at all. Shouldn't he be with his partner? Shouldn't they have knocked on the door like regular policemen?

She understands he saw her at the club and took the opportunity to follow her and Maria. It doesn't make his actions legal, and if it's okay for him to break the law, then it's okay for her. Taking Polaroids of Salami Boy in compromising positions had worked a treat. At least until he'd tried to track them down.

If she threatens to put the Polaroids of Bertolino on the bulletin board at the nearest cop shop, he won't dare show his face again. Will he? She and Maria can continue their search for potential husbands. Even a date with someone halfway eligible might have her mother and the Perry Comb-Over attack dogs backing off.

Her mind made up, Janey loosens Bertolino's brown and orange tie enough to slip it over his head. Next, she undoes every button she can find, spreading the flared collar of his white silk shirt wide and sucking on the inside of her cheeks.

Whoa!

There's not much else she can loosen without untying him and with the amount of groaning going on, it's not a risk she's prepared to take. Here's hoping there are enough condiments in the kitchen for this to show up properly on camera. It's got to look like he's into kinky stuff and not simply basted and ready to barbeque.

· · ·

Loaded with the weirdest assortment of sauces and kitchen paraphernalia she could find, Janey's brought up short in her bedroom. He's conscious, making this a lot harder. Gritting her teeth, she walks jerkily to the bedside table and drops all her goodies in a heap before tidying them, conscious of being watched by a strangely silent Bertolino.

Without warning, his delicious mouth transforms from a grim line into a broad grin and she drops the parcel tape like it's hot. Forgetting the items, she stands rigid at the side of the bed.

"You asked for this. I know my rights and you being here is illegal. My clobbering you was self-defence." Janey pauses for breath, something she's in desperate need of as she looks down at him.

Bertolino doesn't appear in the least worried by her accusations. "I don't need a warrant if I think a member of the public is in imminent danger." He stares past her and out into the gloom of the hallway.

Janey swings away from the bed, following his gaze. Did he follow someone in here?

"Danger? What danger?" Janey tip toes across the room and peers into the dark of the landing. She strains to hear movement. There's nothing. She can't pick up anything. Wait, what? First he sneaks in and now he's telling lies? Is he serious?

She stomps back over and stands next to the bed. "Why are you here? And where's your warrant?"

"Do I need a warrant?"

He's asked while scanning her body in a manner that has a flush spreading from her very core to every extremity, and then some. If this is all it takes to have her knees close to giving out, what's she going to be like when she takes the next step?

She's about to find out.

Scanning the items on her dressing table, she licks her lips in concentration. What'll have the most impact? Does it even matter what she smears across his chest? *Surely, the main damage will be for him to be seen as having been trussed up using his own handcuffs?* It's hardly a good look for a cop.

Decision made, she grabs the squishy plastic tomato-shaped sauce bottle, and holding it above his chiselled, manly, gorgeous… Janey breathes raggedly before squeezing the bottle, hard.

In a single, splattering squirt, he's transformed from the hero on a romance novel cover, to a murder victim. In hindsight, mayonnaise might have been better. She remedies the issue, using a spatula to spread the gloop wide and mixing it with the sauce until it's bright pink in hue. Seeing him opening his mouth to speak, she smears the remainder of the mix across his mouth, gluing his words in place.

Catching her gaze, he flicks his tongue out and runs it first over his bottom lip and then his top, excruciatingly slowly, causing unfamiliar sensations to flood her body. *Oh, my.* He winks at her, and she wishes she'd hit him harder.

Getting Salami Boy drunk and hog-tied was easy compared to this. All she and Maria needed to do was cheat at strip poker while forcing glass after glass of Uncle Luca's rocket fuel down his willing throat.

It does give Janey another idea, though. Marching around to the other bedside table, she pours Bertolino a glass of the high-octane brew.

"Are you sure you want to do this?" Bertolino's words sound loud, even with the thump of music from downstairs.

Pondering the question, Janey's unable to think of a better option. "Yes. Yes, I am" Holding the small glass next to his lips, she hopes he'll drink it without her having to force it on him. The last thing she needs is for him to choke and force her into mouth-to-mouth.

Again, that damned tongue of his flicks out and tastes what she's offering. Her body responds, leaving her well out of her depth. On the bright side, he likes the taste of the brew and lifts his head, allowing her to carefully pour it in. She gets six more glasses into him, before his eyes glaze over.

Lightweight.

Not until he's snoring like a freight train does she gets up the nerve to undo his constraints. She then strips him down to a pair of startlingly white y-fronts. It's not the first time she's been this close to a good-as-naked man. It is, however, the first time she's been this close to a good-as-naked man she's attracted to. Seeing Salami Boy naked after they'd tricked him into stripping had done nothing for her.

She's clipping his right hand back to the bed with the handcuffs when he rolls over. He grabs her with his left hand and pulls her hard against his chest. The tomato sauce and mayonnaise squishes between them.

"And what do you think you're up to, miss?"

His lips are close enough that his words tickle her face.

"But... but... but you were out cold!" Janey struggles to get out of his grip, but other than spreading the mayonnaise and tomato sauce even farther, nothing else happens. Unless you count her heartbeat and body temperature both ratcheting up a notch.

"*Pfffft.* I grew up sneaking Filuferru at family

weddings and funerals. My grandmother could cope with this stuff."

"Then why did you drink it? Why did you pretend to be unconscious?" Janey has another go at escaping his iron grip, earning her a sharp smack on the bum that's fast enough he doesn't lose his hold of her.

"I wanted to see where it was going," he says, leaving his hand on her bum. "I've gotta say, I'm enjoying the direction of things so far."

He squeezes her bum, and it's more than she can deal with. If her mother knew what she was up to, she'd throw a fit. If anyone else knew, even Perry Comb-Over wouldn't go near her.

She doubles her efforts to escape and is surprised when his cheeky grin flips to a grimace and the colour leaches out of his face, leaving him looking distinctly Scandinavian. As she clambers off his lap in a jumble of knees and elbows, he looks as though he's concentrating on not throwing up. She ties his errant hand to the headboard and retrieves the parcel tape.

"Why did you believe that horrible man? What he did to our friend was awful! He's the one you should be chasing, not us!"

Janey's words catch on this last sentence and she wipes her eyes with the back of her hand to clear her vision.

He doesn't answer her question, simply saying, "I will find you."

She slaps a piece of tape she's pulled from the roll over his mouth. This stops any further words right where they are. The room is now as quiet as it'll ever get on a Saturday night. After this, the only sounds in the room are of the photos spitting out the front of the Polaroid camera and the zing of the flashbulb. Not until there are ten photos developing on the dresser does Janey stop.

"If I find out you're following us, these photos will be sent to your superior." She has no idea who this is, but it can't be that hard to find out. *Can it?*

Packing in a flurry–but for her getaway outfit–Janey ignores the grumbling and near-naked Bertolino as best she can. Unfortunately, her eyes have other ideas, and she catches his gaze more often than she'd like. This leaves her in no doubt tied up is the best option for this Italian stallion.

Her sister's dead to the world with earplugs shoved deep inside her ears, allowing Janey to pack for Maria without waking her. Their departure is paused only long enough for the younger girl to stand at the end of Janey's bed. She glares at the good-as-naked cop before screaming, "I hate you!"

A taxi ride into the city takes them to a hotel they'd never consider if it wasn't for the one night. Expensive is an understatement, making the minibar off-limits in a big way. They do however help themselves to all the toiletries and even the disposable shower caps. They've got to get their money's worth somehow, although they balk at stealing the towels. Both sets of rosary beads now missing in action, courtesy of their various moves, it's a step too far.

Without a newspaper, they have no way of knowing the times of trains the following morning. They request a wake-up call for a disgustingly early hour, to ensure they're on the first available train out of Melbourne.

It's not how Janey wants to depart the city. Truth

be told, she doesn't want to depart at all, and knowing what's facing her at the other end of this journey, dread settles low in her abdomen.

8

The train journey home is completed in silence, each of them lost to their thoughts. Janey watches the passing landscape, noting the houses thinning out and the flora and fauna shrinking away from the harsh environment. After the green of Melbourne, home will be barren indeed.

Their journey unplanned, there's no one to meet them at the station. They haven't discussed what they'll say to their parents about why they're home early, and on a Sunday morning, too. Still, maybe this is a good thing. Thanks to the hijinks they've gotten up to over the last week, Maria has a lot to get off her chest. The priest won't know what's hit him.

Closing the door of the phone booth behind her, Janey unclips her wallet and selects a coin. She holds it up and looks at it before sliding it into the slot and dialling home. She's still dithering over the many options she's considered, when her mother answers, panicked. Anyone phoning on a Sunday morning must be in trouble.

"Hi, Mama, it's me."

She doesn't have the chance to say anything further, with her mother going into a full-on panic as to what must be wrong. Listing calamity after calamity, her mother continues until they've escalated to the point of World War III. Her mother pauses to search for more horrors and Janey slides in a few more words.

"Mama, stop, we're fine! We're at the station. Can someone come get us?"

Her mother goes from panicked to suspicious. "Why are you home early? You weren't due for another three weeks. I've written it on the calendar in the kitchen. What have you girls been up to?"

Why, oh, why is Janey surprised? Maybe, deep down, she isn't. Her mother isn't stupid. For her and Maria to think they could turn up early like this and get away with is what's stupid.

Janey knows she's rambling when she lists the reasons for them coming home early, but is unable to stop herself. She lists every one she's thought of during the journey home, and in so doing, makes a lie of all of them. She runs out of words.

"We'll collect you on the way to Mass." Her mother's tone is cold enough for goose bumps to erupt up all over Janey's body.

Exiting the phone booth, she doesn't say anything to Maria.

Maria's shoulders droop. "Oh, heck!"

Sitting on the wooden bench at the front of the station, they discuss where they go to from here, apart from Mass. No decisions are made before their parents turn up. No jolly homecoming here. Their father gets out of the car without engulfing them in a bear hug as is his usual practice. He takes their suitcases and stows them in the boot, slamming it with a finality that's telling. *This is bad.* Able to do no wrong in his eyes, they can usually count on him to side with them against their mother,.

Much as they don't want to, they climb into the back of the car and it's every bit as awful as Janey thought it would be. Sitting behind her father, she tries to make herself as small as possible, not even attempting to say hello to her mother. As a tactic, it doesn't work. Her mother twists around in her seat, spearing first Maria and then her with a look that makes her wish she was even smaller.

The following week is hell. Even convincing their mother they're still 'intact' does nothing to lessen the woman's fury. If they hear it once, they hear it a million times, "I told your father your trip to Melbourne was a bad idea."

Adding to this misery is Perry Comb-Over being invited to dinner twice during the week. The first time is such an unmitigated disaster that Janey manages to fake a stomach bug for his second appearance. Instead, she spends the evening on her bed, flipping through the photos of Anthony Bertolino like a stop-motion movie.

By Friday night, Janey is suffering from a severe case of cabin fever. Their mother hasn't allowed them to leave the grounds since they got home from Mass on Sunday morning.

Even around the house, she's kept such a close eye on them. They haven't even been allowed to phone any of their friends, or even their enemies.

It is, therefore, a surprise when, on Saturday morning at breakfast, their mother announces they'll be attending Bella Carrino's wedding that afternoon. Perhaps the biggest surprise is the girl wasn't even seeing anyone when they left for Melbourne a mere five months earlier. If Janey were to sniff hard enough, she suspects she'd be able to detect the faintest whiff of gunpowder.

Maria stuffs her mouth with another piece of toast. "Who's she marrying?"

Her mother's brow knots; Janey leans closer.

"Sergeant Colaneri's boy." Their mother's lips tighten with disapproval.

Great! They escape house-arrest and it's to an event bound to be crawling with cops. Janey senses another tummy bug coming on while Maria sits frozen, her piece of toast jammed in her mouth, but no chewing going on.

They're relieved when their parents leave them to finish their breakfast and do the washing up. Her hands deep in the soapy water, Janey turns to Maria, who's ready with a tea towel. "I can't believe Bella ended up with him! Talk about opposites attracting."

"It was only a matter of time until someone snagged him."

Janey understands the look of disappointment the girl is wearing. While the groom might not be the greatest catch, he's the best on offer in their town. For him to be off the market, has any remaining produce looking well and truly shop-soiled. She'd like to tell her sister there will be other guys, but she can't do so with conviction. The gene pool in their town is only suitable for paddling.

· · ·

Janey doesn't bother arguing over the outfit selected by her mother for her to wear to the wedding. While her wardrobe might be full of beautiful dresses she'd bought in Melbourne, her mother has selected something that screams 'Little House on the Prairie'. It's the social equivalent of a chastity belt, ensuring she's off-limits to anyone with a modicum of taste. Even Aunty Fina, the chaperone from hell, pales by comparison when it comes to suppressing libidos.

The ceremony is beautiful, if strained, further adding to the impression this isn't a match made in heaven but rather between the sheets.

Janey and Maria's parents bundle them off to the church early and they sit in the row right behind the immediate family. They're well aware of being looked at and talked about by those behind. The girls in town will have labelled them 'failures' for coming home early without a man apiece, something they'd boasted they'd do before their departure.

There's no need to drive to the reception, it's being held in the church hall next door, again smacking of a rushed affair. The speeches are interminable and as boring as it's possible to get. Friends and family scramble for the right words to hide the fact the bride had no choice but to marry her groom.

The atmosphere loosens after they cut the cake and the band strikes up for the married couple's first dance. Never has Janey seen such a miserable pair. Although, if her mother has her way, she knows she'll be fighting for supremacy with Perry.

No sooner has the thought dropped to the pit of her stomach, than the man himself pops up next to her, asking her to dance. And this before the married couple has even finished their turn on the floor. *What an idiot.* There's no avoiding him though, and it's with reluctance she places her hand on his and takes to the floor before the opening bars of the second song.

They're dancing to the fifth song in a row before it dawns on her he won't let her sit. He's too scared she'll be claimed by someone else. She has noticed there are a few out-of-towners amid the wedding guests and even a few who aren't wearing wedding rings.

Ouch! He's trodden on her foot–again. Studying her scuffed shoes and doing her best to swallow another grimace of pain, she sees a guy walk up behind him.

Perry stumbles to a stop, managing to step on her other foot in the process. She'll be lucky not to lose most of her toenails at this rate.

"I'll cut in, if I may?"

Perry yanks his hands off her like she's diseased and Janey looks to see who's saved her. *No!* She'd rather be trampled to a pulp by Comb-Over than dance with his replacement.

Her would-be fiancé storms off the dance floor, leaving her alone, except that is, for Detective Inspector Bertolino. The surrounding noise dies in Janey's ears to be replaced by buzzing. Her vision dances while she remains frozen.

Why, oh why, didn't she leave the photos with Gary or Brian in Melbourne? She can hardly send them to Bertolino's superior when she's locked up.

He claims her nerveless fingers with his own and wraps his other arm tight behind her back, pulling her closer than her mother would approve of. But better this than collapsing in a heap at his feet as she was about to. This close to his chest, she sees it naked in her mind's eye.

Why is it so hot in here?

Quickly, she twigs he doesn't know a soul at the wedding. He's here for one reason and one reason alone. They've been around the dance floor three times without him once standing on her feet, before he speaks to her, "I told you I'd find you. You didn't think I'd let you walk out, leaving me like that, did you?"

Janey leans close to him, ignoring as best she can the hammering of her heart. "Please don't arrest me in here. My mother would never forgive me."

His response is to burst out laughing, drawing the attention of the surrounding couples. Janey's struggling with what he finds so funny when he brings them to a stop next to the wide-open double doors. These lead to the small graveyard in the shadow of the church.

Safely out of the hall and having followed the small path around to the side of the church, Janey hold her hands out. She's got her palms up, in supplication, ready for him to apply the cuffs. Closing her eyes, she waits for the touch of the cold steel that will put an end to life as she knows it. Her mother will be distraught.

Will Perry wait for five to ten years? She hopes not, although chances of him getting a date while she's inside are slim at best.

The detective takes one of her hands in his. Only when his lips press hotly against her palm does she dare open her eyes. *What?*

"But, aren't you arresting me?"

Bertolino chuckles again. "What for?"

Janey is about to list her and Maria's many misdemeanours when she pauses. Not the brightest thing to admit your wrongdoings to a cop. "What about the accusations made by Salami…" Janey chokes on her words, before continuing, "that Greek guy?"

"Ah, yes, about him. He dropped the charges when he was arrested for dognapping and extortion."

Dognapping? Extortion? Janey dwells on this for a second before getting her mind back on track. "But what about, ah…" Janey waves at his chest to put into words what she'd done to him.

"Hmmm. Now that you are going be punished for." His chocolate brown eyes darken further, forcing her to close her own against the onslaught.

His lips have claimed hers in a searing kiss when she hears a gasp from behind.

"Guillerlmina Christina Russo, you stop what you're doing this minute!"

Janey may hear her mother, but she's powerless to comply with the woman's wishes. Her mother's hand on her shoulder has Janey dragging her lips reluctantly away from the detective's. It's impossible to ignore the power of someone who's spent years hand-washing underpants,

"Ah, Mama, this is…" Janey's words die before she can get his official title out.

"Anthony," says the detective.

"Bertolino." Finishes her mother, leaving both Janey and Anthony with their mouth's hanging open. "You're the spitting image of your father."

Seeing the faraway look in her mother's eyes, Janey stares at her in disbelief. "Please tell me we're not related!" She crosses every finger on both hands.

He mother looks first at Janey and then Anthony. "Not yet!"

As fast as she's come upon them, she spins on her

heel and hastens in the direction of the church–most likely to book it.

Stepping behind her, Anthony runs a single finger down the back of Janey's neck. "Now, where were we?"

Unable to think, let alone speak, her whole being fills with lightning when he turns her and carries on from where he'd left off.

THE END

Maid IN CHELSEA

Cleaning for the rich sure
beats a relationship
that sucks.

Andrene Low

1

London - England

This isn't how Vivienne planned her life. Some parts are bang on, while others are unmitigated disasters. Take Kenny. At the outset, he'd looked so good and was her experiment of going 'down market'.

How soon his rock hard abs had softened, along with the rest of him. The only thing hard about him these days is his attitude towards her.

She isn't so much beaten; as browbeaten. Worn down over the preceding seven years and never able to meet Kenny's exacting standards. The longer he's unemployed, the higher these standards become, until she isn't sure there's anything she can do to be deemed successful in his eyes. His meals are too hot, too cold, late. The house is untidy, too tidy and full of tat.

The litany of perceived sins is endless.

One bright spot in her life is her students, not that she ever talks to Kenny about them. If he had any idea how much she loves being a teacher, he'd find some way of spoiling it for her.

No, she'll happily fake lousy days at work and feral kids to keep him in the dark. He'll never know that her hours in the classroom are all that's helping her keep it together.

Looking out at her students, she waits until she has their attention, well as much as is possible at three o'clock on a Friday. "Right, class. Don't forget our field trip to the Museum of London on Monday. If you haven't already given me one, make sure you bring a note from mum or dad to say it's okay. Oh, and don't forget your lunch and some money for the tube."

The other teachers looked at her like she was bonkers when she'd first talked about taking her pint-sized league of nations on an outing into the city. "It'll be like herding cats," was the most popular refrain, followed closely by "You'll lose half of them, mark my words." It was the second sentiment, uttered with such glee that told Vivienne how much her fellow teachers loathed kids.

Sure, her lot can be a challenge at times, ranging as they do from recent arrivals from warmer climes, right through to the 'wide boys' in training from East London. She doesn't need to worry about those ruffians unless it's them nicking stuff from the museum gift shop.

And if they become separated from the group, they'll no doubt make it home in better time than Vivienne and the rest of the class. That they'd more than likely 'borrow' a car for the trip is her biggest concern.

At seven and eight years, they're too short to reach the accelerator, let alone the brakes. However, Viv isn't naïve enough to think this won't stop them from giving it a whirl.

As expected, the class empties like a burst hot-water bottle seconds after the bell, until only a couple of nervous souls are left behind, anguish writ large on their faces. "What are you worried about, Alfred?" Such a big and regal name for so small an Indian boy, the choice of moniker testament to how strong the English influence still is on the Indian sub-continent. As always, whenever she speaks to him, he is sufficiently tongue-tied that a coherent response is ruled out.

Vivienne takes over their conversation in such a way that all he needs do is nod or shake. "Did you get your permission slip?" This is solemnly handed over. "And what about money for the tube?" He unzips his pencil case and shows her a handful of coins and even a few notes stuffed in the bottom with all the pencil shavings. There's more than enough to get him both to and from the museum, even if he wants to catch a cab. "What about lunch?"

This is when Vivienne knows she's found the sticking point. While all the other kids turn up to school with an assortment of sandwiches and junk food, Albert's mum proves herself to be a culinary whiz. The poor kid is saddled each day with a stack of stainless containers that lock together with a band that forms a handle.

There are never less than three courses and consuming those takes up most of his lunch break. This is in comparison to his classmates gaily stuffing sandwiches in their gobs in between running around and screaming.

"You know, you've got enough money there that you could buy a sandwich if you wanted. It could be our secret." Okay, so Vivienne isn't as altruistic as she's making out. Better to get the boy onto the tube without a high-rise of oily Indian cuisine than have to deal with it out in the real world.

She answers questions from the other Nervous Nelly before getting on with tidying her classroom in readiness to head home for the weekend. She's wiping the blackboard clean with a damp cloth when Gareth Jones, upper school maths and science, pops his head through the door. "What on earth did you say to Albert Chaudhary? The boy just skipped down the hallway."

"Hah, told him we'd leave the Tandoori Tower of Doom behind on the field trip and buy a sandwich for lunch instead."

"Excellent, bags first dibs on his lunch." Gareth doesn't bother waiting for a response, taking it as a given and leaving Vivienne to finish up.

Spinning out the tidy-up, Viv is still careful not to tarry too long. If she's late home with Kenny's Friday-night Chinese, her weekend will be hell from beginning to end, rather than hell in places.

One plus is that the Chinese restaurant is near the station at the other end of her journey. She used to have a car, but Kenny said she needed to sell it to help fund their lifestyle after he hurt his back badly enough he couldn't work.

It didn't take her long to see that maintaining their lifestyle involved him buying the biggest telly he could find, and one where the screen had miraculously remained intact when it fell off the back of the lorry.

Even more miraculous was how he'd managed to carry this monster into the house without help. There'd been no point asking where the rest of the funds went, with his dire case of brewer's droop clearly identifying the recipient as the pub on the corner.

Viv's relieved to step straight onto a tube for home rather than waiting, something that could have made her late. Likewise, there's no slowing in her journey when she swings by the Flying Dragon, her usual order already stacked and waiting on the counter. Also as per routine, she hands over a ten pound note and gets exact change in return.

Rather than put the coins back in her purse she slides them into the pocket of coat, only to be retrieved so she can drop them through the letter slot in her neighbour's door.

"I'm home." Viv doesn't need to announce this, but it doesn't stop her. Better to let Kenny know her whereabouts. He doesn't like surprises, something she's learned the hard way.

The only response is a sleepy grunt from the general direction of the sitting room; Viv imagines the arse-shaped dent in the couch already. She'll be lucky if he manages to drag himself upright for dinner, preferring to lie in splendour and eat with his hands 'like the natives'.

Unfortunately, any resemblance to the natives ends there. Viv knows from watching her students eat that they don't end up with food smeared all over them.

And especially not on a filthy singlet that's deemed acceptable attire for dining at home. Only by studiously keeping her eyes glued to the telly is Viv able to eat her meal with any semblance of appetite.

The plastic bag of takeaway containers balanced precariously on the hall table, Viv ditches her trench coat and handbag, slinging them over the newel post on the stairs to save time.

As per routine she nips through to the kitchen, levers all the tops free and slaps them down higgledy-piggledy on a tray. Kenny is all about self-serve, even if half the time he doesn't bother with the plate she gives him, preferring to eat straight from the containers. Doesn't he know how hard it is to get sweet and sour sauce out of Axminster carpet?

"It's about effing time. I'm starved." Kenny stabs his finger at the small coffee table next to the couch, indicating Viv should put his tray there and be bloody quick about it.

As tempting as it is to smash the tray over his head, she puts it down on the china cabinet and sets about clearing the coffee table of empty beer bottles.

Having tidied up after dinner, Viv feigns a headache caused by "those snot-nosed kids she's unlucky enough to be saddled with" and heads for bed. She's not tired, but going to bed and losing herself in a book is bliss. Better this than being stuck in the sitting room with Kenny farting loudly in response to the spicy food he's hoovered his way through.

Viv knows from experience that by ten o'clock, the atmosphere in the front room will be toxic, although never enough to asphyxiate him, unfortunately.

Tonight is different. She's not even a couple of pages into her book when she hears Kenny on the stairs. Her stomach knots in response. Surely he won't try for sex tonight. All it does is make him angry.

Kenny grabs Viv around the throat, yanking her face inches from his. "You useless slag. You being built like a bloke, that's what screws up big Kenny." He shoves her away as though she's a piece of dirt, further reinforcing this with more spit-laden invective.

If this wasn't enough, he jams his foot in the middle of her back and shunts her out of bed. Actual physical violence is a step-up even for Kenny and she tumbles off the mattress, landing hard on her hands and knees.

"You effing bitch, if ya can't get me hard, ya can sleep on the sodding couch."

Yet again Kenny having as much substance as a piece of fried fish left in the steamer for too long is all her fault. He used to like her height and smaller breasts; now he's using them as an excuse for his lack of performance. Faced with yet another night on a couch still infused with the smell of second-hand chow mein, Viv snaps.

She hoped to have more time to prepare, but if she waits any longer, she risks being hurt far worse than tonight's bumps and bruises. Her biggest disappointment will be letting her students down on Monday.

But, if she's getting out, it's now or never and the break needs to be a clean one. All going well Kenny will be comatose before eight o'clock tonight and so this is as good a time as any to escape.

There's no way she can get dressed with him

watching her through slit eyes. The jig would be up then. Instead she grabs her dressing gown off the end of the bed and scurries out of the room as though to do his bidding.

She has no intention of spending another night on their lumpy, stinky couch. Instead she makes her way downstairs and out to the small laundry in the converted coal shed. A quick rummage through the dirty washing has her in possession of a skirt and blouse that will pass muster, just, likewise a bra and knickers.

Back in the hallway she wastes no time dressing, before grabbing her coat off the newel post and shrugging into it. She then buttons it up tight and belts it even tighter. Thank goodness she didn't think to take her coat and handbag upstairs as she usually would.

Viv still has her hand on the highly polished brass knocker on her neighbour's front door when it swings soundlessly open. "I've been expecting you, love. It's time."

That Cecily, her elderly neighbour, has been privy to her and Kenny's 'lovemaking' comes as no surprise. The walls are paper-thin, allowing cold drafts and whispered conversations to find their way through with equal ease. They don't stand a chance when faced with Kenny's spleen-ridden coupling.

Viv waits on the footpath that's right next to the front door rather than follow her neighbour into the narrow hallway. There she sways gently and hugs herself tight in a futile attempt to stop her trembling.

This isn't down to the chill of the evening, but rather a fear of the unknown.

Cecily is soon back and handing over the small suitcase Viv has left there. She's taken months filling it with charity shop finds rather than risk packing her own clothes. Anything to lessen the chance of Kenny noticing her usually meagre wardrobe is even thinner on the rail.

"Are you sure you won't stay here tonight, love?" says her neighbour, grabbing a bulging fabric pouch off the bottom step. She hands this over to Viv, with the coins inside rattling reassuringly.

Viv hefts this into her purse, causing the shoulder straps to drag in protest. "I think it's best I get as far away as possible." She's going to have to be a lot further away from Kenny than next door when he wakes in the morning. "Have you got the letters?"

"Oh. Oh, yes, I have." Cecily collects a bundle of letters from the drawer of a small table that sits snugly against one wall of the hallway.

Viv slides these into her oversized shoulder bag and gives Cecily a tight hug. "I'll be in touch."

Looking up at the smart hotel, Viv worries about paying to stay here. While she has the funds, thoughts of handing over all that coinage in the morning make her redden in anticipation. She'll look like she's robbed a piggy bank, thanks to all change from Chinese takeaways over the preceding months. Kenny spending everything she earns —plus his stipend from the government—it's been hard to scrape together the little she has. It's enough for a few nights in a genteel establishment like this, but only just.

She hopes it's not so genteel they'll balk at a single woman checking in at nine on a Friday night. Even though it's 1980 and women's rights have come a long way since the sixties, there's still oh so far still to go in some neighbourhoods. Weirdly it appears the well-to-do neighbourhoods have farther to go than most.

2

*N*ot since she was fresh out of teachers' training college, has Viv been this nervous. The night porter is everything you'd expect in a private hotel of this nature. He's uniformed, entitled and scary as hell. Looking at her over the top of his pince-nez glasses, she knows he's found her sub-par.

Never mind her dirty clothes are hidden by her tightly-belted coat, a woman not sporting a wedding ring, who's travelling alone and only carrying one battered suitcase, is not their usual clientele.

"A conference, you say?"

"That's right." Viv tries to sound confident, but even with this two-word reply, her voice breaks, popping up an octave and firmly labelling her a liar. Teachers are so much better at euphemisms than out-and-out lies: "Tim can be a challenging pupil and needs to remain focused in class to achieve his full potential."

Better this than the truth: "Tim is a conniving little

toe-rag and the world would be a better place if you'd used a condom seven years ago."

"There are no double rooms vacant." He slams the large, dark green register closed with a finality that has Viv's shoulders drooping in defeat.

She thinks for a moment. *Oh my goodness, he thinks she needs a double because...*

Pulling herself up to her full height, Viv bristles with indignation. "I'm after a single room." Her nostrils flare, but there's nothing she can do about it. Never mind she couldn't afford a double even if one was on offer. A quick glance at the prices listed in a small gilt-frame perched on the front desk has already let her know it's a single, or nothing.

He examines her minutely before slowly re-opening the register. He then runs his finger down a worryingly large number of columns. "We do have a single available. How many nights are you staying?"

The simple question is once again loaded and as much as Viv would like to reply "one night", she knows she can't. "I'd like to book in for the full week, please."

While she might be quaking in her boots about shelling out this much money, she has at least wiped the look of mistrust off his face. She'll be okay, so long as he doesn't demand payment upfront.

Viv doesn't relax until she's safely in her room under the eaves. To call the room a single is generous; she suspects the hostelry term for it is demi-chambre. Despite it being the cheapest on offer, she's honestly been expecting something larger than this glorified broom cupboard.

On the plus side, the single bed is neat and clean and—most attractive of all—doesn't have a drunken and snoring Kenny sprawled across it. The bathroom is along the hall. It's far enough away that she won't hear other guests using it, yet close enough it won't be a mission to use it herself.

The bathroom, much like her room, is also small and clean. She locks the door, delighted to be able to brush her teeth without gagging on the stench of Kenny's most recent bowel movement. She'd even taken to brushing her teeth at the kitchen sink to avoid that poisonous cloud.

Her bedtime routine is also different from usual. The biggest change is having her alarm clock on the bedside table rather than out in the hallway. She learned early on in her relationship with Kenny that he isn't a morning person.

Unfortunately, it took longer to realise he isn't that great in the afternoon or evening either. Peeling the tape away from the back of the alarm clock, she removes the small key stuck there. She slots it into the keyhole and turns it while thinking long and hard about what time to set the alarm.

There's bound to be a queue for the bathroom in the morning, her fellow guests keen to get on with seeing the sights. She settles for 5:00 a.m., doubting many others will be out and about this early on a Saturday. It's early even for her, but better to be washed and dressed and out of the hotel before anyone else is about.

Sleep doesn't come easily, her mind a swirling mire of worry. Will she get a job outside of teaching? Where will she live? Will Kenny find her?

Scant hours later, her alarm clock bellows its way to life, like a newborn, only louder. Exhausted, her eyes gritty, Viv wants to do nothing more than slam her hand on top of the clock, roll over and go back to sleep. Unfortunately, it's not a luxury she can indulge in.

Throwing back the covers, she's on her feet before her body's ready for it abd forced to put a hand against the wall in order to remain upright. All too rapidly, her worries reacquaint themselves with the pit of her stomach and any hesitation on her part is burned away with acid.

Following a quick flannel wash, Viv dons her outfit from the night before. Even though it's grubby, it's better than most of her op shop finds. Until she's had time to visit a laundromat to rid them of the smell of mothballs, these are strictly off limits.

Viv scurries through Reception, without slowing. Dropping her key on the front desk she determinedly avoids eye contact with the night porter. Anything is better than him grilling her as to why she's out and about so early on a Saturday morning.

Not far from the hotel, she spots a red pillar box. Stopping next to it, she drags the bundle of letters out of her handbag and sorts through them. She then posts letters to the few friends who've stuck by her and even the local police station. This way if Kenny does report her missing—when he runs out of food or money—the police will know she doesn't want to be found.

The final letter she posts is to her mother in Edinburgh. Better to explain everything in a letter than phone her up and be stuck with ten minutes of "I told you he was a bad egg." The letter will also be the first contact with her mum in over two years.

The decline in their relationship had been gradual and mostly due in part to Kenny considering Viv's mum to be an 'interfering old biddy'. He'd been right of course, with her mum stressing all his bad points and urging her to come home as a sign off to every phone call.

It wasn't that Kenny was privy to these conversations, but rather that he'd use any excuse to isolate Viv, the better to control her. She can see that now, of course and so doesn't need her mum pointing it out in excruciating detail.

The last letter she holds is for the headmistress of her school. There's no stamp on the envelope because some news is better delivered in person, or at least faster than the Royal Mail is capable of. If she posts it, the letter won't get there until Tuesday at the soonest.

Being as it's far too early to call on Mrs Gregory, Viv's next priority is breakfast. Even though this is on offer at the hotel, a quick scan of the inflated prices had effectively killed her appetite.

Smarter to jump on the tube and head through to a suburb that's both well away from the hotel and her old neighbourhood. She's on the lookout for a greasy spoon offering a breakfast that's large and cheap. Hopefully big enough she won't need to worry about lunch.

A couple of hours and Viv is replete, albeit greasy. A quick glance at the grimy clock hanging precariously above the deep-fryer and she knows she needs to get a move on. How long will it take to get the tube to the other side of London and find Mrs Gregory's house? Not as long as she'd like with the reason for her visit being to break the news she won't be at school on Monday.

Nine on a Saturday morning is a respectable hour to visit, isn't it?

Before she can do that, she'll need to find a toilet. The two large mugs of tea she's taken her time sipping, have hit her bladder and started to trickle south. Thoughts of facing her headmistress with a full bladder have her fidgeting like a five-year-old who's forgotten to pee during recess.

Viv's hand hovers over the door knocker. *Maybe I should just shove the letter through the slot and run? It's not as if Mrs Gregory is at her best during the week, never mind on a Saturday morning.* She's still dithering when the door's opened.

"Miss Morgan?" Mrs Gregory's tone says it all.

Suitably reprimanded, Viv has trouble saying the words she's rehearsed over-and-over on the tube ride here. "I ah, ah was going to send you a letter, but ah, thought it better to deliver it myself."

It's only when she hears crinkling that Viv's aware she's taken the letter out of her handbag.

Mrs Gregory holds her hand out, beckoning for Viv to hand the missive over. Deciding this will be easier than speaking, Viv complies.

Rather than invite Viv into the house as would be polite, Mrs Gregory leaves her standing on the front step. Unable to face the headmistress when she reads the letter, Viv turns sideways to look at the garden. A gnome sits proudly with his fishing rod, amid regimentally planted roses. She doubts this is Mrs Gregory's work.

What's Mr Gregory like.

Spluttering from beside her apprises Viv that Mrs Gregory has got to the meat of the letter.

"But… you can't do this!" Mrs Gregory slaps the letter against her free hand, doing some crinkling of her own.

"I don't want to. I have too." Seeing her words fall on deaf ears, Viv's hands go to the collar of her high-necked blouse.

She's undone a good half-dozen buttons and spread her collar wide before Mrs Gregory rockets from annoyed and confused, to furious.

At first, Viv thinks the anger is directed at her. Only when the headmistress speaks does she understand.

"You'd better come in." This is reinforced by the older woman standing to the side and indicating Viv should lead the way. "Straight down the hall. We're in the conservatory."

We? Viv would prefer not to have an audience for this particular conversation.

Stopping just inside the glass room tacked onto the back of the house, Viv's senses are overwhelmed both by the perfume and colour. So varied and spectacular are the orchids perched on every flat surface that it takes her a second to spot the man slouched in a wicker chair, reading a paper.

"Norman, would you be as kind as to make another pot of tea?"

He lowers the paper and his gaze travels from Mrs Gregory over to Viv. She knows the moment he spots the bruises around her neck. He doesn't say anything, rather his eyebrows raise and he shakes his head slowly.

After folding the paper carefully and popping in into the cane magazine rack next to his chair, he slowly gets to his feet.

His patting Viv gently on the shoulder as he passes is her undoing, taking them all by surprise, especially Viv. She never loses it like this, knowing if she gave into a case of the 'vapours' around Kenny, she'd regret it.

Even more astounding is Mrs Gregory pulling Viv in for a tight, if slightly awkward, hug. This is a side of the headmistress Viv hasn't seen before, with the woman's reputation as a right harridan, extending well beyond the school gates and for good reason.

Spilling her guts is cathartic, albeit humiliating. It doesn't come easy with Mrs Gregory having to prod her on exactly what happened. Only then does Viv admit the abuse has been going on for years and escalating of late.

It's this revelation that has Mrs Gregory insisting she take a sabbatical through to the middle of the first term in the New Year. "Enough time for you to sort things out and avoid that odious man tracking you down."

It's more than Viv could have hoped for and she spends a lot of time on the tube ride back to the hotel shaking her head in disbelief. Sure she knows part of the reason Mrs Gregory has suggested a break is that she doesn't want Kenny hanging around the school.

"Who cares why, I'll take it," Viv whispers to herself. At least she can cross this off her list of worries. Far better her having a sabbatical listed on her CV than abandonment of post. A black mark if ever there was one.

Her main hurdle now is finding a temporary job, plus room and board until the middle of the first term after Christmas; long enough for Kenny to give up and move onto another meal ticket.

As the tube pulls into the next station, Viv stares vacantly at the advertisements for all things Christmas that pepper the curved wall that backs the platform. Her eyes widen on the realisation of how different this festive season will be. For the first time in years she won't have to watch Kenny stuffing himself, in between demands for more gravy and belching loudly enough to drown out the Christmas carols.

As the one responsible for all the cooking and the clean-up after, Viv loves the idea of spending this special day alone. Better this than slaving away in the kitchen for hours while his useless mother does nothing but sit around demanding more bottles of stout.

Viv smiles genuinely for the first time in a long time.

She's still smiling when she walks up the front steps of the genteel hotel.

"Someone's looking happy."

Viv's taken aback at how friendly the day porter is in comparison with his night-time counterpart.

"Ah, yes, I am. May I have the key to room 17, please?"

"Who on earth put you up..." The rest of the sentence stays put in his mouth. "We've got a nice double available on the first floor, if you prefer?"

Viv doesn't need to think long on this. While her tiny room on the top floor might not be the most salubrious on offer, it is the cheapest. "No, I love that room. The view over the rooftops is wonderful."

She knows she's been convincing enough when he hands the key over without another word.

The key safely tucked in the pocket of her coat, Viv heads towards the stairs. While there is an elevator, it's one of those glorified bird cages dating back to the 1920s and would be more at home in a museum than a hotel. Unfortunately as an exhibit.

Without her suitcase to weight her down, Viv's preference is to take the stairs. Before she can put her foot on the first step, she has a thought. Turning back towards Reception, she looks around for a phone, eventually seeing one in a half-booth at the back of the foyer.

"Do you have a Yellow Pages available?" His look of astonishment tells her this isn't a common request in these parts.

"Yes, we do. Somewhere."

He disappears beneath the counter and Viv hears things shuffled left and right with the occasional bump against the polished mahogany that fronts the unit.

"Aha. Here we are." He slaps the yellow directory on top of the counter, its front cover sporting a serious layer of dust. "Just a mo." He pulls a feather duster out and flicks it ineffectually over the cover before sliding it over the counter in Viv's direction.

Up in her room, she puts her large handbag on the bed and retrieves the snacks she purchased on the way home. It's not cordon bleu, but it will be a lot cheaper than eating in the dining room downstairs. While her room is small, she's glad it has tea and coffee-making facilities.

A quick trip to the bathroom to fill the jug and she settles in for some light research and a cuppa. Flipping the large, yellow directory open to 'Employment Agencies', she runs her finger down the columns, reading each of the small ads in turn. She's trawled through several pages before an ad jumps out.

Experience with children?

Tick.

Available for immediate start?

Tick.

Live-in positions available.

Tick.

Rummaging around in her handbag, Viv locates her small notebook. She slides the gold pen that sits snugly in the spine free, and makes a note of the name and address of the agency. It's nearby, she's just not exactly sure where. Thank goodness for the London A-Z. A quick look through its dog-eared pages and she knows where she's going first thing on Monday morning.

All that's left to do now is decide how to spend the rest of her weekend. It's the first in ages that she won't be laden down with housework courtesy of first hosting and then tidying up after Kenny's usual Saturday night session with the boys.

One thing she needs to do is visit a laundromat, even if she has to wear everything she owns in order to get past the front desk without looking likes she's doing a runner.

3

The alarm rattles to life at five on Monday morning and Viv rolls over, wishing she could go back to sleep for a couple of hours. Slamming her hand on top of it, she puts it out of *her* misery.

Rubbing her eyes goes some way towards clearing her view of the room. Her interview outfit is hanging from a hook on the back of the door; everything else remains neatly folded in her suitcase.

The outfit she's picked for her visit to the agency screams governess and so should be acceptable. It's not as though she has a lot of options.

The other thing she doesn't have much choice about is breakfast. It will be the same as dinner last night, consisting of heavy-duty rye bread with cheddar. It's filling, but not even close to appetising.

Hearing movement in the room next to hers, Viv bounds out of bed while stuffing her feet into her slippers and dragging on her dressing gown. There's no way she wants to miss first dibs in the bathroom.

She hurries down the hall with her vanity bag mere

seconds later. In her haste, she'd come close to shutting the door before realising she didn't have her key with her. The last thing she wants is to have to trail downstairs to reception to get a duplicate, dressed in her nightie.

Her ablutions are efficient. The bath, being as big as it is, if she were to fill it, it would drain every hot-water cylinder in the hotel if not the entire block. She's not about to incur the wrath of her fellow guests by doing so.

A mere two inches of water in the bottom of the bath, Viv gets in and kneels rather than sit. The cast-iron is still chilly to the touch and none to gentle on her bruised knees. She flannels all over, cleaning herself as best she can. She can't afford to take too long, with her teeth chattering thanks to the rapidly cooling water.

She's brushing her teeth when she hears boards creaking out in the hallway. When the bathroom door handle rattles urgently, Viv gets enough of a fright to jab the inside of her cheek with the toothbrush. Making short work of spitting out the toothpaste, Viv rinses her mouth and wipes the basin, before collecting her belongings and making a hasty exit.

The flinty gaze of an elderly woman who clearly thinks Viv has stolen 'her spot' escorts her all the way back to her room.

***

"With qualifications like these, why are you interested in the sort of positions we have advertised?"

Viv's been expecting this, her answer well thought out and rehearsed with Mrs. Gregory. "I'm working on a dissertation regarding the use of one-on-one tuition in the modern schoolroom. It's something I can't do while teaching full time."

"Your reference from your current principal is glowing. We'll need to ring for confirmation that it's authentic."

"Certainly," says Viv, smiling, "the phone number is on the school letterhead." Viv was surprised Mrs Gregory had gone to the trouble of writing her a reference. And one completed in longhand on school stationery at that. All of this to a background of Mr Gregory bustling around in the kitchen, making a second cup of tea. Now she's glad of it.

"Excuse me." Leaving Viv sitting there like a common criminal, the women exits the glass-fronted office to use a phone in another similarly public space. Viv's glad not to have to sit quietly by listening to a conversation where her integrity is called into question. She almost feels sorry for the woman doing so with Mrs Gregory.

The agency rep returns, her tail between her legs. She must have got both barrels from the headmistress.

"Everything's in order. Unfortunately, we don't have anything on the books at present, but we will keep you on the top of the pile for the next available position."

Viv fights to keep her spine stiff and her shoulders back. This is not what she expected, given the desperation of their advertisement. The way it's written, she anticipated the agency staff would be fighting over her, not showing her the door. Out on the footpath, she dithers. Should she go left or right? Maybe there's a Post Office nearby where she can look at the Yellow Pages again to see if there's another agency in the area?

"Miss Morgan, a word if you will?"

Viv spins to find another of the agency's staff, head poking out of the door, eyebrows raised in question.

"Yes, of course." Viv follows the woman back inside and through to an office at the rear of the agency. She hasn't even settled herself into the offered seat before the woman outlines a position that sounds perfect. Perhaps too good to be true.

"You'll have one charge. It's live-in, but you will need to start tomorrow."

"Can you tell me more about the position? Exactly where would I be living?"

"Ah." The woman flips through a folder that's full to bursting only finding what she's after at the very back. "Ah, it's in Chelsea, I think," she says, doubt evident in her reply.

Viv scrutinises the woman. It's as if this is the first time the agency staffer has seen this particular folder, strange given the sheer size of the thing. She's no closer to a conclusion when the woman upends the wodge of paper so she can read the cover sheet. That she reads the description line-for-line, again reinforcing her unfamiliarity with the position.

"You'll be looking after one boy, Quincy, plus there are some light housekeeping duties to perform." She peers at the file again, before quickly adding. "Nothing too strenuous."

Viv doesn't have any choice. "Will the interview be this afternoon?"

"No need for that. We'll start you on a temporary basis and if Mrs Harrow is happy with your performance, you may stay on."

"That sounds wonderful." Although Viv's response is positive, she smells something fishy. If she were the boy's mother, she wouldn't want some random person turning up to take care of him. Maybe the mother's as desperate as she is.

Viv leaves the agency with the paperwork completed, the address to report to the following morning tucked safely in her handbag. A quick shufty at her watch confirms it's not even ten o'clock. If she hurries, she can catch up with them. It's also close enough she can walk rather than take a bus or the tube.

She hears the kids before she sees them, their high-pitched chatter bouncing off the walls in the Museum of London. Rounding the corner, Viv is horrified to see a lot of sticky fingers touching display cases. The museum will need to invest in Windolene stocks to put things to rights after they leave.

Clapping her hands loudly ensures she has everyone's attention before she speaks. "Children, what have I told you about not touching the glass."

"Oooh, oooh." A small hand shoots up at the back of the gaggle of children.

"Yes, Christine?"

"Not to, miss."

Viv raises an eyebrow which is enough to have small sticky fingers pulled sharply away from what had earlier, more than likely, been pristine glass. Where on earth is the teacher Mrs Gregory's put in charge of them?

Viv had been so relieved on leaving the headmistress' home the morning after her escape to know the field trip would still be going ahead as planned, even without her in attendance.

A quick scan of the room and she spots Gareth Jones slumped on a bench towards the back of the exhibit hall. He doesn't look happy. Whether it's because he's missed out on Albert's curry lunch or that he's been roped in to look after her rambunctious charges is anyone's guess.

So lost is he in his misery that he doesn't even know she's there until she speaks.

"You look like you could do with some help."

The transformation is immediate and breathtaking. Getting to his feet, he stands tall, sucks in his small paunch and a wide smile splits his face. His "Oh, thank God!" is heartfelt.

Viv can't help smiling in response.

"Does this mean you're staying on at the school?"

Her hand strays to the scarf at her throat before she says, "I can't." She'd like to say more but worries it will have her in tears. It's not a state she wants to be in when around her students, even if they're technically not hers anymore, at least not until the New Year.

His smile falters and he sucks in some air confirming he's not going to let her away with saying nothing.

She doesn't give him a chance to speak, holding her hand up like a policeman on traffic duty. Shaking her head, she turns and flees in the direction of the children where she knows conversation will be impossible.

The rest of the morning is spent answering questions of a historic nature and avoiding Gareth at every turn. The plan for lunch is to spend it in the gardens that huddle next to the remains of the Roman wall that once enclosed the original City of London. After this, there'll be a quick look at the Barbican Centre and then home. For once the weather is on their side, although the closer they get to midday, the more Viv notices Albert fidgeting, his lunch anxiety on full alert.

Seeing him splitting away from the group to check out a cabinet crammed full of old Roman coins, Viv sidles up next to him. She reaches into her large handbag and pulls out a plastic bag, passing it over without a word.

Never have two bits of white bread, some chicken and limp tomato received such unspoken praise. His head lifts and he beams before returning to join his classmates. The small boy has a spring in his step.

"You love them, don't you?"

Viv spins to find Gareth closer than she'd like, his expression is one of bemusement.

Wandering away, she throws "What's not to love?" nonchalantly over her shoulder before being eagerly swallowed up by 'her kids'.

"Harry, if I see you throwing any more pickled onions, I'm going to be exceedingly cross." Viv holds onto her stern expression, although only just, with her laughter fighting for supremacy.

She's thankful lunch is being eaten outside, with Harry and three of his mates deciding the lunches packed by their mums are better used in the re-creation of a Roman battle. By comparison, Albert has savoured every mouthful of the sandwich Viv purchased for him after she finished at the employment agency.

Much as she tried to avoid it, Gareth has scoped out a spot right next to her on a bench sitting hard against the remains of the Roman wall. Leaning back, Viv enjoys the heat of the sun that's stored in the stone, seeping through her coat.

Unable to make her sandwich last any longer, Viv pops the last piece of bread into her mouth and screws up the wrappings. This time, Gareth isn't having a bar of it.

"The Old Dragon said you were on a leave-of-absence. You want to tell me why you didn't mention it on Friday?"

Damn, she should never have joined them here. If it'd been any of the other teachers covering for her, she'd be okay, but she and Gareth go back a long way, having gone to teachers' training college together.

They'd even dated for a short time, just long enough to end up in the sack together after one particularly riotous pub crawl. A night shrouded in mystery for Viv due to an afternoon of drinking games.

"I've been having, ah, trouble at home."

He turns sideways on the bench so that he can look at her properly. Viv, however, keeps staring straight ahead to avoid eye contact. If she looks at him, she'll lose it.

"It's that bastard Kenny, isn't it?"

"Language, Gareth," says Viv.

"Well, you give me a better title, then."

Viv can think of several, but she's not sharing those with Gareth. Settling back against the wall, Viv closes her eyes to the sun, hoping Gareth will leave her alone. She didn't sleep well last night and now she's fighting to keep her eyes open. Maybe it's because it's so warm.

Unbuttoning her coat helps, removing her scarf even more so.

That is, until she hears the sharp intake of breath from Gareth, still sitting beside her on the bench. Damn, she forgot about the bruises on her neck.

4

*E*ven on the tube with Gareth and the full complement of children, a herculean task in its own right, he's not letting it go. He continues to badger her about what the hell went on at the weekend and why she hasn't gone to the police.

Viv doesn't bother explaining that going to the police is the last thing she can do. They'd be more likely to tell her she's lucky to have a bloke and to go home and cook him some dinner. In the eyes of many of the old guard, she's nothing but a chattel. Thank goodness Mrs Gregory burned a few bras in her younger years.

She resorts to putting her fingers in her ears until he finally gives up. It's childish, but it works.

By then it's too late.

He's distracted her and she's forgotten to get off at the station closest to the hotel. She's now far closer to her old domicile than she'd like to be and in real danger of running into Kenny.

How real becomes apparent when the tube pulls

into the station closest to the school and Viv spots Kenny at the same time as he sees her. Even with the tube still moving and solid glass between them, she can tell he's calling her every name under the sun.

"Shit, that's not good."

So shocked is Viv by Kenny's proximity she doesn't even think to reprimand her fellow teacher on his language. She knows his oath has been loud enough for the kids to hear with the most boisterous of them crowing in a singsong chant. "Oooooh, Mr Jones said SHIT!" with their emphasis on the bad word.

The tube is still moving when Kenny runs alongside their carriage, already worming his fingers between the rubber stoppers where the sliding doors meet. Gareth jumps to his feet and places himself in the middle of the aisle between Viv and her ex.

He bounces on his feet, fists already up in a fighting stance. "Harry! You got any of those pickled onions left?" he yells over his shoulder.

Viv has no idea what Gareth's on about asking such a random question. Harry, however, understands, immediately pulling a half-full jar of the noxious snack from his haversack and holding it up like a trophy. Beside him, his mates are busy arming themselves with apple cores and half-eaten sandwiches.

Having removed the lid from his jar of pickled onions, Harry looks to Gareth for direction. "The geezer in the Aston Villa jacket?"

"That's the one. Don't hold back!"

Shoving passengers out of his way, Kenny barges onto the carriage and is lurching in her direction when the first pickled onion hits him in the chest. This is followed closely by any item of food not deemed worthy of lunch and even a few lunch boxes.

Whether this is down to most of her students supporting local football clubs, or the chance to let loose in a public place, Viv doesn't know. As food fights go, it's epic and rather one-sided. However, it isn't an item of food that does the most to halt Kenny's progress; it's a small tartan thermos.

Viv is frozen, watching the mêlée as though in slow motion, when a small hand slides into hers. It's enough to pull her frightened gaze away briefly to see who it is. It's Albert and he looks to be as scared as she is.

"Come, Miss Morgan." Only when he tugs hard on her hand does he break through her terror. This sees her staggering to her feet and following him through the single door at the end of the carriage.

She doesn't dare look back because for such a small boy, Albert is fast on his feet. He's also nimble and it takes every ounce of Viv's concentration to keep up with him without running into passengers heading in the opposite direction. The stairs at the end of the platform are tantalisingly close when Albert yanks on her hand and takes her through a side tunnel.

He doesn't slow and she follows him straight onto a tube heading back towards the city. They don't have time to catch their breath before the doors shut and the tube lurches forward. Looking through the windows, she gets the merest glimpse of Kenny. It's enough to see him slide his finger across his throat in a manner that tightens hers.

Unable to return to the school, there's nothing but for Viv to take Albert home, although only after he's reassured her there'll be someone there. She's still surprised when rather than be greeted at the door by

Albert's mum it's his grandmother who answers. At least that's who Viv thinks she is. Only after the third or fourth polite smile does it occur to Viv that English isn't the old lady's strong suit. Despite the warm welcome, she wouldn't have a clue who Viv is, or what she's on about.

It therefore takes a while for Viv to explain to Albert's grandmother that he isn't in trouble and that he's a good student. It's obvious the old girl isn't taking the boy's word for it when he repeats her words in whatever dialect it is they speak. Thankfully gentle patting on top of Albert's head is a universal enough sign for the old lady to accept the truth of it.

Explaining that the missing Taj-Mahal-of-lunchboxes is Viv's fault is a much bigger challenge, with even Albert struggling for the right words.

When Mrs Chaudhary Senior packs up some curry for Viv to take with her, she isn't sure if this is as a thank you for escorting Albert home or down to a dodgy translation.

The trip back to the hotel is convoluted and overly long with her eschewing the tube in favour of the bus. She sees the inside of a lot of them and has even pounded the pavements before she staggers into the hotel.

Getting past reception with the lunchbox full of reeking curried goodness is only achieved by wrapping her coat around the thing. She then makes sure she gets the key to her room before the receptionist gets a whiff of Albert's gran's cooking.

The food and even her tiny room on the top floor are welcome after the day she's had. It's not even eight before she's enjoyed a curry that's stupendous, even cold and a bath—also cold. After a couple of hours working on a tentative lesson plan, she switches off the light in hopes of a decent night's sleep. If today was big, tomorrow promises to be huge.

The last thing she thinks about before falling asleep is the letter she'd penned on the back of a Chinese takeout menu Mrs Chaudhary had given her. This was handed to Albert for him to deliver to Gareth at school the next day.

Viv finds the Harrow residence easily enough the next morning. It's her first time in what turns out to be Belgravia rather than Chelsea. Mrs Harrow lives in a multi-dwelling building which is something of a surprise.

There's nothing sub-standard about the building, its swathes of red brick and soft grey stone, are high-end through and through. It's more that with an active child in the house, Viv's been expecting a larger establishment, one with some outside space for him to run around and play.

Viv checks the note given to her by the agency once more to be sure it's the right place, before walking up the front steps and between the imposing columns that frame the entrance. She drops her suitcase on the ornately tiled top step and pushes the single doorbell that sits to the right of the front door. She then waits, although not for long.

"Hah, you the latest, then?" a man's voice says from beside her but below ground level. "Name's Jack. Be with you in a tick."

True to his word, the front door opens a moment later and he swings it wide to allow her to enter. She's in front of the elevator doors at the back of the foyer when there's a discreet cough from behind. The doorman stands next to a narrow door off to the side, his waggling eyebrows indicating it's where she should be going.

Servant's entrance it is, then.

This sees her following him down a set of narrow stairs and through a rabbit warren of even narrower passages. A bigger woman than she would be pushed to make her way through some gaps. As it is Viv has to hold her suitcase out awkwardly in front because it wouldn't fit beside her without catching on the multitude of pipes that dot the passages.

Inexorably they make their way to what feels like the next block over before he stops next to a set of elevator doors. These are utilitarian compared with their public-facing counterparts.

Viv's standing at the back of the large, obviously freight, elevator, when the doorman leans in, pushes the '6' button and pulls back out again.

"Aren't you coming with me?"

"'ell no. Mrs Dunning, the 'ousekeeper, would 'and me my balls in a bag if I was ta access the private quarters."

As slow as the doors have been to close, the elevator is even slower. So slow in fact, it takes a moment for Viv to realise she's even on her way up. It does, however, give her time to work on settling her nerves.

Licking her index finger, she first sweeps it first across one eyebrow and then the other. Patting the bun on the back of her head, she checks for loose hairs, before straightening her already-straight skirt. All of this is done by feel. There aren't any mirrors in the beast she's travelling in and its metal walls are so dinged and scraped as to kill off any reflections.

Even though she's expecting it, she's still surprised when the doors open straight onto a small service area. She's even able to see into the kitchen of the apartment through an open door opposite the elevator.

The doors haven't had time to death-rattle their way shut before a large woman storms out of the kitchen. She throws an autocratic "follow me" at Viv and disappears through another door, leaving Viv scrambling to follow.

If she didn't know the matron from her old boarding school to be long dead, Viv would swear she's following Miss Cabot. Hard military bearing, steel-grey hair, face like a baboon's arse? Yep, it's all there. Here's hoping the woman doesn't also prove herself to be an out-and-out cow of the first order.

"In here." The woman, who can only be Mrs Dunning, the doorman's nemesis, slams her hand hard against the door she's standing next to. This reveals a room as neat as a pin and about the same size, making the demi-chambre at the hotel look palatial by comparison. Viv inches her way in and drops her suitcase next to the bed, all while eyeing the battleship grey uniform laid on the counterpane.

Viv is both relieved and dismayed. Relieved she doesn't need to worry about the meagre contents of her small suitcase being up to snuff. Dismayed that the uniform looks to be one of the housekeeper's cast-offs. She will swim in it. Thankfully, it's something Mrs Dunning sees.

After a masculine-sounding *"Hummpf"*, she leaves Viv on her own. But not without telling her to "Wait!"

is a tone more commonly used at dog obedience classes. It's as though Viv is a Scottish terrier rather than simply Scottish.

The woman takes her time returning, leaving Viv unsure of herself. *Should she unpack or is she meant to start work immediately?* It's already gone nine and so any charge of hers should already be at their lessons.

Viv still thinks it's off that a seven-year-old isn't enrolled at one of the up-market schools in this area of London. Or failing that bundled up and sent to a prep school in readiness for Eton or Cambridge.

Uncertainty is wiggling its way under the skin of her psyche before Mrs Dunning returns with another uniform. This one is closer to Viv's size and the grey less gunnery sergeant in hue.

"Once you've changed, make your way to the kitchen along the hall and I'll brief you on your 'other' duties."

Viv is alone before she notices the older woman's stress on the word 'other'. Nothing she can't handle.

It's a sentiment she revises, when on walking into the kitchen in her uniform. Mrs Dunning hands her a rubber apron and nods at what looks like a dinner party's worth of washing up. A large dinner party.

A VERY LARGE dinner party.

Light housekeeping duties my bum.

"Oh, I thought I'd need to start young Quincy's lessons by now?"

"Hah, right. No, he and 'her ladyship' will still be abed until at least eleven."

Viv analyses this seemingly simple statement while running hot water into a sink large enough to bathe a baby. Horse.

What did Mrs Dunning mean? It isn't so much what she said as how she said it.

So far as Viv is aware her new employer isn't titled, with the woman at the employment agency referring to her simply as Mrs Harrow.

While a title wouldn't be uncommon in this neighbourhood, the way Mrs Dunning said 'her ladyship' implies this is self-imposed rather than the real deal. There's also the fact a seven-year-old boy is allowed to lay abed until eleven on a school day. Even if he's home-schooled, it's not healthy.

It takes Viv an hour to clear the kitchen bench of dirty dishes, dry them and, through trial and error, put everything away. By her estimations, there had to have been at least twenty people at dinner the night before. Thankfully all the dishes had been rinsed before they were stacked or her task would have been even more onerous.

She's barely hung the rubber apron on a hook next to the door that, presumably, leads to Mrs Harrow's quarters, before Mrs Dunning speaks again. Not that the woman is verbose, by any means.

No, she hands Viv a bucket full of cleaning equipment, the word "Come" tossed carelessly in her direction. There's nothing but to follow the woman along a narrow hallway and through a swinging door and to be smart about it for fear of losing her guide.

Their destination is a bathroom larger than the front room at the terrace house she'd shared with Kenny.

"I'll be back in half an hour and I expect it to be clean enough to eat off. If it's not, your trial is over."

And this, right here explains why that file at the employment agency is as fat as it is.

5

*V*iv isn't sure whether Mrs Dunning is referring to the floor, the bath or the toilet when it comes to porcelain suitable for culinary purposes. Either way, she doesn't waste time getting stuck in.

Who'd have thought all those years of trying desperately to keep Kenny happy would come in handy? Still, better to be slaving away in solitude, than doing it to a background of Kenny telling her to hurry up because he needed to take a dump.

She'd once suggested he might like to do this before she cleaned the toilet. It was something that saw him shove her so far down the bowl that her face was worryingly close to the water.

Sadly not so far that she didn't hear, "Would you want your arse near that mess?" The irony that the skid marks in question were courtesy of his poisoned digestive tract had been lost on him. Or maybe not.

Viv is finishing the mirror when Mrs Dunning returns. The place sparkles enough that Kenny wouldn't think twice about relieving himself here. Viv is confident it will also pass the culinary purposes test of her new boss. While Mrs Harrow might technically be her employer, Viv's under no illusions as to who calls the shots.

Again all she secures is a *"Hummpf"* and the bucket being snatched from her hand. This then being dumped unceremoniously behind the door suggests Viv is up to snuff. This is doubly confirmed when Mrs Dunning says "I'll take you through to meet Lady Harrow."

Interesting, her new boss does carry a title. Viv crosses her fingers the woman isn't as entitled as some nobility are, considering themselves well above the likes of her.

Viv again follows Mrs Dunning as best she can. Seeing how far along the parqueted hall her boss has gone, Viv trots to catch up. She's close on Mrs Dunning's heels when the woman swerves through the last door on the left.

The only occupant in the ornately Georgian room is a softly-rounded woman sitting on a straight-backed seat, upholstered in a self-stripe gold fabric. She looks to be crowding eighty, so there's no way she can be mother to a seven-year-old. Even in retrospect, her ovaries would have been like shrivelled raisins at the beginning of the gestation period. *Maybe the wee chap is adopted.*

It takes Viv a second to see Lady Harrow isn't alone after all. A small, and unnaturally blue, poodle is curled up next to her.

"You may take my darling for his morning constitutional now." Lady Harrow leans over and kisses the small dog on top of his head and Viv's wiped her mouth with the back of her hand before she's conscious of doing so. Brought up to think of dogs as dirty creatures, seeing someone choosing to put their mouth this close to one, sets her stomach roiling.

That Lady Harrow then flips the mutt onto his back and peppers his tummy with more kisses has Viv close to gagging. The aristocratic old girl is a circumcision away from going down on the dog.

It takes Viv a second to see the diamante-studded lead Mrs Dunning is dangling in front of her face. It's a moment longer before she understands she's not going to meet her charge just yet. Most kids would be bouncing off the walls by this time of day, never mind still in bed.

Out in the hall with the blue dog under her control, Viv is escorted to the front door by the housekeeper. Typical. The dog has better access privileges than she does.

"The key to the park is on the leash. I'd suggest you hurry unless you're keen on cleaning poodle piddle off the parquet."

Viv's out in the foyer before she's able to find the words she's looking for. "Ah, when will I get to meet young Quincy?"

Mrs Dunning doesn't bother responding other than to glare at Viv and then slam the front door in her face.

"Well, that's rich," says Viv to the empty foyer, although the poodle does look up at her, his expression saying he agrees.

She's never been in charge of a dog before and isn't sure of the protocol. At the very least she's undoubtedly supposed to know his name if she's to call him when he's off the lead. *Should she even do that?*

Being careful to avoid actually touching the dog, Viv twists his collar around until she's able to read his name tag.

"What!?"

She's being paid fifty quid a week plus board and lodging to take a poodle out to pee in a park? *So much for all my lovely lesson plans.*

Viv settles in over the next month, worked to the bone by Mrs Dunning, who doesn't appear to do anything but cook meals. And, there's not much work involved in these either, with them being distinctly lacklustre to appeal to Lady Harrow's limited palate.

Viv is also responsible for greeting all guests at the front door, given the housekeeper's 'old bones' aren't up to hurrying. She can't complain; the work is easier than putting up with Kenny. And because she doesn't leave the apartment, other than to take Quincy out for his thrice-daily constitutionals, she's managing to save more in one month than she had in the previous six. That her wages are paid in notes that smell strongly of mothballs also means she gets to keep it all with Lady Harrow not bothering about anything so trifling as tax.

It'd all be great if it wasn't for Rupert, Lady Harrow's nephew. He's the wrong side of both forty years and fourteen stone, balding and has personality quirks most commonly seen in locked wards. His biggest delusion is the one about his artistic talent.

Unfortunately, it's a delusion shared by Lady Harrow. This sees Viv stuck with dusting an assortment of paintings she'd grudgingly award a single gold star and then only out of sympathy for the student responsible.

Dusting his amateur paintings is the least of her worries when it comes to the honourable Rupert Smythe-Brown. No, as luck would have it, he's also got the remnants of a British public school education. Namely, a longing to be deemed naughty enough to have his bottom paddled, 'til pink and preferably by someone with the bearing of Mrs Dunning.

Before Viv knew this, she caught Rupert looking in her direction and had glared at him using her best schoolmistress mien. A pity then that grumpy schoolteacher is like catnip to this particular member of London the slap and tickle set.

Now, if she hears his voice or gets a whiff of the cloying aftershave he bathes in, she's off to the farthest reaches of the apartment. And if he tracks her down, she's fully prepared to spray herself with enough furniture polish that he won't be able to get a good grip.

Hearing a firm knock at the front door, Viv can tell it's not Rupert. The *rat-ta-tat* is too forceful and given his preferred-nephew status, he has a key.

Viv opens the front door and is faced with two young women who look to be in their mid-twenties. Next to them stands Jack, the odious doorman who haunts the downstairs foyer as though it's a bridge to his troll.

Because there's nothing in the book about visitors today, Viv keeps her welcome on the chilly side of reserved and is pleased to see the visitors' chirpiness wilt. This does nothing to shut them up though, with the blonde wittering on about a coat for Quincy.

So ludicrous is this notion Viv's about to give them

the heave-ho when Lady Harrow trills out that she's been expecting them. Good of the old girl to tell her staff about it.

Viv shows the visitors to the drawing room; all while imagining Quincy decked out in a canine version of something from Saville Row. It's about as ludicrous as her students turning up to class in high-end formal wear.

Leaving the visitors—who aren't offered refreshments—with Lady Harrow, Viv goes in search of some morning tea. She's down to dregs and crumbs when the drawing room bell rings, announcing the doggie tailors are ready to leave.

She's glad their visit hasn't been too long as it's time for her and Quincy to go to the park in the middle of the Square. Viv now looks forward to these outings, liking the fresh air after the over-heated stuffiness of the apartment and a chance to be alone with her thoughts.

Timing is also critical if she's to avoid the perfectly alliterated 'poodle pee on the parquet'. Cleaning it up would have her far closer to a dog's private parts than she would ever want to be.

Having overhead the young visitors talking about the elevator playing up, Viv collects Quincy from the drawing room. There's no way she's going to risk getting stuck like they were. After a show of opening and shutting the front door, she sneaks him through to the back of the apartment and into the service elevator. Better to risk Lady Harrow's wrath than be stuck in the elevator-equivalent of an upright freezer with a dog that's bladder is full to the brim.

Something that's blissfully empty is the park itself, with none of the other regular dog walkers in attendance. It's just her, the barren winter landscape and a blue poodle. That is until Viv hears her name shouted.

This isn't good.

No one around here knows her name other than Mrs Dunning, Lady Harrow and Jack the doorman. The voice doesn't belong to any of them.

Spinning, Viv slips off the edge of the narrow path, landing heavily on her knees. She crouches down even further, hidden by a small brick wall. She's safe for now but effectively trapped in the private park.

It's been over a month since she escaped and with his lack of energy, she thought Kenny would have given up trying to track her down by now. As to how he's found her here, she doesn't have a clue. On a more positive note, he can't get to her without a key to the wrought iron gate that ensures the park stays private to the Square's residents.

There's not a chance he can scale the chest-height fence. At least, not without catching his gut or a goolie on one of the spikes that guard the top as assiduously as a Rottweiler with a bad tooth.

The cold is seeping into her bones before she hears her name again, this time from right behind her, in a hoarse whisper. Flailing around, relief floods through her to see it's Gareth. That Quincy rushes over to stand between her and her fellow teacher is the biggest surprise.

Do toy breeds even do this? Isn't this sort of protective behaviour the predilection of the bruiser classes?

Gareth takes a big step back and Viv realises the bark end must look a whole lot more intimidating than the end that's worryingly close to her face. It takes a moment for her to understand what's happening.

It's so blasted long since she laughed; the sensation sits awkwardly on her frame. It takes hold when Gareth joins in and, as if sensing Viv is no longer in danger, Quincy joins in, barking joyously and jumping on the spot. Only when the dog trots over and sniffs Gareth's shoe does the Welshman put his hand down so the poodle can nuzzle it.

He must pass the sniff test, because Quincy is soon all over him, unfortunately, in a rather amorous fashion.

"Get a room, you two," says Viv, before dissolving into giggles again.

Gareth looks at her. "Oh, I'm sorry. Here, let me help you up."

On her feet, Viv dusts herself as best she can. "What are you doing here? Shouldn't you be in class?"

"I was told to get in touch with you, urgently. Because you don't have access to a phone, I thought it best to come in person rather than write to you."

Viv's not surprised Gareth knows where she lives, as she'd included it in the letter she'd handed over to Albert Chaudrey all those weeks ago. This had been handed to Albert with instructions to give it to Gareth so he could in turn pass it on to the Mrs Gregory. The last thing she's been expecting is to see him here in person.

It's more that Mrs Gregory asked Viv to stay in touch and she didn't have the heart to get Albert to hand a letter over to the headmistress personally. It would have been more than the small chap could cope with.

"Where's the fire?"

"Huh? Oh, right. Your ex has been hanging around the school asking the kids if they know where you are and generally being a nuisance. Mrs Gregory wanted to make sure you didn't give into the temptation to drop by for a visit because you were missing your kids."

The headmistress knows Viv well, as she's been thinking of doing this very thing on her next day off. She's missing the scruffy little tearaways like crazy. "Didn't the school call the police?"

"They did, but he's always gone by the time they arrive. We gave them your old address, but it looks like he's no longer in residence. The windows are boarded up, apparently."

Viv closes her eyes for a second before they snap open again. There isn't a chance Kenny will have moved on, with that involving far too much effort on his part. More likely he's stopped paying rent and the landlord has boarded the place up in an attempt to stop him from squatting.

Despite being a lazy bastard, there's no way a few boards would stop Kenny from getting in. Especially not when his living there rent-free would mean he can spend the entirety of his benefit on beer and takeaways.

Viv knows for sure his mum isn't gullible enough to allow him to move back in with her. The woman had been positively gleeful when Kenny and Viv moved in together all those years ago. In hindsight his mum muttering that he was her responsibility now should have been a warning.

"Hang on. What if he saw you leave in the middle of the day? He knows you know me. What if he followed you?"

Viv no longer feels like laughing. Now she feels exposed, with a freshly painted target on her back.

"Oh, shit. I don't think he was around."

"But you can't be sure?"

"No." Gareth scans the footpaths around the edge of the Square as frantically as Viv.

A couple of full rotations confirm the Square is mercifully free of grubby, overweight, geezers. Viv worries it might not stay this way and makes short work of clipping the lead back onto Quincy's collar and dragging him over to the gate.

Gareth keeps apace with them, even accompanying them through the Mews to the back of the property. He even escorts her and Quincy inside the portico where she presses the button for the service elevator.

Although they've been vigilant about keeping an eye out for Kenny, Viv doesn't relax until she's seen Gareth disappear around the corner of the Mews and she and Quincy are in the service elevator.

She's about to push the button for the top floor when her hand stills. What if? Deciding to err on the side of caution, she presses every button so that if anyone does happen upon the back entrance to the building, they won't be able to tell on which floor she's got off at.

6

The service elevator is slow at the best of times. Stopping at every floor, it appears to take forever. Each time it stops, Quincy gets to his feet, ready to leave.

"Not yet, boy."

The dog looks at her as if she's barking, but her sixth sense has saved her from Kenny's wrath on more than one occasion. The hairs on the back of her neck being strictly at attention – it's a warning she won't ignore.

The lock on the back door downstairs will be child's play to her larcenous ex and so the elevator is the next best barrier. This way, he'll be stuck searching all the floors before he reaches the sixth. Her hope is this will give the building's other occupants plenty of opportunity to intercept him.

"You took your sweet time. Her Ladyship won't be happy to see Quincy shivering like that."

Viv hasn't been aware of the state of the dog until it's pointed out by Mrs Dunning, her own personal Sergeant Major. The woman's right though, the dog looks to be perishing.

Being responsible for an animal is a challenge compared to looking after kids. Unlike a dog, they'll tell you loudly and often what they're feeling at any second of the day, whether you want to know, or not.

"Come on, Quincy, let's get you toasty."

Normally, Viv's go-to for warming someone or something is hot water, but there's no way she's going anywhere near that immaculate poodle clip. Her luck of late will see her screw it up. No, much safer to take the pooch to her box room and turn the fan heater on full-bore. The dimensions of her private space being what they are, it'll be tropical in no time.

She watches the dog unfurl in front of the heater and it occurs to her that only a few weeks back, the thought of choosing to have the dog in her bedroom would have been anathema to her. Maybe it's that he smells better than a lot of her students and doesn't appear to shed hair at all.

Quincy is positively glowing when Viv hears a commotion in the Mews. It's not the usual clatter of deliveries or the rubbish collection and even from up here, she recognises Kenny's bastardisation of the English language.

No!

Scrambling to her feet, she sidles over to the small window until she's jammed hard up against the curtains. She looks at an oblique angle down into the small space behind the building dreading what it is she's going to see.

A quick glimpse and she jerks back. It's been

enough to see Jack grasping Kenny firmly by the ear. Given the disparity in their sizes, the doorman shouldn't have been able to keep Kenny under control like this. He must have hidden skills because Kenny is howling in pain and tottering along behind Jack, his head bent to the side in an apparent attempt to keep the pressure off his lug.

Another quick gander is enough to see Kenny her lumpy ex dragged down the Mews in the direction of Eaton Place. There's no way Viv's missing out on what happens next.

"Come on, Quincy, you'll be warm enough now."

She flips the knob on top of the heater to the off position and is surprised to see the dog's shoulders visibly droop. Hah, such a human emotion from the little fur ball.

Grabbing her coat off her bed, Viv opens the door of her bedroom and is surprised at how cold the hall feels by comparison. It's something Quincy obviously picks up on too with the amount of stalling that's going on.

"Come on, mister. It's not that bad," she says, clicking her fingers to get him moving again. If she's to see what happens to Kenny, they both need to get a wriggle on. Lucky for her, the dog is close behind her when she walks out into the hallway. Leaving him to trot to the drawing room, she nips out of the front door, opening and closing it as quietly as she can.

Racing across the foyer, she throws herself through the door that leads to the stairs, racing up them two at a time and scrambling to get the key to the door at the top from its hiding spot. Opening it, a blast of cold air takes her breath away. The park is sheltered by comparison and she had no idea it would be this polar up here. Her lack of a hat, gloves and scarf will see *her* defrosting in front of the fan heater after this escapade.

She makes it to the parapet that backs the building in time to see Jack and Kenny clear the Mews. At this point, Viv's expecting Jack to send Kenny on his way with a boot to his flabby arse. Instead the pair round the corner into Eaton Place as one and disappear from view.

Where on earth is the doorman taking him? Do they even need a police station in this neighbourhood?

Viv flies across the roof to the other side, her nose now running as fast as she is. Her hands stuffed in the pockets of her coat, her fingers curl around a long-forgotten tissue. It'll have to do.

She blows her nose and shelters behind a chimney stack, all while watching Jack and Kenny stumbling along the footpath away from the heart of Belgravia. Her vivid imagination envisages a border of sorts.

They don't get far before a black and white police car pulls up next to them. Whether this is by design or coincidence, Viv isn't sure, but Kenny is having none of it.

Yanking hard against Jack's hold on his ear, he bellows in pain, before taking off at a sprint. An officer explodes from the police car and is in pursuit seconds later.

Jack, meanwhile, dusts his hands together in the sign of a job well done, salutes the police officer still in the car and turns towards home. All the action now well out of sight, Viv wastes no time in hightailing it off the roof. She doesn't bother waiting for the world's dodgiest elevator on the sixth floor.

Instead she flies down the stairs to the ground floor

in hopes of intercepting Jack. She's in luck, entering the foyer at the same time as he does, although he's nowhere near as out of breath as she is. His examination of her is clinical and then critical. "So, you're the one he was bleating on about."

"Not here." Viv's gaze darts in the direction of the door leading to the lower level.

Rather than acknowledge her request for privacy, he walks towards the door and then through it. His leaving it ajar is the only indication she's to follow him. It's an invitation he doesn't need to repeat.

Gossip that he is, Jack's spilling the beans on what's transpired with Kenny before the door's even shut properly. Jaqueline Fortescue's butler caught Kenny snooping around on the first floor and gave him into Jack's care soon after. Apparently Smithson's ex-army and there wasn't a chance Kenny was getting away from him.

"Your bloke kept saying 'e was after his fiancée, 'cause she'd stolen somethin' from 'im. I said to 'im that unless his fiancée was the wrong side of seventy, he 'ad the wrong building."

"Thank you for that."

Jack pulls himself up to his full height, a good head below Viv's own. "Didn't do it for you, love. Can't 'ave the old girls being upset by riffraff the likes of 'im skulking about."

This leaves Viv in no doubt of her place in the pecking order. "Do you think he'll come back?"

"Not a chance. Not with the local coppers being on the lookout for 'im. They might well have collared 'im already. PC Walker doesn't live up to 'is name."

It takes Viv a moment to deconstruct his sentence. She hopes he's right because it would be a huge relief to think Kenny's next domicile is Wormwood Scrubs prison. She'd be able to get back on with her life, at least for the foreseeable future.

Shame then, that the hairs on the back of her neck say this is a big, fat, no, that he's still at large and will bide his time. Waiting is something Kenny's good at when it comes to getting even. Shame he hadn't displayed the same patience where she was concerned.

Viv is vigilant over the next week, scuttling to and from the park as quickly as possible and not giving Quincy the opportunity to so much as sniff the same piece of ground twice. The quicker he does his business, the better she likes it.

Warming them both up in her room afterwards is now a regular part of their routine. It doesn't matter that the small dog is now sporting a smart new coat courtesy of Samantha, the doggie tailor. The closer they get the Christmas, the colder it gets to the point Viv wouldn't mind a new coat as warm as those Quincy now trots around in.

The other new addition to the household is a gorgeous little painting of Quincy that sits in the guest bathroom. This had been a gift to Lady Harrow from the doggie tailor's friend and a true masterpiece in miniature. It was also something Lady Harrow refused to have sitting on the mantle next to 'Rupert's works of art'.

'Works of arse', more like it.

Instead her ladyship had asked Viv to deal with it—posh talk for binning the painting—and something that had upset Jennie, the artist. Viv at first thought of hanging it in her own room, but then decided it would be better in the hall bathroom.

Here it can be seen by any guests of Lady Harrow and no doubt compared unfavourably to Rupert's daubs. Anything to show the upper crust English git in as dim light as possible is a plus in Viv's eyes.

Having expected a break by accompanying her Ladyship, Quincy and Mrs Dunning to the family's country pile for Christmas, Viv's disappointed not to be invited. Apparently, the groom at the country place takes care of Quincy's needs when he's down there, so her services won't be required.

No, Viv can keep an eye on the house and do a bit of dusting while she's about it, this last instruction courtesy of Mrs Dunning. Perhaps the biggest disappointment about not being taken to a safe place is that because her charge won't be on the premises, her wages will be halved.

Viv isn't sure if this is down to her ladyship or the penny-pinching Mrs Dunning with any savings going straight into that battle-axe's pocket. Still, Viv can't complain too much, with her accommodation still being free.

The day after her Ladyship and Mrs Dunning leave for the country Viv discovers the heating has been turned off. Whether this is by accident or as another cost-cutting exercise by the housekeeper, she's not sure. Either way the place is perishing.

"Good lord, how many layers do you have on?"

Until Gareth mentions it, Viv hasn't been aware she's done up like a strudel, although thinking back; she'd been surprised on leaving the apartment to find it as warm outside as it had been in. Or was that the other way around? Certainly the fan heater in her box room has been working overtime to stop her from freezing to death overnight.

In the warmth of the pub, Viv can't shed the layers fast enough. It's that or be overcome by the heat. Down to jeans and a sweatshirt, the bench seat on her side of the booth is now piled high with her scarf, hat, extra jumper, coat and gloves. By comparison, there's a single coat on the seat next to Gareth.

"Lady Harrow had the heating turned off when she left for the country. At least I think it was her."

"She what!"

Viv shrugs. "Mrs Dunning told the caretaker there's no point heating the whole place for one person and to shut it down until their return."

"If it's too cold, you can always stay in the spare room at my place until she gets back."

"Gareth, we've talked about this." Viv has many reasons why she doesn't want to stay at his place, the foremost being Kenny more than likely knows where it is. She also doesn't want Gareth to get the wrong idea. Sure, university was a long time ago, but feelings don't change that much. Do they?

Gareth opens his mouth as if to press the matter, but rather than do so, he stands. "Name your poison."

"I'll have a cider, please."

"Beef or lamb for your main?"

"Beef, please," says Viv, her mouth already watering at thoughts of a full roast lunch complete with Yorkshire pudding. She looks briefly at the blackboard on the wall above the bar. Yum, the set lunch comes complete with Spotted Dick and custard for dessert.

Viv watches Gareth push his way through the crowd towards the bar where he places the order for their Christmas lunch and drinks.

His paying doesn't sit well with Viv but neither does she want to make a scene by arguing about it. She'll make it up to him when she's back on her feet and Kenny is nothing but an unpleasant memory.

Watching her fellow teacher at the bar Viv can't help but notice how good-looking he is. She can't remember why they hadn't carried on dating back in the day. Maybe because she wanted to focus on her studies? Turning away from him to stare at their battered tabletop, she's at a loss. Maybe once she's over Kenny?

She's still deep in thought when a glass of cider appears in front of her. It's a pint glass.

"Good heavens, I won't be able to drink all that."

"Give it your best shot. It's not like we're going back to work after this."

"No, but I do want my wits about me if anything should happen." Kenny is never far from Viv's thoughts. Her neck hairs are twitching ninety to the dozen and that's never a good sign. "Have you seen any more of him?"

Gareth opens his mouth to speak, then shuts it again. His internal battle is as evident as if he were having an open punch-up with one of the other patrons.

"Spill."

"Okay, but don't freak out."

Viv's already disobeying orders.

"Yeah, well, he was following me by the time I got to the tube station …"

"And."

"I managed to give him the slip."

"Managed or think you managed?"

"Last I saw, he was on the tube heading for Wimbledon. Short of him being able to stop the train, there's no way he could have followed me."

"What about the emergency brake? The guy's crazy enough to pull it."

"I, ah. Oh, shit."

Viv's appetite is replaced by her gut churning so hard she'd be a fool to let it anywhere near food. Without thinking, she picks up her pint of cider and gulps half-a-dozen mouthfuls. This burns its way into her stomach and she's worried enough about its return that she has to wait a second before speaking. "We can't stay here." Rubbing the back of her neck does nothing to settle her nerves.

"Come on!" Gareth's already on his feet and even struggling into his coat.

Viv follows suit, although she's nowhere as quick to match him, having to deal with far more items of clothing. Hot on his heels, she's surprised when, rather than heading to the front doors at the corner of the building, they force their way over to the bar. Once there he lifts the flap at one end and disappears through a door behind it without slowing.

Viv looks sideways at the barman as she follows in Gareth's stead, expecting a protest. All she gets is a wink as he reaches for the flap to return it to its closed position. She's only taken a step in Gareth's stead when light floods the place courtesy of the front doors being thrown open.

Looking over her shoulder, a primordial part of Viv already knows who it is she'll see. And she's not disappointed, excepting that she is. Very.

Viv crosses her fingers he hasn't seen her, ducks low and shoots forward through the door, pleased when this is closed behind her. Gareth who's marching down the hallway they've entered disappears around a corner and she hurries to catch up.

She catches sight of him again as she rounds the same corner, in time to see him opening a door, the light streaming in telling her it's the way out. He turns and beckons to her to get a wriggle on.

"Come on." He holds his hand out and grabs hers, tugging her through the door. He then slams it behind them and drags her along the alley as though their lives depend on it.

Any hopes that Kenny hasn't seen her are dashed when the outside door crashes open behind them, followed by footsteps thundering in their direction. These are interspersed with ragged breathing and a gasped out, "Effing bitch." It's all the prompting she needs to dig deep and find muscles she hasn't used since sports day at primary school.

$\mathcal{V}$iv's breath burns her throat and she doesn't dare look back. Instead she concentrates on keeping her hand in Gareth's as he pulls her along at a speed she'd never be able to manage on her own.

She comes close to taking a tumble when he swerves around a corner, crosses a narrow delivery lane and takes them down yet another alley. Only some fancy footwork keeps her on hers. She doesn't have time to gather her wits before he's off into another alley and another.

It's as though he knows where he's going.

Only when he opens a gate set into a tall brick wall and drags her into a small yard, does she think he's made a mistake. They're trapped! That is until the backdoor of the property opens to reveal an elderly lady in a pale pink, quilted house coat.

Expecting the old girl to scream or yell for help, Viv's stunned when she smiles broadly. Gareth doesn't give the woman a chance to speak, putting his finger to his lips and sssshing quietly. She complies, standing aside to allow Gareth and Viv to walk into the house, straight through it and out the front door, although Gareth does check both ways before he steps out onto the footpath.

Expecting the pace to slacken, Viv's disappointed when Gareth is off again at speed, crossing the road and leading her down yet another alleyway. She's now totally lost and reasons if she doesn't know where the heck they are; hopefully, Kenny won't either.

A few more twists and turns and they stumble into another pub and through into a small bar before Gareth finally stops allowing Viv to catch her breath. He even goes so far as removing his coat letting her know their mad dash is over and she can finally relax. It's not until she peeled off all her own layers that Viv drops into a seat at the nearest empty table.

Actually, a quick look around, shows all the tables to be empty, and even the small bar at the end of the room doesn't have anyone standing next to it. However, the rumble of voices through a solid oak door next to the bar tells of patrons in another part of the building.

They're sitting grinning at each other when two meals are plonked down in front of them. Viv isn't even sure where the woman has come from until she spins around in her seat and spies a gently swinging door behind them.

Viv looks up at the woman. "What? We didn't order these."

"Yes, we did," says Gareth, before cracking up laughing.

"Wait? What? We're back in the same pub?"

"Last place he'll look for us is here and especially in

the snug." Gareth stabs a large piece of beef with his fork, swipes it through a veritable lake of gravy and stuffs it into his mouth. He then raises an eyebrow in Viv's direction when she doesn't immediately get on with her meal.

"He's right, love, you can relax. We're down a coupla of staff today due to a nasty dose of 'Christmas Cheer', so the snug's closed." Following on from this, she steps over and turns the key in the door they've entered by, effectively sealing them in. "You enjoy your lunch." She disappears back through the swinging door, leaving them alone.

Viv's only just started working away on a thick slab of beef when the same woman returns with the drinks they'd abandoned earlier. These are placed on the table next to theirs to give them elbow room. While it might have felt like they'd been running for hours, there are still bubbles rising in their glasses.

"So," Viv swallows her piece of beef, "You're familiar with the area?"

"Grew up here."

"You never told me that."

Gareth shrugs as though it isn't important.

"And the old lady?"

"My nanna."

Viv nods slowly while savouring a piece of soggy Yorkshire pud. While most people like it crisp, soggy with gravy is Viv's favourite.

"You're sure he won't come back here?"

"As sure as anyone can be, although now people know what he looks like, he might have trouble."

His reassurances are enough for Viv to settle in to enjoy her meal and drink. After all the running, she has no trouble getting through her pint of cider, experiencing a nice buzz as a result.

She hopes Gareth is right about Kenny giving up, because there is no way she'd want to run into the world's best contraceptive in her current state. Never mind getting away, she'd be lucky not to throw up over him if he rough-housed her. Okay, that she could cope with.

She refuses a second drink, conscious she needs to get home, including time to check the way is clear of Kenny. She also needs to ensure her room is nice and toasty before she turns in for the night to avoid hypothermia. When she makes noises about this, Gareth tells her to relax, that he's got it sorted.

"And anyway, you haven't had your Spotted Dick yet."

Despite hoovering her way through a pub-sized roast meal and feeling full to bursting, her mouth still waters. How could she have forgotten about her favourite part of any meal? That's right, being chased through the streets of London by her looney ex.

Leaving the pub, Viv supports her tummy like she's pregnant. Thankfully there's no sign of Kenny outside as there isn't a chance Viv could run as full as she is. She's also a couple of sheets to the wind on the alcohol front with Gareth swaying her into having another cider. Even though it was only a half pint, it's enough to have the tube station looking to be farther away than her waddle is up to.

Concentrating on putting one foot in front of the other, Viv's unaware Gareth has stopped next to a beat-up panel van until he calls out to her. "Where are you off to?"

"The tube."

"No need. Gary, the publican, said I could drop you home in his rust bucket. I'm coming back here to spend the night with nanna. Can't very well run through her place and then not call back for a proper visit."

Viv's wrinkling her nose in confusion when he adds, "Old girl hasn't got a phone."

There's no conversation on the drive back to Eaton Square; mostly down to the mechanical quirks of the engine. Adding to this cacophony of nuts and bolts in a dryer soundtrack is the heater being on full-bore. Without this, the van having been stripped of all its linings would be as cold as an ice-box. Despite the best efforts of the asthmatic heater, it's still a close run thing.

Because of how loud the vehicle is, they park a couple of blocks away from Lady Harrow's place. This way they won't get complaints from the neighbours and if Kenny is skulking around, they're more likely to see him before he sees them.

A quick peek around the corner of the Mews is enough to spot the waste of space leaning against the back wall of Viv's building.

This puts the kybosh on her going in the way she's supposed to. "I'll need to sneak in the front way."

"Do you even want to go inside with him there? He's picked the locks before, hasn't he?"

"After the reception he got last time, I don't think he'd dare break-in again. He'll be hoping to nab me outside."

Even to Viv's drink-addled brain, it makes sense

that Kenny wouldn't push his luck if cops are involved. He's been in close contact with too much stuff acquired dubiously to be comfortable around them.

Viv's lost all feeling in her toes before Kenny moves. With him busy emptying his bladder against the wall next to the entrance, Viv and Gareth dart across the open end of the Mews. They then make their way around and into the Square proper without alerting him to their presence.

Viv's unaccountably nervous when she rings the front door bell. Gareth rather than Quincy beside her, she's not supposed to enter the building this way and she's sure this breach in protocol will get back to Lady Harrow, or worse, Mrs Dunning the housekeeper.

"Sorry, Jack. I tried to go in the back way, but my ex is out there."

"Is 'e now." Jack puffs out his chest. "We'll see about that, won't we? My mates at the station will be well pleased to 'ear about this. By the back door, you say?"

Viv nods vigorously until the rattling of her brain forces her to stop. One and a half pints of cider—okay it was Scrumpy—and she's a mess. What a lightweight.

Jack having disappeared back downstairs to his lair presumably to call the cops, Viv feels safe to push the 'up' button for the lift. She even feels safe enough to get inside. She's surprised, however, when Gareth joins her and this must show.

"There's no one home, is there?"

He has a point, but that doesn't make Viv feel any less like she's sneaking her boyfriend into the family home, after lights-out. He's right though. Lady Harrow isn't due back for another week and she's only coming home then because Rupert has a solo art exhibition.

Doubtless, it's being held in a condemned

warehouse somewhere in the East End as no gallery worth its salt would want his *masterpieces* within a bull's roar of their hallowed walls.

"No, just me."

"I want to see you safely to the front door. No telling what that bone-head ex of yours is capable of."

"With luck, the local coppers will have collared him by now." Despite voicing this, Viv knows the chances are slim. Just as she's got a sixth sense about knowing when Kenny is around, he's got even sharper powers when it comes to knowing when he's anywhere near someone sporting a badge, even if it's hidden under plain clothes. How else would he have gotten away with his larceny for so long? Not because of superior brain power, that's for sure.

She lets Gareth leave the elevator first, knowing the exact moment he declares the foyer safe by the way he settles back on his heels. Crossing the foyer, however, she can't help but notice her senses are on high alert and she wastes no time opening the apartment door and scuttling inside, beckoning for Gareth to follow.

Incredulous, his eyebrows shoot up until they're hidden by his shaggy fringe. "The front door's not locked?"

"Ah, no. Not with Jack downstairs." Even as she's saying it, Viv knows the doorman isn't up to the task of keeping a determined Kenny at bay.

"What about the back entrance?"

"I thought with the cops already having scared him off once, he wouldn't try that again." Viv hugs herself, even going so far as to rub her hands up and down her arms in search of warmth.

"You know what *But* thought?"

"He thought his arse was hanging out of bed, so he got out to put it back in again." Viv finishes the adage for him. She doesn't get any further, frozen to the spot and not wanting to venture any farther into what she has thought of up until right then as her safe space.

Thank goodness Gareth escorted her up here. Without him questioning the security, she'd have gaily waltzed in without a care in the world.

Other than freezing to death, that is. The inside of the apartment is icy enough for her to see her breath, noting absently how rapid this is. The temperature outside must have dropped while they were at lunch. She thought it was simply down to a complete lack of insulation in the van that it had been so cold on the way home.

"You cannot stay here. If Kenny doesn't get you, the bloody frost bite will."

"I can't stay at your place. What if any of the kids see me leaving there? And we know Kenny knows where you live." Viv doesn't voice the main reason she doesn't want to lodge with Gareth; she's already feeling differently about him.

"Not there, with my nanna. At least until your boss gets back and you're not on your own." Gareth blows on his hands and rubs them briskly together. "And until the bloody heating is back on."

This, Viv can live with. She's already met the woman, sort of, so it wouldn't feel too strange spending a few nights there. "I'll need to collect a few things."

"And risk running into the crazy man, heck no." Gareth grabs her by the hand and she's back out in the foyer a moment later, its warmth a welcome relief.

The elevator only stalls three times on the trip to

the ground floor, leaving Viv filling the silence with mindless chatter. It feels awkward until she asks how the kids in her class are coping. The elevator goes from being chocker with jagged-edged topics best avoided, to rocking gently with their combined laughter as Gareth goes through what happened on the tube after Albert had urged her to make a run for it.

"Harry is going to get a gold star for that when I'm back. I might even pull a few strings to see if I can't get him onto one of the rugby teams."

"You might need to get Suzie Cooper a new thermos while you're at it."

"That was her?"

"Yep. Watching that thermos spinning through the air and scoring a direct hit to Kenny's noggin was poetry in motion."

They're still laughing about it when they exit the elevator into the ground floor foyer, although once again Gareth leads the way. Their chuckles die when they see the look on Jack's face.

"They didn't get him, did they?" says Viv.

"No. The scruffy lard-arse managed to leg it before the boys in blue could cut off his escape."

Gareth's nanna straightens in her hard-backed chair and grabs the handle of the teapot. "Another cup of tea, dear?"

"No thanks, Mrs Jones. Four is my limit for a morning."

Actually, this is an understatement, with Viv awash after two cups of the badly stewed tea. She's only been drinking cups three and four to be polite.

Gareth's nanna on the other hand is able to work her way through a canteen-sized aluminium teapot of the tannin-laden brew every morning. At least this has been the case for the week and a half Viv's been staying here.

Viv has no cause for complaint, with the old girl taking her in as if she's family rather than a virtual stranger thrust upon her over the holiday season. This had included making Viv welcome on Christmas Day in a way Kenny's mother never had.

It was also nice to have someone to share the cooking with, although it had taken a lot cajoling for

Gareth's nanna to agree to this. But there wasn't a chance Viv was going to stand-by while Mrs Jones did all the work.

There's also the plus that the small terrace house is kept at a constant temperature the likes often experienced in greenhouses and saunas. Viv is basking in the heat after the perishing cold of the apartment.

She's also enjoying not having to look over her shoulder every minute. There isn't a hope of Kenny being able to find her here, especially if Viv keeps her wits about her. With luck, he'll have been back hanging around the apartment and Belgravia's boys in blue will have nabbed him. This is long shot, but Viv is still crossing her fingers for a Christmas—or at the very least—New Year's miracle.

"Are you in for tea tonight? I'm planning a nice beef stew." Gareth's nanna smacks her lips in anticipation of a dish she's yet to cook.

Viv isn't far behind in this anticipation, with experience telling her it will be as good as everything else she's eaten since she's been in residence. Sure Mrs Jones might do terrible things to tea, but she's no slouch in the kitchen.

"Yes, I am." She smiles to herself that Mrs Jones, Bronwyn, has even asked. Viv hasn't left the house since moving in, apart from the odd dash to the corner shop to buy basics. The last thing she wants to do is scrounge off an old lady. She's not that broke.

"That's good. Gareth's coming over, too." The old lady looks sideways at her, which doesn't go unnoticed. It's not the first time there's been a hopeful look cast in Viv's direction with her hostess obviously harbouring dreams of the romantic kind.

Viv leans away from the table and straightens her tummy as much as the kitchen chair will allow. "Oh, my goodness, I'm so full. I shouldn't have had seconds." It's the beef suet dumplings that have done her in. Despite them being light and fluffy, atop a huge bowl of stew, light and fluffy is never going to be up to the challenge.

"I'm with you," says Gareth, letting his belt out a couple of notches and getting a death glare from his nanna. "You want to go for a walk around the block to make room for dessert?" Gareth is already on his feet indicating he's going anyway.

"What are we having?" Viv can't help but ask even though she's full to bursting.

Mrs Jones pauses briefly in her collection of the empty dinner plates, smiles broadly and states with a certain degree of glee, "Sticky date pud."

Viv groans. "We might need to make it five times around the block if my uniform is to fit when I return to Lady Harrow's tomorrow."

"All ready?" Gareth sounds as disappointed as his nanna looks.

Viv, however, is ready to return to her boxroom in Belgravia. With Gareth making her leave the apartment without packing, she's been stuck washing her smalls every night and drying them on the radiator in her room.

Along with this, she's been alternating between her own clothes and some of Gareth's nanna's. Sure they're the perfect disguise for trips to the corner shop, but despite not being a slave to fashion Viv isn't keen on looking like an old-age pensioner either.

. . .

In the end, it takes six circuits of the block before Viv and Gareth feel ready to face what will surely be a double helping of sticky date pud. And, this most assuredly with an unhealthy amount of ice cream, finished off with whipped cream and shaved chocolate. But it's worth it because Viv is going to miss all this delicious cooking when she clocks back in.

Mrs Dunning's food being of a utilitarian nature and deliberately bland to keep Lady Harrow happy it's got more in common with space food, than cuisine. Enough to keep you alive, but never up to tickling your taste buds.

Perhaps the funniest thing in all of that bland stodge is the old girl doesn't have any tummy troubles when it comes to polishing off a fifth of scotch every couple of days. There'll be no need to embalm her when she goes, with any cremation positively volatile.

The first thing Viv notices on entering the apartment through the service elevator the following evening is that the temperature is positively tropical. "You'd better go," she whispers to Gareth who's escorted her to give the place the once over.

"If you're sure?" he says, directly into her ear. "What if she's had the heating put on in readiness but isn't here yet?"

He voices Viv's own concern, but she's not about to risk him running into her Ladyship, or worse, Mrs Dunning, if they are indeed in residence. It would be a case for instant dismissal and something neither woman would think twice about.

No, with Kenny still on the loose, Viv needs this job more than ever. She wants a decent nest egg saved up for when she goes back to teaching. Setting herself up in a new place won't come cheap, with a bond, furniture and the like to purchase. Heck, she'll even need to purchase more clothes with the charity shop bits and bobs still in her tatty suitcase not up to snuff for a teacher.

There's just one almighty road block to all of this.

If Kenny is still making a nuisance of himself hanging around the school when she's due to start back, she'll have to apply for a transfer. It was something she discussed with the headmistress all those weeks back.

And the longer Kenny lingers, the closer it will be to the middle of the first term. By then any transfers still open will see her buried deep in the countryside; the positions not filled because no-one wants them. Thoughts of steaming piles of cow manure and not seeing her little tykes again has a lump sticking in Viv's throat.

Watching the service elevator doors shut on Gareth, she's unable to stop her hand straying to her cheek, where he kissed her. It had been so natural she hadn't even thought to blush. Maybe there'll be love post-Kenny after all, something she hadn't dared think about. It isn't like she's pining over him – anything but.

Again this will all depend on how tenacious her ex proves to be.

· · ·

There being no need to unpack, Viv gives the apartment a quick search, showing neither her Ladyship nor Mrs Dunning to be in residence. Because the heating is on, she knows they have to be home soon, and anyway isn't tonight the opening night of Rupert's solo exhibition? A quick check of the calendar next to the fridge confirms this and that the fridge is chock full of fresh fruit and veg.

Being alone does cause a flicker of unease, but Viv tamps it down when it becomes obvious Kenny isn't in residence either. It also means there are no duties for her to perform; leaving Viv free to get ready for bed. She's not long turned the light off when she hears clattering in the kitchen.

Her immediate thought is how inconsiderate Mrs Dunning can be at times, but a quick check of the luminous hands of her alarm clock tell her it's only 9.30 p.m. and not the middle of the night. Gareth's nanna likes to have dinner on the table bang on five, meaning the rest of the evening passes slowly at best.

Only when it sounds like someone has emptied the entire contents of the pot cupboard onto the floor of the kitchen, does Viv think she should go and say hello to her boss. It sounds like the woman is ticked off about something, so far better to deal with it now than wait until the morning.

Viv's tying the belt on her bathrobe when her hands still. Does she really want to face her boss while still in her pyjamas? That'd be a big, fat no, although she forgoes her uniform with today technically being her day off. No, smart casual will suffice to pop her head into the kitchen and say hello and welcome back.

· · ·

Viv runs her fingers through her hair and ties it up into a knot on top of her head, before opening the door to her room and padding along the hall to the kitchen. There's no way she's putting shoes and socks on. And, anyway, chances are the woman won't see her slippers, especially not if she stays on her side of the huge island that dominates the kitchen.

Seeing the fridge door wide open and no sign of her employer, Viv coughs her presence. It's not loud, but enough to see a hand appear around the fridge door. The hand is decidedly masculine in size. Honestly, the woman should think about a manicure, even if she eschews polish. The door shuts and Viv knows a manicure is the least of the late-night snacker's issues.

"'bout effing time you turned up. Nothing to eat in this effing hole."

Any response to this nonsense jams firmly in Viv's throat. While her power of speech might be frozen, thankfully her feet aren't and she backs slowly out of the room. Not slowly enough.

"No, you sodding don't. I'm starving here, bitch."

It's been nearly two months since anyone has spoken to Viv like this and her Pavlovian response is to do what he says. Anything is better than a thrashing followed by other 'pleasantries'. Her feet, however, have other ideas and before she knows it, she's out in the hall. She thinks for a second. Back way out: she'll be trapped waiting for the elevator to arrive.

Front door and hurtling down the stairs it is.

Spinning as fast as her slippers will allow, Viv is off heading for the posh bits of the apartment. She doesn't need to look back to know Kenny is after her, his footfalls echoing loudly through the narrow hallway that twists and turns through the servants quarters.

Despite tripping along as fast as her slippers will allow she's not making much headway. It's something that has her kicking them off, preferring cold feet to a lack of traction.

She hits the swing door out into the main hall of the apartment without slowing and races down it. From the amount of swearing from behind, she knows Kenny hasn't been lucky with his timing of the swing door. Lord knows she's nearly connected with the thing a couple of times after following Mrs Dunning through it.

Good, it's all the lead she needs. She yanks hard on the front door handle and is horrified to find it doesn't turn. What? The front door's never locked. Not with Jack guarding the main entrance downstairs and she knows she didn't lock it.

Damn it, why isn't there a key in the lock?

Turning, she races back down the hall. At least this way she can lock herself in one of the spare bedrooms and scream holy murder out a front window. If she stays next to the front door, she'll be trapped well and truly.

She hasn't made it more than a couple of feet when Kenny staggers out into the main hallway, his hands clamped firmly over his nose. He's weaving slightly and blinking rapidly, telling her the door has hammered him in a big way.

His gaze darts around wildly until he spots her. His hands drop to his side and he fists them ready for action, seemingly oblivious to the blood now dripping down his face. "You're gonna pay for that, bitch."

He walks towards her, his paces measured, each

step ratcheting Viv's heartrate up another notch. She soon matches him step-for-step, the only difference being, she's retreating, taking her closer and closer to that locked front door.

She knows she's running out of room when an evil smile alights on Kenny's face. "I've got you now, you slag." He doesn't hurry, instead taking his time and going into details Viv would rather not be privy to.

That he bullet points each nasty deed by punching his right hand into the palm of his left has sweat prickling all over Viv's body.

A quick glance to her left and Viv knows she's only got one option. Sure the door doesn't have a key, but if she can jam herself between it and the bath she'll be safe for now.

Trapped, but safe.

Then all she'll need to do is stay there until Lady Harrow gets home.

Over his game of cat and mouse, Kenny bounces on the balls of his feet, readying himself. He darts forward, his hands already outstretched in anticipation. Viv waits until the last possible second. She's throwing herself to the side and into the guest bathroom when she hears the front door open.

Unable to stop his forward momentum, Kenny sails past. She's not even had time to slam the bathroom door when she hears Kenny and another male shouting. This is followed by a huge thump, and finally silence.

Viv's quietly easing the bathroom door shut, ready to jam herself behind it, when Lady Harrow's cut glass tones shatter the silence. "Who is this vagrant?"

This is followed by someone who sounds remarkably like the Honourable Rupert Smythe-

Brown screaming, "Get him off me. Get him off me!" Based on this soundtrack, Viv has to assume Kenny must be taking his frustrations out on Lady Harrow's nephew.

Better him than me.

Looking sideways under the door doesn't shed any light on what's happening, with the gap simply too narrow to see what's going on.

Do I really need to go out there?

She's still unsure when there's a bellow of pain, followed by Rupert screaming, "No, no! Leave him where he is!"

The suspense is killing Viv and unable to resist any longer, she slowly gets to her feet and opens the door a sliver, all without anyone looking in her direction. Even able to see going on she's none the wiser, unable to make sense of the debacle in front of her.

For starters Kenny is laying full length on top of Rupert Smythe-Brown. That they've run into each other is easy to understand. Less easy to comprehend is why Rupert appears to be starkers. Next to this pile of human misery stands Lady Harrow, her top lip curled, nostrils flared.

If there's a plus in this scene, it's that Kenny is hiding the worst Rupert can offer in the way of family baubles.

But why isn't Kenny getting up? And why has Rupert changed his mind about moving Kenny, apart from the purposes of modesty, something that's been sadly lacking in that individual up until now?

"Your ladyship, if you could hold Quincy, I'll take care of this larrikin for you."

Until he's spoken Viv wasn't aware of Jack lurking out in the foyer with her charge.

The leash handed over to her ladyship, Jack steps into the hallway, ready to grab Kenny by the scruff of his neck. The East London wide boy isn't having a bar of it, shaking his head violently and attempting to scramble to his feet and escape.

He doesn't get far with Rupert lifting off the floor along with him like a freakish Siamese twin. They hover for a second before slamming back down again, the hall ringing with the unmistakable sound of flabby English arse connecting with polished parquet.

It's now obvious the pair is somehow glued together at the chest and places further south. It's enough to have Viv quietly gagging and fighting the urge to speak on the big white telephone behind her. Tonight's dinner thankfully staying put, Viv takes a quick sniff of the air in the hallway. It reminds her of something. She sniffs again, deeper this time.

That's it! After new Lino was laid in her classroom during the summer holidays it smelled exactly like this. Even a week later, the only way to keep the glue fume headaches at bay was by having the classroom door and all the windows open. No wonder the two of them can't get apart. That glue was vicious.

On seeing Mrs Dunning thundering along the hall, her sensible shoes living up to their name, Viv ducks behind the door just in time.

"I've called the police, Lady Harrow. They're on their way."

This news has Kenny redoubling his efforts to get free, ably assisted by Jack. It's all to no avail with him still stuck firm when two cops exit the elevator what feels like seconds later.

"My goodness, officers. Such marvellous service." Lady Harrow sounds as surprised as Viv at the promptness of their arrival. There isn't a chance the boys in blue would respond this quickly to a domestic in her old neighbourhood, preferring to let things run their course. Mostly while they stayed snug and warm back at the station.

"We were following up on the report of a break-in downstairs."

Jack kicks one of Kenny's flailing legs. "And this 'ere is the bloke you're after. 'e's been making a right nuisance of 'imself, 'e as."

This confirmation is good enough for the coppers, one of them wasting no time in slapping cuffs on Kenny. A task made easy by him already having assumed the position courtesy of an obviously sticky Rupert Smythe-Brown.

It is not until his rights are read by the officer still standing out in the foyer, that the one who cuffed Kenny, speaks his mind. "You mate, are going down."

Viv's whispered "Yes!" is loud enough to have everyone looking in her direction.

Lady Harrow's eyes narrow. "Do you know this person?"

"Unfortunately, yes?"

"She'll vouch for me, won't you, love?" Kenny's eyes are pleading with more than a hint of "and if you don't, you're gonna know a world of pain."

Viv doesn't need to dwell on her reply. "No, Kenny. I won't. What I will do is tell these nice officers about your lock-up in Poplar. The one registered in your mum's name. You know, the one full to the rafters with stolen goods. That's what I'll do."

No sooner have these words left her mouth, than one of the officers hands her a card. He doesn't say anything and Viv's nod is enough of a response for him. Busy as she is reading the details on the card, it takes a moment for Viv to comprehend what the grinding sound is she can hear. It's Mrs Dunning's teeth.

"I always told her Ladyship you were no good. You can pack your things and leave, now."

"She can't leave yet." Lady Harrow's tone brooks no argument. "Run the bath and get your cleaning products. He's your friend. You're responsible for getting them unstuck."

The thought of donning pink rubber gloves and scrubbing away at Kenny and Rupert is too awful to comprehend. One of them on their own would be bad enough, but the pair of them stuck together?

A huge shudder wracks her frame.

She's thinking hard on a polite way to tell her Ladyship to get stuffed when the impasse is broken by the arrival of Gareth. Never has Viv been so pleased to see an individual.

"Like hell is Viv scrubbing those two." Skirting around the pile of English git in the middle of the hallway, he takes Viv's hand. "Come on, let's get your stuff and get the hell out of here."

Gareth is already leading her down the hall, when she stops in her tracks. "Hang on a second. I need to grab something from the bathroom." Getting dangerously close to the now-thrashing Siamese twins, Viv nips back into the bathroom.

It takes but a second to grab the portrait of Quincy off the shelf above the bath and stuff it up her jumper before legging it. She knows she won't be back here and wants a reminder of her charge. She's surprised to find she's going to miss the small dog.

"Bye Quincy, you be a good boy." Viv is surprised

when her voice breaks on this simple request. Adding to her heartbreak is him howling in response, his mournful tone filling the hallway and haunting her all the way back to her box room.

She's close to tears when Gareth does something that lifts her spirits. At first she doesn't see what he's dangling in front of her. Only by swiping at her eyes is she able to see it's a key.

"You know that day I met up with you in the park."

Viv nods in response.

"You didn't think I scaled the fence, did you?"

Thinking back on that day, Viv remembers she hadn't given much thought to how he'd gained access. She'd been more relieved he wasn't Kenny to study the logistics of the visit.

"Some numpty on the other side of the square left their key in the lock. You can visit the little rascal when your replacement starts, if you like."

"Yes, I'd like that a lot."

Watching the doors on the service elevator close for what Viv knows is the final time; the giggles hit the pair of them. On reaching ground level, their eyes are streaming, they're holding onto each other to stay upright and their bellows of laughter fill the space.

A reality check hits Viv at the same time as the cold night air. "But where am I supposed to go?"

"What about your old place? It's not like Kenny will be there."

Gareth's tone says he's unsure of this option and it is one Viv says a categorical 'no' to. She'd rather stay in a pay-by-the-hour-hotel than venture back to her old life. No, the only reason she'll be going back there is to pick up the contents of her wardrobe and anything of sentimental value she left behind.

This presupposes Kenny hasn't flogged all her things down the market to supplement his income. With the place apparently boarded up, she makes a mental note to purchase a hammer before returning. She also needs to pick up some chocolates for her old neighbour. Without the woman's help, Viv suspects she'd still be stuck back there.

"You could come back to my place."

"Gareth, we've been through this."

"What if I told you I moved while you were staying with my nanna? I found a basement flat in Chelsea, a place outside the school district. Would that make a difference?"

"It could." Viv slips her hand inside his as they walk to where he's parked the van.

"What if I told you it's a two-bed place and we can take our time. Start over rather than pick up where we left off at Uni?"

They stop beside the van and Viv looks up at him under the light afforded by the ornate Georgian lamppost they're standing next to. "I think … I think I'd like that."

Gareth sighs in relief, drops her suitcase on the footpath and drags her into a crushing embrace. Viv revels in the heat where their bodies connect, her head resting against his chest allowing her to listen to the steady beat of his heart.

How could I have been so stupid all those years ago?

Only when their embrace shows no sign of ending

and her toes are numb, does she lift her head. "Aren't we going to get in the van?"

"Bloody thing died on me. That's why I was still here when the cops turned up."

His look of disgust is all it takes for Viv to start laughing again. It's not that it's funny as such; more that she's relieved the hell her life has been looks to finally be over. She can go back to teaching and she can forget about Kenny for at least two to three years, maybe longer with the information she'll hand over to the police.

She hopes his cellmate won't be as disappointed with the performance of 'Big Kenny' as the man himself.

THE END

Gold DIGGER

**Finding the gold is easy.
Keeping it will be
the challenge.**

Andrene Low

1

London - England

Stef twirls the paddle to check its weight, unable to stop a snigger. If it wasn't for all the studs peppering one side, she could be getting ready for a game of ping pong.

Instead, she's readying herself for a game of *paddle pops*. The spanking paddle atop her haphazardly folded clothes, she closes the lid on her suitcase. Once she's checked it's properly locked, she rolls it out onto the landing.

The old-school metal skates taped to the bottom with a bucket-load of electrical tape are the work of her dad. He'd learned a thing or two in his years as a London cabbie, and how to avoid lugging bags was top of the list. Sure, it looks a sight, but it works.

Back in her room, Stef lifts the blankets on her bed and, sliding her hand in underneath the bottom sheet, retrieves a dog-eared manila folder. It's the only one she kept after she, Brenda, and Julian lifted a whole pile from Wallace Smythe-Brown's London town house. Its current condition isn't how they'd found it but courtesy of the number of times she's flicked through its contents.

She doesn't need to read through everything again, pretty much knowing it all off by heart. However, this doesn't stop her from a quick skim. She probably knows the contents better than Wallace *Shit-Brown* and that pug-ugly nephew of his, Rupert. These two being the reprobates who'd compiled all the dossiers.

Just like the others, the papers she's flicking through were used to blackmail a member of the British aristocracy out of his hard-earned coin. But with her about to visit Cecil Percy-Ryder, the subject of this very dossier, she can't risk taking it with her. She's going to have to rely on her memory this time.

Her gaze keeps going back to the one term that pops up over and over. It sounds so familiar, but she can't for the life of her think why. "Arthur's Folly? Arthur's Folly?" No matter how many times she says it aloud, or in her head, she still can't get the connection. The memory of hearing these words spoken when she was a child has stuck, just not the setting or who it was who said them. She shakes her head, hoping to rattle some brain cells free, but it does no good. On shoving the file back in its hiding spot she's none the wiser.

A quick shufty at her new, upmarket watch—a recent gift from Cecil—and Stef realises she needs to get a wriggle-on. She'll cop grief from her dad if she's not downstairs and ready for him to take her to the train station. After struggling down the stairs with her suitcase, she marvels at how quiet the house is. The unearthly hush down to nearly all the inhabitants either being out of town or even out of the country.

The only exceptions are Flo and Bert, the live-in help, and Eadie, her landlady and mentor.

Her case next to the front door, Stef taps gently on the sitting-room door. Last thing she needs is to scare the old girl and have to resort to her recently acquired CPR skills. "You awake, Eadie?" An unladylike snort from inside the room is all she needs to feel comfortable pushing the door open and walking in. "Right, I'm off to Cecil's pile in the country."

"You've got everything?"

Stef nods, part of her still in disbelief that the genteel looking octogenarian sitting in front of her is the one who's been responsible for her dominatrix training. Although even she realises, she's still got a lot to learn. Never in a million years could she have seen this future for herself when she was approached by that crazy Aussie bird, Brenda, a mere couple of months back.

Still, it beats living at home in a moth-eaten part of East London where all the household appliances are hot. Not temperature wise, rather due to a dad who keeps finding things before they've even been 'lost'. It's also a lot better than working as a barmaid; with less time on her feet, and tips a zillion times greater.

Perhaps the biggest surprise, or is that another plus, is that she doesn't have to shag the old guys, just paddle their flabby arses. Her telling them they've been a very bad boy in her sternest voice possible doesn't go astray, either. The hardest part is not laughing when they respond like a schoolboy who's been caught doing something naughty.

And being paid in cash or trinkets also has her managing to save, for the first time in her life.

After clocking the half-empty decanter on the

small table next to Eadie's chair, Stef asks, "You all good for sherry?"

"If you could just top up my glass that would be wonderful. Flo will be back from the shops soon and she can take care of things after that."

Even with Brenda's school for girls no longer in operation Eadie's domestics, Flo and Bert, have continued to live on the premises. It's something all the girls are happy about. Knowing that Eadie, who they all love and who's got crippling arthritis, has round-the-clock support gives them peace of mind.

Stef does as she's asked, before bending down and kissing the old lady's cheek, surprising both of them. "You take care of ya-self while I'm away."

Rather than respond in words, Eadie waves toward the door, shooing Stef out of the room to a background of jaunty beeping from her dad out front.

Stef pauses on the front step, waiting for it to dawn on her dad that she's not lugging her suitcase down the path to his car. This takes longer than it should, perhaps in part due to his general avoidance of hard work.

"Blimmin' 'eck, love, whatcha got in here, a body?"

"That's why I needed a ride. Didn't want to hav'ta deal with it on the tube."

She's close enough to hear him muttering about 'a bloody hearse' when he manhandles it through the back door and onto the seat. His avoiding putting her bag in the boot means one of two things. He doesn't fancy lifting it up and into the boot or the boots chocker with stuff that's hot enough to blister the paintwork.

They're nearly at the station before Stef broaches the subject she's been mulling over and the whole reason she wanted a ride with her dad. "Da?"

"Yes, love."

"Do the words *Arthur's Folly* mean anything to ya?"

His reaction is such that she immediately regrets asking him while he's driving. They're lucky there's no-one next to them when he swerves wildly.

"Where the bleedin' 'ell?" He chokes off the rest of his comment, takes a couple of deep breaths and starts up again. "Why'd ya ask love?" His tone is suspiciously neutral.

This is part of what Stef has been contemplating over. Her pulling the wool over her old man's eyes is never easy, and with him on high alert like he is now, it'll be even harder.

"Relax, would ya! I had a dream about it. Last night."

If there's one thing Brenda's taught her, it's that there's nothing like going on the attack to throw someone off the scent and so she goes in for the kill. "Da, you carryin' on like this has me thinking I musta heard it from you."

Damn, his eye's twitching. Wait for it. Wait for it.

"Not me, love. You musta imagined it."

Now she knows she's onto something. While Brenda has taught her how to run a good offence, it's her mum who's shown her how to run defence. That woman can get information out of her dad even when he doesn't want to give up.

Her suitcase safely stowed in the baggage car, and herself ensconced in a first-class compartment, Stef sinks back into her seat. Her mind full of whirling images of what her dad told her in the car. It's unbelievable and a sure thing that Wallace and Rupert Smythe-Brown don't know about it, or they'd have blackmailed her elderly friend into coughing up for sure.

Fortunately, with those two reprobates in the pokey, it leaves the way clear for her to snoop around at Cecil's without risk of being sprung. She'd be nervous if they'd simply done a 'Lord Lucan', with the number of purported sightings of that supposedly dead peer indicating there's no way he's topped himself; just faked it.

The trip is uneventful. The train leaves ten minutes late proving that, even with a first-class ticket, British Rail lives up to its reputation. Perhaps it's because it's two in the afternoon on a Tuesday, but Stef has the compartment to herself for the entire trip. Perfect as far as she's concerned, saving her from having to make small talk with people she's got nothing in common with. It's not as if she can come clean on what she'll do while she's in the country. Well, not without having her fellow passengers jumping off the train next time it so much as slows down.

On disembarking at the small station Cecil told her is close to Ryder Hall, Stef drags her bag from where it's been dumped. She tugs it along the platform, doing her best to ignore the squeaky wheels, and into a small, but surprisingly tidy, waiting room.

And there she waits.

And waits.

Surely Cecil doesn't expect her to spring for a taxi,

if such a service is even available out here? Dammit, she doesn't even have a phone number for the house. If he's not here soon, she'll teach him a lesson by catching the first train back to town.

She's worn quite the groove in the wide wooden floor boards when a man explodes into the waiting room, looking wildly around. Thanks to the size of the room, and her being the only one in it, his gaze locks onto her immediately.

"Stefanie!?"

She tilts her head back in order to examine his face. It's an unfamiliar action for her when she's wearing stilettoes. Unable to respond verbally, her words jammed firmly in her throat, she gives him a curt nod. It's enough to have him grabbing the handle of her large suitcase and lifting it as though it doesn't weigh a ton. And yet another reason to have her heart beating double-time.

Steff trails him out of the waiting room, all while struggling to get herself under control. It's been a long time since a man's affected her this way, and especially not after he's only barked one word at her. *Could it be because I've only been interacting with submissive older gents for the past couple of months? Yes. That must be it.*

Nothing at all to do with the guy being built like a brick shit house and too rough around the edges to appear on the cover of a romance novel. Watching the muscles in his back ripple when he hefts her suitcase into a beaten-up Land Rover, Stef's unable to stop a sharp intake of breath. It's something that has him turning and examining her in a manner that leaves her feeling uncomfortable.

Might he know why I'm here? For the first time since she started down her new career path, her profession doesn't sit comfortably, a rampant flush starting between her boobs and travelling north. The brow he arches in question isn't easy to spot, hidden as it is under an unruly mop of dark hair.

"Must be coming down with something."

He doesn't appear to be buying it. Instead he passes deliberately close by her on his way to the passenger's door. He then gestures with his free hand for her to get in, all with a smug grin plastered on that chiselled face of his. *Damn.*

On taking in the state of the front seat, Stef stalls. There's no way she's getting in there and sitting on all that crud in her brand-new Burberry trench coat. A heartfelt sigh from behind her, she steps to the side. She's relieved when he reaches over the back of the seats and grabs a towel. After ridding the seat of dirt and grime, he gives the towel a vigorous shake before folding it carefully and placing it on the seat for her to sit on.

Despite all this, she knows that she won't be comfortable sitting this close to him during the drive. Not when she's on her way to cater to the sexual needs of an old bloke, using a paddle and handcuffs. Unfortunately, the Land Rover doesn't have any back seats, and she sure as heck isn't riding in the tray with her suitcase.

And being strapped across the bonnet is definitely not happening, unless it's Cecil and she's in charge of the rope.

The cab feels even smaller when he climbs in the driver's side and settles himself behind the wheel. It's odd being cast in the subservient role after playing the 'Dom' for the preceding two months. She can't work out whether she likes it or not, and isn't keen on examining it too closely.

The drive is completed in silence, neither of them saying a word until the Land Rover swings through the gates at Ryder Hall. Then there's not a hope she can stay quiet. "Bleedin' 'ell!" The drive goes on forever, protected from the elements by a colonnade of ancient oak trees. But it's not this that's been responsible for Stef's oath, it's that through the trees she's got a gander of the main house and it's humongous. Even bigger than the place she'd visited with Brenda, Julian, and the other girls for the country house party.

It's not a friendly house, with nothing wedding cake about it. It's shrouded in 'glum', the stone dark with age and featuring enough pointy bits to give off a dangerous vibe simply sitting there. If it's this dismal from the outside, gawd only knows what it'll be like inside.

She quietly soaks everything in, and boy is there a lot of it. She was aware Cecil was rich, but this is not what she's been expecting. As foreboding as it is, she can understand why he chooses to spend most of his time in the city. Other than at the height of summer, or over Christmas when family are in residence, he steers clear of the place.

Obviously, he's making an exception for her visit because it is neither the height of summer nor Christmas time. She can't complain, with fewer people she can check out what her dad told her about in the car. Jeez, if he knew what information he'd innocently handed her, he'd blow a gasket.

They're driving across the broad expanse of gravel that fronts the house when she spots a Roman ruin off to the right. There's no doubt the hillock it sits atop is manmade. "What's that?" She's 95% sure she knows, although she's unable to stop herself from holding her breath until it's confirmed.

Her driver turns in the direction she's pointing. "That?" He harrumphs in disgust before continuing, "That's Arthur's Folly."

2

It's no surprise the B&D paraphernalia Eadie has lent her is as heavy as it is. There's nothing cheap about any of it, with everything made out of thick leather and sporting enough buckles to keep the naughtiest of boys under control.

From what Cecil had said, he's got everything she needs, but Eadie had insisted she pack things she's comfortable with. Her as new to the scene as she is, it's her preference too. Thank goodness the driver had carried it up to her room, or she'd be a heaving, sweaty mess right now. She still doesn't know what his name is and she's damned if she'll ask.

Stef lays her equipment out on the large four-poster, a smile flickering across her face. By the time she's finished with Cecil, he'll be gagging to tell her all about Arthur's Folly. She knows she didn't get the complete picture from her dad because, even while he'd been spilling his guts, that damned eye of his had never fully quietened down. Her mum said if it was flickering, he was holding back. No, it will be up to her

247

to put the pieces together. If the treasure is what her dad makes it out to be, she's gonna need a blasted wheelbarrow to move it all.

She's had a good nosy around her room, unpacked her suitcase, slid it under the bed and is lying back taking in the room when there's a discrete knock at her bedroom door. About time the old codger turned up. She's already been here nearly half-an-hour.

Once again standing, Stef gives herself a mental shake, and dons her dominatrix persona. It's show-time. Stalking across the bedroom in ground-eating strides, she wrenches the door open wide and yells "Where the hell have you been?!"

The driver doesn't respond other than opening and closing his mouth a few times.

"Oh shit, sorry. I thought you were Cecil." This does nothing to explain away her oddball behaviour, at least not if the puzzlement on his face is any indicator.

"Drinks are being served in the conservatory, if you'd like to make your way downstairs."

With his tone brusque and his departure immediate, Stef's none the wiser as to where the conservatory is, or even if he's accepted her apology. She couldn't have accompanied him anyway. She's wearing little more than a leather corset and lacy knickers underneath the Burberry coat that's, thankfully, still buttoned up.

Unaware if there'll be anyone else at the drinks, Stef flies over to the freestanding wardrobe and yanks the door open. She then flicks through the clothes she's just put in there. Thank goodness Eadie had told her to pack a few dresses, with it being a demure dark plum number she grabs now.

The trench coat tossed over the end of the bed, she

doesn't bother removing the leather corset before throwing the dress on. She's still buttoning it up on her way out the door. She manages to retrace her steps to the main foyer but, as to where she's meant to go from here, she's at a loss. Well, not completely. She's watched as many BBC period dramas as the next girl and knows the conservatory will be at the back of the house. Question is how to reach the back of the house without going out the front door around the side of the building and finding it that way.

She's opened the fifth door leading off the main hall before she strikes gold, with the room she's entered opening out onto the conservatory. The murmur of male voices as she crosses the lushly carpeted room has her glad she's wearing the dress over her B&D get-up.

Stef pauses on the threshold to the conservatory. This gives her eyes time to adjust to the increase in light. Only then does she walk down the wide concrete steps and between towering palms in the direction of the other guests. She recognises Cecil's voice but is unsure who it is he's talking to, with their conversation having stopped abruptly when her heels had first clattered against the tiled floor. Long enough though for her to hear Cecil say, "Arthur wouldn't like that". There's that blasted name again.

On turning a corner on the meandering path she's been following, Stef feels like she stumbled into a scene from a Somerset Maugham play. Cecil sits at his ease in a large fan-backed cane chair, a cigar in one hand. What looks like a glass of whisky is gripped in the other.

"Hello dear, I was thinking about sending young Liam in search of you."

Next to Cecil's chair, Stef bends down and gives him a daughterly kiss on the forehead. It's only when she straightens that she gets to see who the occupant of the other Peacock chair is. She's not often surprised, but seeing the driver sitting at his ease and armed with a cigar and a glass of whisky does it. Isn't that taking fraternising with the staff a step too far?

Cecil waves his cigar in the younger man's direction. "I believe you've already made the acquaintance of Liam, my sister's boy."

"Not officially," says Stef, unable to stop herself from sounding a little sniffy. *Why the hell hadn't he said who he was when he picked me up at the station? Hmmmph, letting me think he was the hired help.* A brief glance in his direction and she knows full well the bastard's done it on purpose.

"Help yourself to a small libation, dear." Cecil once again uses his cigar as a pointer. "We're not hung up on protocol down here in the country."

Small libation? Stef could murder a pint of Watney's bleedin' red barrel but a glass of whisky will have to do, given this is all that's on offer. She doesn't hold back, filling her glass indecently close to the top. She thinks twice about nabbing a cigar from the case but decides no before taking the only unoccupied cane chair.

Cecil proceeds to lead their conversation, covering off the weather, her train journey down, and gossip about people they both know. Liam doesn't utter a word, instead keeping his gaze on Stef whilst drinking his whisky and drawing on his cigar, to the point she's squirming. She's used to men checking her out, but this is more closely aligned to a scientific examination than ogling and she doesn't like it.

"Well Liam, we won't keep you any longer. I'm sure you've got better things to do than sit here chewing the fat with us."

There's nothing veiled about Cecil's dismissal of his nephew, with it being blatant enough that the most socially inept would catch on.

"No, I'm fine. Been rushing all day." The younger man reinforces his intention to stay put by topping up his drink and even waving the decanter around in invitation.

"Come my dear," says Cecil. "Let me show you around the place."

Watching the old bloke dragging himself to his feet is painful, but Stef isn't about to offer any help and blow her dominant role. She does however worry if the cane chair is up to the challenge of him leaning fully on it. It's creaking alarmingly; almost as much as the old codger himself.

Only when he's safely on his pins and holding his arm out to her, does she stand, taking the opportunity to glance in Liam's direction. He's still staring at her.

What is his problem?

Cecil doesn't say another word until they're safely out in the front hall. "I do apologise for our unwanted company. Pops up like the harbinger of doom every time I want to have a little fun."

Stef's guarded in her response, only giving a small shrug. Not for a second does she think Liam won't follow them. Nope, until she knows what the full story is with that one, she's staying mum.

Cecil keeps up a running commentary on every bit of masonry on show, plus a few bits that aren't. All while walking determinedly across the hall toward a set of double doors on the far side. Rather than walking through them, he stops bang in front of the wall to the right. After some sleight of hand she hears a soft click, after which he pushes on a panel and stands back to allow it to swing out. He puts his finger to his lips and gestures for her to walk through the gap.

She wastes no time stepping into the relative dark, with Cecil close on her heels. The panel has only just clicked back into place when they hear a door opening out in the hallway and hurried steps. That it's Liam is confirmed when they hear him cursing, followed by a lot of opening and closing of doors. This is soon followed by the front door slamming hard enough to rattle the glass in the side panels.

Stef's about to speak, when Cecil places his finger over her lips, and she nods to let him know she's understood. Sure enough, another minute or two pass and then they hear the front door open and close again, this time more sedately.

"Right, let's get this show on the road," says Cecil, keeping his voice low as though still unsure if the coast is actually clear. The space is then illuminated when he clicks on a torch, flashing it around wildly and nearly clobbering her with it in the process.

Worried he's getting over-excited, Stef growls deep in the back of her throat before gritting out "Behave yourself!" It's enough to have him settling down, squeezing past her and leading the way down some stairs just beyond where they've been standing. The further they descend, the colder it gets and Stef wishes she'd worn her trench coat to drinks and stuff what Liam thought about it.

On stepping down into a dank cellar, Stef's relieved when Cecil flicks on some lights and hangs the torch on a nail sticking dangerously out of a nearby post.

The extra light does nothing to help make the space cosy. Cecil must notice her shivering, because the next thing she knows a musty cape is draped around her shoulders. Watching him don a similar cape, she ties the ribbons at the neck of her own to hold it in place. When he pulls his hood up, Stef follows suit because, while it reeks of mould and days of old, the cape is fur lined and already warming her up.

What follows is a forced march, along a brick-lined passage that goes on for ever and is cold enough that her breath is visible in the dim light. Her stilettos no doubt make it feel further than it is, and she's careful where she puts her feet. And it's a challenge avoiding all the gaps between the flagstones. Of as much concern as ruining her new shoes, is Cecil's breathing. It's getting worse by the yard and Stef's giving thought to chucking the old chap over a shoulder and legging it, when she spots steps ahead.

There are a lot more steps at this end of the passage than there had been at the other. For once she avoids her dominant role. "Mind if we take a small breather before we tackle that lot?"

That Cecil doesn't answer other than to nod his agreement doesn't come as a surprise. If Stef was wheezing that hard, she wouldn't be able to talk either.

They have to stop twice more before they make it to the top of the steps and along a short corridor. There, Cecil pushes on a door, swinging it wide and standing to the side to allow her to enter first.

"Welcome, my dear. Welcome to Arthur's Folly."

*N*ope, it's not what Stef has been expecting at all. Rather than a high-end summer house, as the outside design would suggest, the inside is set up like a shrine. A shrine to having your arse paddled 'til pink.

To having weights and pulleys attached to bits and bobs that shouldn't have weights and pulleys attached to them. To featuring more stuff designed to inflict pain than is commonly seen outside the Tower of London.

She is way out of her league with this lot.

No wonder Eadie had suggested she bring her own gear. Liam would have a fit if he knew about this place. *Shit.*

"Liam doesn't know about this place, does he?"

Cecil, who's reclining on a fainting couch as if he's about to use it for its intended purpose, rouses himself enough to answer. "Good god, no. Not when the place got its name, courtesy of his father's actions. Mind if I have a little shuteye?"

He doesn't wait for her to answer before closing his eyes and snuggling into the depths of the fur-lined cloak that all but smothers his small frame.

Now what?

Stef wanders aimlessly around the room to a background of Cecil's gentle snoring, then there's nothing aimless about her actions. Despite searching Ryder Hall extensively, none of her dad's ah *colleagues* had ever been able to find their way into the Folly and so it's virgin territory in some respects. If it moves, she moves it. If it lifts, she lifts it to the best of her abilities, which are many after years of manhandling casks of beer in the basement of various pubs in London. Things that can slide are slid.

Nothing. Not even a bloody dust mote meaning someone on the staff knows about the place or Cecil likes to play maid while being whipped.

And if that's the case, I should get him around to clean my room at Eadie's place. Hell, Eadie would probably be happy if he cleaned the whole place from top to bottom.

Only two things are certain. She needs to get a fire going if they're to avoid freezing to death and, when she's done that, she's ditching the heels. No point being dominant when your submissive is out for the count and likely to remain that way for some time.

Half an hour later and there's a fire going that's got the combustive powers of something able to roast a whole pig. Even then, it doesn't stand a chance against the cold in this mausoleum of pain. Cecil peacefully asleep, Stef drags the chaise, with him atop, nearer to the fire without waking him.

For herself she shoves a small rack closer to the fire

so she can sit on the end of it. There being sod all firewood left in the basket on the hearth, she'll use it for fuel if push comes to shove.

Even though she's sitting her feet still hurt. Sure, putting her shoes back on when Cecil rouses himself will hurt like the dickens, but better to have relief now while he's out for the count. After taking them off, she puts them carefully to one side and slides her feet out toward the flames, wiggling her toes to get some blood flowing. It's only when she's sliding her feet backward and forward to massage her heels that she notices something.

She bends forward, touching first one tile and then the other.

That's weird. They appear the same. *Shouldn't they all feel the same?*

Not until she's down on her hands and knees is she able to see the difference. While one is terracotta, the other is only painted to mimic terracotta. Stef swings around and unhooks one of the clamps from side of the rack. She then gets stuck into the grout, all while keeping as quiet as she can. This way she'll both avoid waking Cecil and hear if there's a hitch in his breathing to show he's about to wake up of his own accord.

It takes close to a half an hour to free the tile, but it's the highest hourly rate she's ever achieved. While the top of the tile gives the impression of terracotta, the weight and sheen of gold on the bottom tell her it's anything but. It's a few years' pay, that's what it is.

Now what? Stef turns the tile over and over in her hand, her mind whirling just as much. It's heavy, but not that heavy. And if there's one, there could be more. The way her dad had told it, the robbers had gotten away with a truck-load. Not literally, just in matters of the overall value.

Cecil snorting and fidgeting is enough to let her know she doesn't have the luxury of time. Without pause, she lays the tile on the floor, ditches the cape, and unbuttons the front of her dress. Once free of it, she slides the tile down the front of her leather corset resulting in an intake of breath sharp enough to have her coughing.

She's only just managed to get the cape back in place when Cecil opens his eyes. There's only one way she'll avoid killing the old geezer today, and that's by playing her dominant role to the hilt.

Stef leaps to her feet, puts her hands on her hips and opens the cape enough that he can clock her red and black corset. "How dare you lay there like an odious slug while I wait!?"

"Sorry mistress."

"Do you know what I do to odious little slugs who keep me waiting?" Stef doesn't care what he answers; she'll do what she wants, anyway. And that's ignoring any of the B&D gear scattered around the Folly like toys abandoned after an ice cream truck passes the house.

"Whip me?" Cecil's voice if full of hope, as are his eyes.

Boy, are you in for a major letdown.

If Stef was to get physical now, the tile of gold would likely drop out the bottom of her corset, breaking a toe. Only by pushing her tummy out is she able to keep it nice and snug under her boobs.

"No, you little weasel. I've been waiting on you for over an hour. You'll get nothing tonight."

His disappointment is palpable and Stef pauses and

sighs dramatically. It's enough that the gold tile slips just a smidgeon letting her know she's got no choice if she wants to keep her mitts on it. Who knows when, if ever, she'll gain access to Arthur's Folly again? "How dare you stare at me that way! For that, you can walk all the way back to the cellar in *my* shoes. Let's see how you like that."

Stef walks down the stairs ahead of Cecil, her feet snug and comfortable in Cecil's fashionable brogues. They're loose, although not so much she's unable to walk in them. Shame the same can't be said for Cecil, who's following behind her. He'd been unsteady and uncomfortable in her heels in the Folly, having her decide to lead the way. If he took a header from top step to bottom, there'd be no way he'd survive.

They stop for a breather five times on the way back due to a combination of Cecil's breathing and the crippling tightness and height of Stef's heels slowing him down. But damn her if the old bastard doesn't seem to be enjoying every second.

Shame the same can't be said for her shoes.

Stef is horrified when he returns them to her. There isn't a chance they'll fit her now, and never mind the scuffs to the heels, have them beyond repair. "You'll buy me a new pair. No, make it *two* pair. You may keep these."

She drops them negligently before stalking over to the stairs that lead to the front hall, grabbing the torch on her way. Still slopping along in Cecil's shoes, she tiptoes up the stairs in case Liam's lurking in the main hall. She only slips out of the brogues when she's right beside the secret panel.

That Cecil has to remove her shoes to put his back on has her smiling inwardly. He's a right demon for pain, just as Eadie warned her.

Stef has always prided herself on her hearing, but is surprised to see Cecil put his finger to his lips after straightening from putting his shoes back on. He takes the torch from her and clicks it off, leaving them to stand in the dark. At first Stef doesn't hear anything other than their combined breathing, but then she does.

How are they supposed to get back into the hall with someone lurking out there? Whoever it is, is methodically working their way around the hall, knocking on the walls, waiting and then continuing on, marking it firmly as Liam.

He's getting ever closer to their hiding spot, meaning it's only a matter of time before they're discovered. She's getting fidgety when she hears a loud bong from further away in the house. This is followed by a gasp of exasperation from frighteningly close by, before they hear footsteps retreating and a door slamming on the other side of the hall.

"Come on, my dear, we'll need to motor if we want to get free and clear."

Luckily for Stef, Cecil's idea of motoring is a brisk walk for her. However, on reaching the stairs, she flies up them two at a time to get to her room as quickly as she can. One hand on the bannister, the other hard across her stomach to keep the gold tile in place. No way can Liam catch sight of her barefoot and wearing only a leather corset and a fur-lined cloak.

She'd only realised she'd left her dress in the Folly when they reached the cellar and she was stuffed if she was going all the way back to get it.

No, she'll use it as an excuse to get Cecil to take her back there tomorrow. And this time, she's taking note of where it is that he pushes to release the panel in the hallway. Heaven only knows how many other floor tiles are gold like the one now sitting under a mountain of make-up in her toiletries caddy.

Stef pokes the perfectly rounded mound of gelatinous goo that sits proudly in the middle of her plate. No food she's aware of is this pink, naturally. Or this wobbly. "What is it?"

"Salmon mousse."

Cecil sucks a glob of the stuff off his fork before it can splatter back down onto his plate like several before. It's all Stef can do not to gag. The only upside to all of this is that Liam is as unimpressed with their starter as she is. After moving the parsley garnish a few times, he drops his cutlery with a clatter and pushes his plate to the side as far away as he can. The three of them clustered around the head of a table that's over twenty feet in length, this is a good long way.

"Oh, that's a shame. I'm allergic." Stef puts on her best disappointed expression, hoping she won't be pushed too much on what her allergy is. She doubts an allergy to food that resembles a pimply arse cheek is a real thing.

"So, Liam, how long will we have the *pleasure* of your company?" Cecil sits with a forkful of 'bum' precariously poised, waiting for his nephew to answer.

Rather than looking at his uncle, Liam gazes at Stef, raises an eyebrow and says, "I'm not so sure *this time.*"

Stef stares back just as hard, giving no measure.

What does he mean this time? Does he always pop up when his uncle has visitors? Is she the reason he's staying?

This would all be so much easier if he was pug-ugly. As it is, she's not sure if she's checking to see what he's up to, or simply because he's easy on the eye. She wouldn't go so far as to call him devastatingly handsome but, boy-oh-boy, he does do something for her. Shame he's off limits, in a big way.

Much to Stef and Liam's delight, the main course is a Beef Wellington that's firm to the bite without being tough. It's accompanied by vegetables that haven't had any colour boiled out of them; that the gravy isn't lumpy like her mum's is also a plus in Stef's eyes.

She's seen firsthand what's on offer in the pudding department in these big country places and wants an iron-clad excuse to get out of it. She stuffs herself with the main until her corset is ready to give at the seams, anything to prove her point of being full to bursting.

On seeing a chocolate gateau placed on the table in front of her, she could kick herself. Little wonder Liam hadn't hoovered his way through the main. If she was to swallow even the smallest sliver, she'd bring it all back. Not a good look.

There isn't another word out of Cecil as he ploughs his way through a slab of gateau that the size of your average house brick.

Liam then swallows another huge mouthful and taunts her further by licking his spoon. "Not hungry?"

Oh, she's hungry alright.

But he'll keep.

4

Stef thinks back over the evening while luxuriates in an enormous claw-foot tub that's just short of being Olympic in length, if not depth. Despite increasingly pointed comments from Cecil, Liam had proved as tenacious as cat fur on black pants when it came to refusing to leave her and the old chap alone.

It's this that sees her now relaxing in a hot bath before it's even gone nine pm, which is just as well as Cecil hadn't been up for anything too strenuous. He'd gone into what amounted to a food coma after polishing off most of the gateau.

The old geezer must have hollow legs.

She's working on how to get to and from the Folly without being caught by Liam for the umpteenth time when there's movement in her bedroom. Stef smiles broadly. Could it be Cecil isn't as tired as he'd seemed after all? Shame she's not at her dominant best lying as she is under a mountain of bubbles.

Even starkers would be better than this.

Stef eases herself out of the water and stands in the tub until the bulk of the bubbles have sluiced down her body. Clambering over the side, she grabs one of the enormous fluffy towels stacked on a chair at the end of the bath and dries herself rapidly and efficiently. She thinks for mere seconds before dropping the towel in the laundry hamper, swinging the door wide and striding out into her bedroom.

That's weird, there's no-one here. Now.

A quick scan of her belongings is enough to know they're not as they were before she took her bath. How long had whoever it was been rummaging about before she was aware of them?

She doubts it was Cecil as he'd have no reason to sneak about like a thief. Or more likely, he'd want to be caught doing so and thus earn himself a good spanking.

No, there's only one person it could have been. And damn if she isn't a little disappointed he's no longer here. Thank god her make-up bag with its golden secret had been in the bathroom with her. If it wasn't, she'd be back to being as poor as she had been on arrival.

It means one thing though, if she's retrieving more tiles, she'll need to find a bang-up hiding spot. But first she needs to get her mitts on the tiles and that'll involve a lot of hard work. Shame she hadn't thought to pack a boiler suit.

Stef stands in the middle of her room deep in thought. "I wonder?" The room doesn't answer back. That doesn't stop her striding over to the large coffin of a chest tucked into one corner of the room. She twists the key in the lock and lifts the lid and is immediately assailed by a cloud of camphor. One plus is that it's toxic enough to ensure any clothes in there will be in good shape.

She's been hoping for men's clothes. Far more practical for prising the gold tiles free in the Folly, lugging them out through the house and burying them for collection later. What she finds is almost as good. There are at least half a dozen riding habits in there, all ancient. Fortunately, they're serviceable and, more importantly, appear big enough that she won't have buttons popping at the first sign of exertion. Even better is they're all in dark jewel colours, perfect for skulking around the hallways of a pile like this.

Quarter of an hour later and she's ready. Not just a habit, but also riding boots, with a crop that fits snuggly in a pocket on the side of one boot. She decides against wearing one of the veiled hats. Instead she pulls her hair back in a solid plait that hangs down the middle of her back and well out of the way.

Then she waits.

And waits some more.

She's unsure which room Liam is in, if he actually has a room, or if he simply spends his time lurking in the hallway trying to catch someone at something. Her bedroom light switched off, she's able to tell the lights in the hallway are still burning bright. This will make it impossible to sneak around without that bastard Liam spotting her.

Turning, she leans her back against the bedroom door and allows the dark to close in around her. After shutting her eyes, she wills herself to think through the problem. What would her dad do? Hmmm, he'd probably jam a screwdriver into the nearest power point in hopes of shorting the lights in the entire place. Best not.

Only on opening her eyes does Stef see what she would otherwise have missed. It makes sense though. If there's one secret passage in a place this size, there are bound to be more. After pushing away from the door, she stalks across her room. Not once does she take her eye off the slivers of light that show another exit from her room. Is this how Liam got into her room earlier and left without her hearing her door opening and shutting?

Does she risk running into him back here as much as in the main hall itself?

Stef pushes the middle of the panel.

Nothing, apart from the light sneaking its way through the slits, fading until it's gone altogether.

Turning on her bedside lamp, Stef runs her hands over the wall in search of any protuberances; she pushes, prods, attempts to slide and generally gives the wall a good old grope.

Nothing.

Stef gazes down at her bedside lamp and then at the wall sconce that's right above it, she wonders. It makes no sense having two lights that close to each other. It's far too Agatha Christie, surely? She grasps the brass upright that's been fashioned to resemble a candle, and uses it as though pulling a pint of beer.

Nothing.

She twists the brass candle first one way and then the other and is finally rewarded with the faintest of clicks. This time when she pushes on the centre of the panel, it opens smoothly without so much as a whisper. No wonder she hadn't noticed him sneaking into her room.

Only a couple of steps into the space and her worry about her boots making too much noise are allayed.

While the carpet is undoubtedly old and threadbare underfoot, it'll still muffle her steps perfectly. She gropes around in the dark until her hand falls on what she'd hoped. A small torch, hopefully with batteries that aren't flat because who knows when this one was last used. She's thinking Liam would surely have brought his own with him.

Phew. While small and not particularly bright, the torch will at least stop her from falling arse over tea kettle. It will also allow her to pinpoint any panels she can use to access other parts of the house.

She's not gone more than twenty feet when she hears noise off to her left. She switches off the torch without pause and stands stock still. Hardly breathing, she waits for her eyes to adjust to the pitch black. Just as back in her room, she can eventually make out the slivers of light that outline the panel.

However, this panel is different. This panel has peep holes, although none of them are at eye level. Nope, if she's looking through them, she'll need to hunker down. Down on her hands and knees while gussied up in a Victorian riding habit isn't easy, but she manages it without falling over or dropping the torch.

Unfortunately, what she sees on peeking through the small, round hole has the torch dropping from her nerveless fingers. The sound of it hitting the carpeted floor, although soft, is enough to have him swinging away from the bathroom sink and staring hard in her direction. Holy hell, he's a big boy. Especially from this angle and with him being naked and all.

It takes a second for Stef's addled brain to realise the reason he's getting bigger is that he's getting closer. Her head pulled back to give herself some space to think, she gives it a shake to clear it of erotic thoughts involving Liam as naked as he is now. *Bloody hell. What if he knows how to open the panel?*

A flustered grope around her feet, and Stef's hand lands on the torch. She flicks it on, trusting he won't see the light through peep hole, before swinging it wildly around. She's needs something to jam the door shut with, apart from herself, that is.

She slides a wooden peg into place seconds before Liam pushes against the panel, hard. "I know you're in there," he hisses through the gap between the panel and the wall. "And when I get hold of you."

He doesn't continue, instead putting his efforts into getting the panel to move, and causing the peg to groan as much as Liam himself. Stef's not waiting to find out if the peg's got dry rot or even the wet kind. After struggling to her feet, she takes off down the passage away from her bedroom. She's keeping as quiet as she can in hopes he won't know which direction she's gone in.

Her natural reaction was to head back to the safety of her bedroom, which is exactly why she's now flying in the other direction. She turns at random as she comes to each intersection, hoping to throw him off the scent.

She's lost count of how many corners she's turned and staircases she's gone up and down when she's dismayed to hear movement nearby. She accelerates, glad all those years spent standing behind bars have given her leg muscles with more power than most women. It's something she's using to her advantage.

After five more minutes of concerted twisting and turning, she again fights instinct, and stops and listens hard. There's still noise coming from the behind her, but it's definitely fainter than before. *Excellent.*

She races off again, and, after taking a couple more corners, chooses a panel at random and slides the pegs holding it in place quietly to the side.

She repeats the process with half a dozen more panels before missing a couple and then exiting into the library. At least it is if the mountains of books are any indicator. Even better is that it shows her to be on the ground floor, with French doors opening onto a patio. She opens these wide, making sure they stay open, and then scarpers in the other direction. She inches the door to the hall open in case Mr Well Hung is lurking out there.

Finally, she's in luck. The hallway is empty and, more importantly, dark.

Even better is that the library is on the side of the foyer with the secret passage to the basement.

A couple of quick breaths to steady herself and Stef strides out into the brightly lit foyer. She grabs the wall sconce beside the panel, twists it, and disappears through the gap. It swings closed behind her a second later. Only then does she breathe.

Any luck and she's left Liam tripping around in the passages, or even searching for her outside. Either way he will have missed her disappearing act.

She isn't taking any chances. She locks the panel in place and grabs the larger torch and pocketing the smaller one. Sure, her dad had never actually taken her on a job, but she'd overhead enough planning sessions when she was little for some basics to stick.

.   .   .

Stef stuffs the tile into the pocket of her riding habit, pleased it's large enough. Without her corset on it's the safest place to carry it. She can hardly stroll through the main part of the house holding what ostensibly looks to be a floor tile.

She's located half a dozen more by walking around the space in bare feet, although only prising this one free. Safer to leave them where they are than risk running into Liam while weighted down like a pack horse.

There's no time to waste. She skips down the stairs and takes off along the passage toward the house, her way lit by the large torch. As tempting as it had been to turn the lights on, she'd decided against this in favour of subterfuge. Last thing she needs is for Liam to stumble upon the subterranean cavern because it's lit up like Christmas.

Only when the passage starts to angle up does she slow her pace. She even goes so far as to turn the torch off and creep along the last few feet by feel only. She knows from having seen the floor of the passage in electric light that there's nothing for her to trip over.

Surprise then, when on taking another step forward, the toe of her boot catches on something, sending her flying forward into the dark.

Damn, this is going to hurt.

It's not the floor of the passage she's tripped over. Rather, it's a solid mountain of flesh, with a quick grope letting her know it's definitely not Cecil. The other discovery is that Liam didn't bother getting dressed before starting his pursuit of her.

5

If there's one thing Stef's old man has taught her, it's how to take care of herself. A skill that's helped her eject many a drunken punter after closing hours, now comes in handy. It allows her to free herself from Liam's grip, likely breaking one of his fingers in the process.

Her stumbling to her feet has the heel of one of her riding boots in contact with a bit of him not used to being treated like a stirrup. She doesn't bother fighting the grin at his shouted oath.

She's turned the corner and has started up the stairs when she hears enough movement behind her to know he's already on his feet. Impressive, but not fast enough to catch her before she's unlocked the panel, raced across the foyer, and shot up the stairs as though the coppers are on her tail.

She isn't heading for her own room. She'd be bonkers to do that. Instead she nips around the corner and opens the first door she comes across, closing herself into the darkness seconds later.

The room doesn't remain dark for long.

She's still turning the key in the lock when a light across the room flares into life. Cecil is struggling to sit up in bed and blinking in an effort to wake properly. He's not sleepy for long when he takes in her outfit.

The familiar gleam showing in his eye, Stef decides to make the best of a bad situation. She retrieves the whip from its pocket on the side of her boot and whacks it against the leather for good measure. It's then she realises that somewhere between her encounter with Liam and reaching the safety of Cecil's bedroom, she's lost the second blasted tile. Damn it, now she really needs to whip out her frustrations.

Lucky for her that Cecil enjoys nothing better.

Breakfast the next morning is a quiet affair with no sign of Liam, although a set of used dishes and a half-empty cup of coffee indicate he's eaten earlier.

"Do you have to stand there like that?"

Stef feels like a right plonker sitting at the over-sized table on her own, while Cecil stands, eating his bacon and eggs at the side board. It wasn't as though she'd whacked the old codger's flabby arse that hard. Nothing he'd said he couldn't handle, at any rate.

"My dear, you simply don't know your own strength." Cecil's tone is one of admiration.

"Sit!" Stef nods toward the chair at the head of the table.

"But," Cecil pauses with a fork-full of scrambled egg, ready to shove it into his mouth.

"Now!"

Stef's tone brooks no argument and is authoritative

enough that he swallows hard, before putting his fork and uneaten egg back down on the plate. He then gathers everything up and walks meekly to take his place at the table. He isn't able to stop a hiss of pain when his bum hits the softly upholstered carver chair.

Surely I didn't hit him that hard?

She's having second thoughts on the effort she'd put in when Cecil interrupts her thoughts.

"I thought we could take another gander at the Folly this afternoon."

Hah, so much for him being in pain or, more to the point, in too much pain to be uninterested in a further paddling. Stef isn't keen on visiting the shrine to B&D with the old bloke in tow any time soon. While on the quest for tiles the night before, she'd had a chance to check out the *toys* there and didn't want a bar of them. If she was to wield half the items in that room, Cecil would be Cecilia quicker than you could say *castration* three times in a row.

Stef stands so abruptly that her chair is thrown backward clattering to the floor. She leans over the table, towering over him. In a low voice, full of as much menace as she can rustle up, she growls at him. "How dare you tell me what to do?"

Actually he hadn't, but close enough for her purposes. "I'm leaving."

She follows through on her promise by storming out of the room as dramatically as she can without risking laughter. Her own. Shame her exit is ruined when she collides with Liam just outside the door, hard enough that he sends her back a couple of steps.

"You going somewhere?"

"Home. I'll need a ride to the station."

"I'm busy!" Liam's response is at abrupt as her

request has been, with his broad smile irritating in the extreme.

Stef doesn't say a thing, instead swinging back to face Cecil and spearing him with a glance that has him squirming.

"Afraid I'm not able to, my dear. If the local constabulary catch me behind the wheel, there'll be the devil to pay."

"That's if he doesn't end up in ditch first," says Liam.

"Grrrrrr." Stef's unable to stop vocalising her disapproval. She's stuffed if she's staying here with Liam in residence. Better to come back another time when she'll be free and clear to grab as many tiles as she can.

But how am I supposed to get to the train station? It's too far to walk.

The solution comes to her when she's stomping her way up to her room. It won't be the easiest option, although worth it even if she won't be around to see the expression on Liam's face. Watch him try to smile then.

In the end, the easiest part of her departure is hot-wiring the Land Rover. Just as well, because after finding the heap of junk and lugging her suitcase down from her room, she's ready to drop.

Any exhaustion on her part falls away as she sweeps past the front doors of the house and sees Liam exploding out of the front doors. While the Land Rover isn't the fastest vehicle around, it's thankfully faster than Liam's ground-devouring strides. He then gives up and runs as fast in the other direction. This has her abandoning her plan to only use the Land Rover to get as far as the train station.

There's only one reason he's running as fast as he is, and that's because there's another vehicle on the property. Not that she noticed one parked in the garage.

"Come on ya bucket of bolts!" Stef stomps her foot down on the accelerator as hard as she can, thankful she's wearing the riding boots rather than her stilettos. The Land Rover lurches forward, albeit sluggishly, increasing in speed ever so slowly until she's going a respectable 50 miles an hour when she passes the station. As to where she goes from here, she relies on instinct. It's always served her well in the past, so hopefully it'll do so again.

Stef's feeling good about her choices of left and right turns when Liam's disembodied voice fills the cab and she nearly steers off the road.

"You can run missy, but you can't hide."

"Hah! Just watch me," shouts Stef, even if she understands he can't hear her. Nor is she picking up the mic and responding as he's probably expecting.

"Do you know what I'll do when I catch up with you?"

Stef's imagining all sorts of bad things when his rich chuckle rumbles out of the speaker and touches her in places it has no right.

"Bloody 'ell." Stef snaps the radio off; worried she'll have an accident, or climax, if she keeps listening to him.

She can't help but sigh with relief when she stumbles upon the A40. After that it's plain sailing into London, with her tension easing enough she's able to hum a tune to herself. That is, until she spots a motorbike in her rear-view mirror. It's not the first time she's seen it but it's not gaining on her, just staying half a dozen car lengths behind her. Despite her plan being to head straight to Chiswick, that's so not happening. If it is Liam on the motorbike, there's not a chance she wants to lead him there.

After checking to see if she isn't just being paranoid, Stef takes four right-hand turns in a row and, sure enough, the motorbike is still showing in the rear-view mirror.

Blast him.

What starts out as a small smile soon morphs into a full-on grin. Let's see how he likes it when she leads him on a merry chase through the East End. It's an area where she knows every shortcut and alley, and where there's also a particular builder's yard.

It's one that she'll be able to sail straight through, but he won't. Well, not if her Uncle Reggie has anything to say about it. She's got her fingers crossed he's actually there and not out on some 'job' with her dad.

Stef swings the Land Rover around another corner and into what appears to be a dead-end alley, pulling to a stop just short of the large gates that span the road.

Three short, followed by three long, beeps on the horn have these swinging open, allowing her to drive straight in. She doesn't stop, only slows enough that she can wind the window down and yell out

"I'm being followed by a geezer on a motorbike. Stall him as long as you can!"

On receiving a nod of understanding from her Uncle, Stef accelerates across the yard and through the double gates on the other side. These slam shut not long after her exit. Rather than heading straight for Chiswick, she takes the most convoluted route she can, something made difficult by the lack of agility on the part of the Land Rover.

It takes an hour to get to Eadie's place. Much as she'd like to do nothing more than to put her feet up and have a cuppa, her new plan doesn't give her time.

"Hey Eadie, flying visit!" Stef dumps her bag in the hallway and bursts into the sitting room.

"Good lord, what happened? Why are you home early?"

"This!"

Stef sucks in her stomach and is rewarded when the tile drops out the bottom of her corset, landing with a bounce on the plush carpet.

"What on earth?" Eadie holds her hand out.

"Careful, it's bleeding 'eavy." Stef places it carefully in Eadie's lap to avoid the old girl having to take the weight.

"Gold?" Eadie's expression now matches that of Stef when she'd first discovered the tile in the Folly.

"Solid! I think."

"But where on earth did you find it?"

"Arthur's Folly."

Stef explains how she'd come to discover the tile and the fact it was only one of many. "Liam will know about it by now. I dropped one by accident in the secret passage."

"He may know about the one you dropped but you can be sure he doesn't know about the rest."

"Why'd ya say that?"

"Because if he knew, they wouldn't still be grappling with the crippling death duties Arthur's unfortunate death encumbered them with.

"Unfortunate?"

"Erotic asphyxiation," says Eadie, absently. "He was a gasper of the extreme variety. Ginny Roberts was never the same after. Arthur hated using his safe word, so it was always touch-and-go between his coming and accidentally going. His timing and hers were off something chronic that day. By the time the doctor arrived, there was nothing for him to do but sign the death certificate."

"That's how the place got its name, isn't it?"

"Yes, Liam hates it, but the name has stuck with a select few."

Stef retrieves the tile from Eadie's lap. "Damn, this means I'll have to take this back, doesn't it?"

"Are you mad? If this gold comes from where I think it does, then one missing tile will be neither here nor there. No, you keep that as a little nest egg and tell Cecil about the rest."

"Bugger. I'd better get moving then. Lean forward."

Eadie doesn't hesitate to comply and Stef drops the tile safely behind the pillow at the back of the old lady's chair. She plumps the pillow and helps her mentor settle back down again. "Safe as 'ouses back there. I'll deal with it when I get back."

The return trip to Ryder Hall is accomplished relatively quickly. Not because of the performance of the rusty Land Rover, but more to Stef knowing where she's actually going. There also no need to take evasive action to shake Liam and she's certainly sitting more comfortably without a gold tile shoved down her underwear.

As the miles disappear, she rehearses her return.

Going through every argument, complaint and bitch that Liam can come up with. She's not worried about Cecil. Him she can settle with a well-aimed glare.

What a disappointment then to swing into the garage without encountering an irate Liam. To be able to lug her suitcase back up to her room without so much as a peep out of anyone. She then searches the house for Cecil, finding him in his favourite spot for this time of day; in the conservatory with a glass of whisky.

On seeing her, Cecil goes from being hunched over his drink, to sitting up straight and smiling broadly. "You came back!"

"Someone's gotta keep you in line!"

Stef helps herself to a drink—lord knows she needs one—before taking the seat next to Cecil. "Where's Liam?" Stef knows it's only a matter of time before he pops up behind a palm.

"Not sure. Haven't seen him all day."

"He's not here?"

"No."

Stef slugs her drink back, slams her glass down on the small cane table and then leans over and takes Cecil's drink away from him. She puts it next to her empty.

"Come on, I've got something to show you and you need to see it before Liam's back."

They're not even halfway to the Folly when Stef loses patience. At this rate the bloody gold will have been reclaimed by the earth by the time they sodding get there.

She squeezes past Cecil, stops in her tracks, and hunkers down. "Get on!"

"What? I can't ride you like a brood mare."

"If you don't get on, I'm turning around and I'm leaving. For good!"

The second part of their journey goes a lot faster, although Stef rips strips off Cecil when he gleefully calls out "Tallyho". She's not reversing their roles that much.

Only once he's settled on the fainting couch in the Folly does Stef get down on her hands and knees and peel the carpet back. There's no reaction from the old gent, proving again whoever painted the gold tiles to imitate terracotta did a bang-up job.

"Give me a second." A nipple clamp grabbed off a nearby table and Stef can't help but laugh at the look of hope from Cecil. "Think you're gonna like what I'm about to show ya a lot more than that."

Working away at the grout surrounding the tile she's found purely by feel, Stef's aware of Cecil leaning forward, his elbows on his knees, his attention firmly on her hands. His gasp when she works the tile free is exactly as hers had been when she'd found both the first and second.

She hands it to him and can tell he's as surprised by the weight as she had been.

"Gold?"

"Yep. And probably enough to deal to some death duties plus change for a holiday."

Stef hopes there's enough left for a holiday as she doesn't want to spend her tile on anything like that. No, she'd like to put it toward a small flat. She's lived in cramped quarters most of her life, a space she can call her own is something she covets. A place where the landlord can't put the rent up at a moment's notice or decide he's evicting her because she's a week behind on it. A haven.

"I wonder if Liam knows about this," says Cecil.

"If he didn't before, he will now."

At least Stef thinks he knows. She hadn't even bothered to check the floor of the passage for the second tile, sure that Liam would have grabbed it soon after she'd lost it.

"Wait here!"

Stef doesn't want to be slowed down by Cecil. All she wants is to run to the other end of the passage, scramble around on the floor, and then race back. Indeed, she doesn't even wait for him to acknowledge her comment before legging it, making good time without an aging lord draped over her like a cheap coat.

Now that she knows what she's after, it makes finding the tile easier. Maybe having landed terracotta-side up is why Liam hadn't spotted it. If it'd landed other side up, he'd have seen it in a heartbeat. Fortunately the passage had only been lit with the light borrowed from the cellar area.

She's about to pick up the tile when she's overcome by a foreboding. It's one that sees her leaving it where it is and returning to the Folly at belting speed. She'll be able to try out for the Olympics at this rate. The light switch at the top of the stairs flicked off, she plunges the passage behind her into a Stygian marathon for anyone on her tail.

She listens carefully, even pausing her breathing. Nope, she can't hear any movement, although that's not to say there isn't anyone behind her.

"Is there a key to this lock?" Stef taps the door quietly for emphasis so he knows which lock she's talking about.

Cecil takes a moment to answer, engaged as he is in levering another tile free of the floor.

"Yes, on a hook behind the curtain."

Then he's straight back to beavering away on saving his estate from taxes.

Stef locks the door and then, for good measure, draws the deep red velvet curtain across it. This ensures any light from inside the Folly won't be seen out in the passage. There only remains one problem. If Liam does track them down here, and he's already proven he knows where the passage is, they're trapped like rats. It's not a feeling she likes.

Quarter of an hour passes before Stef allows Cecil

to move again. Enough time that Liam would have been able to reach the Folly, even if he'd had to crawl in the dark on all fours. Then it's all go, with both of them working away in different areas of the Folly.

After digging up a dozen tiles between them, they notice a pattern emerging. This makes finding more tiles a lot easier although the digging part remains as painful as ever. If she'd thought this through, they'd have come here armed with appropriate tools. But she'd been concentrating on getting here before Liam got back.

It's while Cecil is taking another breather on the fainting couch that Stef asks about something that's been bugging her. "Is there another way out of this place?"

"Apparently. Although I've never worked out where it is."

"Right, you keep digging, I'll work out how we can get out of here without the risk of running into your nephew."

To a background of tapping and scraping, Stef examines every inch of the place. Twice. Without finding so much as a loose bit of wooden trim. "Shit!"

"Nothing?"

"No. I'm damned if I can see another way out of this place."

"Maybe a closer look at the altar?"

Although not consciously, Stef finally admits to herself she's been avoiding this centrepiece of the room. Chances are, with it being made out of solid marble and all, there won't be any panels sliding to the side any time soon.

Stepping up onto the plinth, she circles it, taking in the various manacles and chains that are bolted to its sides. There's not the slightest gap anywhere that she can see, even after her third lap of it. It's not until she slaps her hands down on top of it in frustration that the bleeding obvious becomes, well, obvious.

"It's hollow! And it sure as hell aint marble."

"Ah, yes. It's rococo. Marble's far too cold for old bones," says Cecil, glancing up from his scrabbling. Soon after he holds another tile triumphantly aloft and adds it to the mounting pile beside him.

Stef, who has no idea what he's on about, turns back toward the altar and pushes against it tentatively. Any hope that the whole thing will simply swivel to the side are quickly dashed. Now she knows it's made out of wood, she'll smash the bleeding thing if she has to.

But she might not have to. A proper examination of the chains dangling down either side of the altar has her spotting something. It's something she would have missed if she hadn't been specifically hunting for it.

"Bingo!"

Stef twists what seems like a length of chain and is rewarded when the whole altar slides backwards to reveal a stone staircase descending to lord knows where. The stench of mould and damp that wafts out, points to it not having been used in a good long time. Close to twenty-five years if what her dad was saying is true.

"You stay here and I'll go check this out." She grabs the larger of the two torches and, switching it on, aims it down into the dark. She's hoping beyond hope that there aren't too many creepy crawlies lurking down there. Thank goodness the riding boots will keep anything on the floor well away from her toes.

"Be careful, my dear."

Stef's so careful, she's just this side of crawling, taking her own good time to descend the steps. The passage at the bottom must be a lot deeper underground than the one leading from the house. Even better, when she reaches it she's pleased to see she's able to stand tall without the cobwebs hanging from the ceiling catching in her hair. It's also wide enough for two people to walk abreast without scraping the bricks that line it.

"Right. Let's see where you're gonna lead me to."

Stef starts out slowly, but when the floor of the passage changes from slippery bricks to fine gravel, she increases her pace knowing she won't slip on this. It still takes an eternity for the passage to start to slant upwards, letting her know she's getting closer to an exit. Hopefully one she's able to open.

Even expecting the end of the passage as she is, being faced with a solid wall of boards and battens comes as a surprise. That there are wooden pegs at regular intervals down the right-hand edge is a good sign, meaning it's unlikely to be locked from the other side. Question is, where will it open up to? Hopefully not straight into the living room of some worker's cottage, or the main bar of the local pub. She sure feels like she's walked far enough that she could even be on the outskirts of London.

Sliding the pegs out of their holes isn't as easy here as it had been with the panels in the house. It takes a good amount of jiggling before she's able to work each of them free. Not knowing what's on the other side, she's keeping the squeaking to a minimum.

Even so, if there is someone on the other side they'll be standing on a chair by now. Or armed with a broom.

Finally the last peg gives up its hold and Stef puts it on the ground next to the others. Grabbing the torch, she points it towards the panel, grabs the handle, and, after flicking the torch off, pulls the whole thing toward her.

It moves a tiny bit, but then jams. She shakes her head to clear it of images of everyone in an unseen bar suddenly stopping with their pints, staring horrified at the wall and wondering if it's time to call it a night.

After turning the torch back on, Stef once again points it at the wall. She must have missed something for the panel to have moved as little as it did. She directs the torchlight first down one side and then other, there are no obstructions she can see. She sweeps it across the top, even running her hand along the edge of the panel in case there's a hidden mechanism.

Still nothing.

It's not until she shines the torch on the floor and checks it out it properly that she spots the problem. She stomps hard on the brick, trying to bed it down like those that surround it. All this does is send a shooting pain up her leg. It also has a loud boom reverberating through the passage.

Bugger. Shame she doesn't have a nipple clamp handy. For sure she'll have to dig the blasted brick free if she wants the panel to swing wide enough for her to squeeze through.

Her cussing and swearing does no good, but it does tamp down her level of frustration enough that she can think logically about the problem at hand. It's only when she goes to hang the torch back on the spike in the wall, that it all becomes clear.

She doesn't even have to try hard to remove the spike from the wall. This is down to it having been jammed in a gap in the oak upright rather than hammered in place. After that it's mere seconds' work to remove the brick and stack it to the side with the wooden pegs.

Once again she grabs hold of the wooden handle on the panel and turns the torch off.

This time when she pulls on the panel, it swings wide without so much as a squeak.

But, on seeing what's waiting for her on the other side, there's no way Stef can keep quiet. Anything but.

7

Liam sits there like he owns the place, a whisky in one hand while the other casually grips the trigger of the shotgun that's sitting across his lap.

After slugging the contents of the glass, he drops it beside his chair before hefting the shotgun up and swinging it in her direction. While this is bad, it's the black eye he's sporting that gives her pause. Looks like Reggie and his boys have been a little heavy-handed when it came to stalling him back at the builder's yard.

"What have you done with my Uncle?" he barks at her.

Staring down the double barrels, Stef sees red. "What the bleeding 'ell do you mean, what 'ave I done with 'im?"

Damn it, Eadie would give her a right bollocking if she could hear all these dropped H's they've worked so hard to rid her of.

"We can't afford another scandal like that my unfortunate father caused the family. I refuse to be the laughingstock of the county, again. So I'll ask again. What have you done with my Uncle?"

"I aint snuffed 'im, if that's what you was thinking."

The shotgun drops a little, but not so far that she wouldn't be knee-capped. In an effort to avoid any damage to her person at all, Stef adds "He was alive and kicking when I saw him half an 'our ago."

Liam leans to the side to peer around her into the darkness of the passage behind. "Where is he then?"

"Relax would ya." Stef nods at the shotgun for emphasis. "When I left 'im, he was on his hands and knees in the Folly. He was getting stuck in with a nipple-clamp like there was no tomorra. Happy as a choir boy receiving a private communion."

"He was what?!" yells Liam, surging to his feet and storming across the room to tower over her, the gun now a lot closer to her head than she'd like. "If you've harmed him in any way, you will pay dearly for it."

This is interesting. The bloke seems genuinely concerned about the welfare of his uncle. If he's simply holding out for his inheritance, surely he'd be happy to see the old codger popping his clogs. Perhaps just not from erotic asphyxiation given the family history.

Any further thoughts are scattered when he nudges her with the gun, forcing her to turn back down the passage and retrace her steps.

If she'd thought the trip out was a nightmare, being prodded in the back every time she much as slows on the return journey, isn't fun.

Finally, she's had enough. She stops dead, and reasonably sure she won't end up that way, swings toward him, shining the torch directly into his eyes and grits out. "If you bleeding nudge me with that sodding gun one more time, I'll take the bloody thing off ya and shove it where the sun don't shine. We clear!"

Only on receiving the slightest of nods in response does she storm off, leaving him to follow as best he can, given she's the one with the torch. Thankfully she doesn't get any more prompting of the steel kind before reaching the stairs to the Folly. She doesn't slow, instead climbing the stairs as rapidly as she can. If she can just make it through the gap and slide the altar back into place, she'll be home free.

Unfortunately, Liam's long legs once again work in his favour. She's unable to click the altar back into place before the barrel of the gun is slammed through the gap.

"Ah, I see you've brought company," says Cecil, who's once again taking a breather on the fainting couch. When she sees how many tiles are sitting under it, Stef's not surprised he's knackered. He's been busy.

The altar smashes back hard with the unholy racket having both Stef and Cecil covering their ears. Liam then stands tall on the plinth next to the altar, his gaze darting about wildly as though expecting to find his uncle tied up and tortured.

How very disappointing for him.

After slamming the gun down on top of the altar, he's at his uncle's side in seconds. "You're hurt?"

"Hurt? Why on earth would I be hurt?"

"Her!" spits Liam, over his shoulder. "That's her stock in trade, isn't it?"

Cecil gazes up at her, his face a picture of guilt. "Stefanie, promise you won't take this the wrong way."

Stef's unable to stop, her hackles rising in readiness. A warning like this and she knows damn well she won't like what he's about to say. She's unable to stop herself from crossing her arms in readiness.

Cecil turns back at Liam. "Stefanie's a kitten."

"A kitten!" Both Liam and Stef explode at the same time.

While Liam is looking at her in disbelief, she's staring daggers at Cecil, her mind already whirring on him pretending to be in pain at breakfast only that morning. The crafty old bugger. No way will he need to pretend he's in pain after their next session.

That's if there is another session. And taking a peek at Liam, she doubts it.

"Hang on a goddam second." This has both men gaping at her. "Why on earth are you letting this pip squeak tell you what you can and can't do?"

"Pip squeak!" Liam draws himself up to his full height, showing he's anything but. "Has my uncle not explained to you that the estate actually passed to me on my father's death?"

"To you?" Even though she's addressed her question to Liam, she waits on Cecil to respond and is gob smacked when he nods.

"And one of the provisos to my uncle receiving his stipend from the estate is that he's not to indulge in the abominations he so enjoys."

"Oh my god, that's what the Smythe-Browns were using against you, isn't it?"

The old man nods briefly.

Blackmail aside, Cecil's addiction to pain must be something else. Enough to risk losing his home and income, all for the sake of a few stolen moments with someone like her. "Cecil, why didn't you say something?"

"And pass up the opportunity to use the Folly?" All

that's missing from his response is the "Are you mad?" that remains hanging in the air.

"Hell yes if it stops this arsehole kicking you out."

"That's it. I will not be insulted in my own home. You!" He points at Stef to confirm she's about to get the old heave-ho, "Leave now. And no, you can't use the Land Rover. As far as I'm concerned you can walk to the damn station."

When she doesn't move fast enough for his liking, he grabs her by the arm and frog marches her across the room, unlocks the door and shoves her through it.

"I'll help my uncle back to the main house. When we get there, I want you gone."

Knowing how slow Cecil moves, Stef wastes no time in scarpering, flicking the lights on at the top of the stairs. It's not that she's scared of Liam, but more that she's got things to do. Without the need to slow for Cecil or because she's walking by torchlight, Stef makes the most of the weak lightbulbs. They allow her to all but jogs to the other end of the passage. Let Liam think she's in awe of him.

The floor of the passage has started to slant upwards when she slows. She's now scanning every square inch of the floor from side to side in a sweeping motion.

"Bingo." She says quietly to herself before bending over to retrieve the second tile.

She'll be stuffed if she's handing this over to Liam now that she knows he's the one facing the crippling death duties. Maybe if he hadn't proven himself to be such a pain in the bum, she'd be feeling more benevolent. "I wonder?" she says into the quiet of the passage.

She doesn't bother waiting to find out, instead

shooting up the stairs to the foyer and then not wasting a second in getting up to her bedroom. She's soon dressed in the Victorian riding habit of the night before and has shoved everything back in her suitcase.

Rather than lugging this downstairs, she drags it around the corner and dumps it in Cecil's room before hightailing it down the stairs and out the front door.

Hot wiring the motorbike isn't necessary, with the key still being in the ignition. She's only ridden one once before, but it's enough to see her already a good distance down the driveway before Liam explodes out the front door. Well, he did say not to take the Land Rover. He didn't say a damned thing about half-inching the motorbike.

Back at the house in Chiswick, Eadie looks up as Stef walks into the sitting room. "Where did you get the motorbike from?"

"Borrowed it off a friend."

"Oh yes, and who would that be?"

"Goes by the name of Liam." Stef's unable to stop her lip from curling in disgust.

"Arthur's boy?"

"That's him. Self-important bastard and the rightful owner of Ryder Hall."

It's not often Eadie is shocked, but Stef can see that she too has been unaware of this titbit, with her face writ large with disbelief. "And Cecil confirmed this?"

"Yep."

"This certainly changes things."

"How's that?"

"Well, for one thing, it's Liam who's got access to

the money and not Cecil as we'd thought when Brenda and I suggested you strike up a friendship with him."

"Damn. I hadn't even thought about that. Just as well I got this then, isn't it?"

Stef again sucks in her tummy and the gold tile drops out the bottom of her corset. It then slides down the leg of the divided skirt, and lands with a thunk on the carpet.

"You got another one?"

"More than one. Last I saw Cecil had dug up at least a dozen or so."

"And Liam knows about them."

"Now there I can't help you."

The rest of the evening is spent in contemplation of where Stef should go from here. It would be a complete waste of time to flirt with Liam. She's well and truly blotted her copy book by borrowing first the Land Rover and then the motorbike.

"The easiest solution," Eadie pauses to take a large gulp of sherry, "is to wait until Cecil is back in town and simply ask him."

"And then what? There's no way I can go back there and just waltz in the front door like I own the place and grab 'em. I'd need a bleeding wheelbarrow."

"What about the other exit from the Folly?"

"Wouldn't have a darned clue where it was. I only saw the one room and with Liam sitting there with a shot gun, I didn't like to go any further."

"But it was an old building, you say?"

"Yeah, near derelict, if you ask me."

"Well, that's got to limit it. I'm sure Cecil can point you in the right direction if he wants to get his mitts on those gold tiles. At least before Liam stumbles upon them."

"Shhhh. Do you hear that?" Stef jumps up, getting her ear as close to the curtained front window as the couch will allow. Damn, she'd recognise the tappets doing their thing on that bucket of bolts anywhere. But how on earth did Liam find her here? It wasn't like he was on her tail when she left the property and she definitely didn't see him on the trip to London.

"Stef, the tiles!" Eadie hisses from behind her, breaking her out of her reverie.

A couple of giant strides and Stef scoops them up off the coffee table. Eadie tilts forward as far as her arthritis allows and the tiles disappear down the back of the old lady's chair.

No sooner has the pillow been plumped than there's an urgent banging at the front door.

"Show time!" says Stef, shaking the tension out of her shoulders before bending over and grabbing the horse whip out of the pocket on the side of her boot.

8

Stef forces herself to walk to the front door, the riding crop at the ready to do some damage to Liam if he decides to forgo manners. It's almost a disappointment, when on opening it she has to adjust her line of sight down about a foot.

"Ooooh, I've been bad. So very, very bad," says Cecil, his look of contrition having a practiced air about it.

Stef stares over the top of his head, but can't see any sign of Liam. "Did you drive here by yourself?" A quick check of the Land Rover shows it to be in the same shape as last time she'd seen it. "Without crashing?"

Cecil skips past her and disappears into the front room without answering, leaving her to shut the front door and follow him. There's a problem, though. A very large boot is in the way, stopping the door from closing. Unfortunately, it's attached to Liam.

"Not so fast… Kitten."

That he grins broadly after calling her this has Stef

lifting her arm. She's ready to give him a right walloping, but he's too fast. He grabs her by the wrist and gently takes the riding crop off her. He then uses it to point her in the direction of the sitting room as though he's the host and she's the guest. *Bloody cheek.*

Stef throws herself down on the couch, making sure to hog as much space as she can in hopes Liam will remain standing. No such luck. He starts lowering himself ever so slowly and Stef knows if she doesn't move she'll end up with the smart arse sitting on her lap. *Never a hat pin handy when you need one.*

She's only just settled herself as far from Liam as possible, when Eadie speaks.

"Stef, would you be so good as to ask Bert to rustle up a pot of tea for us and maybe a few biscuits?"

"Ah, yeah. Sure." Stef clambers to her feet, unable to keep the puzzlement off her face. Eadie drinking tea after ten in the morning isn't something she's seen since living here.

What is she up to?

Something smells fishy, Stef races through to the kitchen, tosses the request for a cuppa in Bert's direction and is back in no time at all. But, long enough for Liam to be sitting smack bang in the middle of the blasted couch.

Much as she'd like to use his own tactic on him, she doubts he'd move and she does not want to end up on his lap. Instead she grabs the hoop back chair that sits at the small escritoire in the corner of the room. She drags it over next to the coffee table, swings it around and straddles it.

On hearing her elderly mentor's sharp intake of breath, Stef laughs. "Relax would ya, Eadie? It's a split skirt." Stef flaps the material, showing she's not about to flash her knickers to anyone. She leans forward, props her chin on the hoop of the chair and looks at the other two. "So, who the 'ell's telling me what the bleeding hell is going on?"

"We always knew the gold was somewhere on the estate, but we couldn't find it." Liam has the nerve to seem peeved that she's found it rather than him.

"Yes, well." Cecil scouts around for the right words. "The sticking point is that it's not exactly ours."

"Then who does it belong to?" Again Stef turns to each of them, but it's Eadie who is busting to tell her. "Go on."

"It was never reported in the papers, but the rumours were rife."

"And," says Stef, prompting her to continue, because so far she's no further ahead in understanding what's going on than she was five minutes ago.

Cecil coughs to gain her attention. "Arthur used to drink at the Oakley pub. Supposedly they used to pop in there for a quick pint when they got sick of being holed up at the farmhouse."

Stef's had enough. "Who's they? What didn't the papers report? Where the 'ell is Oakley?"

Cecil and Eadie start talking over the top of each other in an effort to give her as much information as they can, as quickly as possible. They only stop when Liam whistles loudly enough to have the figurines in the china cabinet rattling.

With everyone's full attention, he speaks. "Ryder Hall is near Oakley. Also near Oakley is Leatherslade Farm, where the robbers holed up after they'd committed the greatest train robbery of all time. My father, Arthur, used to like to pop down to the pub at Oakley for a quick one and apparently got talking to one of the gang there. He bought the chap enough drinks that he let slip about some gold that hadn't been on the manifesto. Gold that they'd had a devil of a job getting back to the farm because it weighed a ton. To this day there's never been any mention of missing gold and the police have never reported its recovery."

"So you think Arthur helped 'imself when the crims were all locked up or in South America."

"We do," says Liam. "In fact we know he did, because he told me himself."

"Just not where it was," adds Cecil.

"So that's why he bought Leatherslade Farm when the crown auctioned it off," says Eadie. She stares up at the ceiling before continuing. "It made no sense at the time, and Arthur was always cagey as to why he'd acquired it."

"We all thought he was barking," says Cecil. "He paid through the nose for the place."

"But what my Uncle and I would like to know is what *you two* are doing about it?" Liam glances first at Eadie and then at Stef.

"From the sound of things, we've got a lot of work to do." Eadie's eyes are alight with excitement and if her hands weren't so crippled with arthritis, Stef knows she'd be rubbing them together. As it is, she gets a puzzled look from Liam.

"What my nephew would like to know is, will you go to the authorities?"

Eadie snorts, as is her way. "And do what? Report finding some gold that isn't missing?"

"Stuffed if I'll be dobbing you in. I'll need a finder's fee though," says Stef.

From the sound of things, there's a lot more gold than the few tiles she and Cecil have managed to dig up. Her two tiles are chicken feed compared to what could be on offer.

"One percent. No more." Liam leans back and crosses his arms, telling her it's not open to negotiation.

Naïve sod. Stef smiles broadly and is rewarded when he relaxes, thinking she's agreeing to this paltry cut. Like hell she is. If it wasn't for her, they'd still be searching for the sodding gold. There's also the fact she's more than likely already got that percentage stuffed down the back of Eadie's chair.

Her casually uttered "Ten percent and not a penny less," has him tense enough you could bounce pennies off him. Stef wishes she had a few handy, just to test her theory out.

Liam thrusts himself forward to the edge on the couch, his body angled in her direction in a manner that's just shy of threatening. "That's robbery!"

"No, that's what your dad did. Even though he didn't flog the gold 'imself, he still 'elped 'imself when no one was about. Mates of my dad know people who are still inside for that job. Trust me, they won't be pleased to find out your dad helped himself to their hard-earned brass." This is actually a wild summation on Stef's part, but something her dad had said in the car made her think she isn't too far off the mark.

"Hard-earned brass?" Liam has the nerve to look indignant, conveniently forgetting the fact his dad hadn't earned it either.

"How about five percent?" says Cecil, his voice hopeful. Whether this is of her accepting the offer or avoiding a full-on stoush, who knows.

Five percent is actually what Stef's been after all along, but she's seen her mum haggling over the price of fish down the market enough to know how it's done. Gold, fish, goldfish, didn't matter what it was, premise was the same. Start high.

"Deal." Stef thrusts her hand in Cecil's direction, both because he's the closer of the two and she doesn't trust Liam not to crush her hand in spite.

"Fine, five percent," agrees Liam, "but you get to help us dig it up."

And so it is, Stef finds herself down on her hands and knees in the Folly being whipped into shape by Liam. He's proving himself to be quite the drill sergeant. Stef squints at yet another ripped and torn fingernail. Damn it, it was the last one still intact. She should have pushed for ten percent. Cecil is still up in town with Eadie, leaving her and Liam to do the heavy lifting. The older pair is working on how to convert the tiles into cold hard cash and more importantly where that should go.

Stef knows Brenda has a Swiss bank account and thinks that's what she'll do with her cut. Far enough away that her mum and dad won't be constantly hitting her up for loans that never get repaid, but close enough she can buy that place of her own. Stef holds up yet another tile and flips it over to reveal the gold showing on the underside. A penthouse would be nice.

A noise from the centre of the room has Stef glancing up to see Liam stagger out of the stairs usually hidden under the altar. The boilersuit he's wearing is unzipped all the way, with the sleeves tied around his waist, leaving his muscled chest open for inspection. Shame he's still wearing a t-shirt, although it's wet enough with sweat that he could win competitions in pubs.

He's lugging a backpack that is close buckling under the strain of its contents. Once clear of the plinth, he shrugs out of it and lets it down to the ground with a loud muffled clunking. "There are even some more tiles hidden under the gravel."

"Bloody 'ell, your old man was busy."

"It took him years from what he was able to tell me."

"Yeah, now that's what I don't understand. If he could tell you how he did it, why couldn't he tell you where the bleeding 'ell he'd stowed them?"

"The timing of his death was rather, ah unfortunate. I only had minutes with him before he passed."

Liam acts uncomfortable to be discussing this and after what Eadie had told Stef about how Arthur shuffled off, she can't altogether blame him.

"Where's your mum in all of this?"

"Couldn't stand the shame of how father died. Took her own life not long after."

Sheesh, as embarrassing as her dad can be after a few pints, he's never done anything that would have her mum topping herself.

"That can't have been easy."

"It wasn't. So you can understand why I'm not keen on my uncle risking the same method of demise."

"Not dying on my watch, that's for bleedin' sure. I've even got a handle on mouth-to-mouth."

Liam pausing on his unpacking of the backpack and arches a brow. "Have you now?"

"Not like that, ya dirty sod." Stef's unable to stop the giggle that follows.

"Right!" says Liam, suddenly straightening from his task. "Let's call it a day."

Stef doesn't need any encouragement to abandon the floor, even if she's surprised they're stopping early for the day. Well, earlier than the previous two days, but not soon enough in her books. Barmaid work is easy compared to this.

Stef's not long been in the tub with the water deep enough she could learn scuba in here, when the door to her bathroom swings open. Liam walks in as though it's this most usual thing in the world. It's not as far as she's concerned and she makes quick work of corralling the bubbles until they're covering all the bits they should be.

This proves futile when Liam shrugs out of the robe he's wearing, showing himself to be starkers, and steps into the other end of the tub.

"Don't look at me like that. I wasn't the one who used all the hot water."

Stef's got two choices.

She can get out of the tub and leave the room in a huff.

Or she can threaten to do him damage if he comes down her end of the tub.

Tired as she is, she opts for the latter. Let's be honest, the bloke is easy on the eye and he's loaded to boot.

Maybe it's time to retire her whip.

Or not.

Liam's a little too cheeky for her liking. He needs someone to take him in hand. Or take a hand to him.

Either works for Stef and the smile she's getting in return suggests he won't be averse.

Hmmm, it must be hereditary.

I hope you had as much fun reading these blasts from the past as I had writing them. If you did, I'd be thrilled if you could give it some **STAR LOVE** before you leave.

Read on to discover others in this series. For a heap of fun with your friends, check out the **BOOK CLUB QUESTIONS AND EXTRAS** at the very back. There may be cocktails involved.

ABOUT THE AUTHOR

Andrene is a multi-genre author who writes edgy chick lit under her own name, and paranormal cozy mysteries, as Andie Low.

She also writes short and steamy curvy girl romance under the pen name Hope Malone. If you'd like to stalk her, you can sign up to her newsletter on her website.

THE LOW DOWN comes out once a month and includes new releases, special offers and comps.

www.andrenelowauthor.com

EDGY, RETRO CHICK LIT

Written in British English, the series is a lot like the late seventies, in that it's full of bad language, bad behavior and Farrah Fawcett hair. There's also a lot to laugh about.

COOGAN'S BREAK
CURVY ROMANCE SERIES

HOPE MALONE

Welcome to Coogan's Break where the girls are curvy, and the guys hotter than hell. If you're short on time, but long for romance, this series of short and steamy romances might just be what you've been looking for.

Meet Frankie Bonny, a jinxed witch with Bruce Lee moves. With the 'help' of Dex, her snarky Jack Russell, she's out to solve murders, mysteries, and more. Add in Zane, Frankie's mystical, but equally gorgeous, neighbor, and things are about to get interesting.

BOOK CLUB QUESTIONS

- What was your favourite part of the book?
- What was your least favourite?
- Did you race to the end, or was it more of a slow seventies-style burn?
- Which scene has stuck with you?
- What did you think of the writing style? Are there any standout sentences?
- Do you think the author captured the animal's personalities authentically?
- Do you think the author captured the seventies authentically?
- Would you want to read another book by this author?
- What surprised you most about the book?
- What's the worst way you've ever been dumped?
- Have you ever had revenge on someone who's treated you badly? If so, how?
- What's the best revenge you've ever heard of? (My boss's current wife sending the

marital bed to the girlfriend's office is up there for me. Not sure if it still had the sheets and duvet in-situ, although that would have made it funnier.)

- Do you think Samantha was responsible for a lot of the problems that befell her?

Just as you can pair a fine wine with fabulous cuisine, we believe in the perfect drink to accompany a spirited book club discussion. Read on for a few seventies-inspired drinks and recipes to get you started.

GRASSHOPPER

- 1 ounce green crème de menthe
- 1 ounce white crème de cacao
- 2 ounces heavy cream

DIRECTIONS

- Combine all ingredients in a cocktail shaker filled with ice
- Shake well
- Strain into a martini glass

DISCO DANCER

- 2 ounces freshly squeezed orange juice
- 1 ounce Galliano
- 1 ounce vodka
- Dash orange bitters
- Ice and Cold club soda

DIRECTIONS

- Combine orange juice, Galliano, vodka, and bitters in a cocktail shaker with ice and shake.
- Strain into a chilled cocktail glass, top with a splash of club soda, and serve.

TEQUILA SUNRISE

- 2 oz tequila Lots of ice
- 3/4 cup orange juice
- 1/4 cup pineapple juice
- 2 oz grenadine syrup
- 1 maraschino cherry for garnish

DIRECTIONS

- Pour the tequila in tall glass, then top with ice.
- Pour the orange juice over the top without mixing. Then pineapple juice.

- Finally carefully pour in the grenadine, which will sink to the bottom.
- Top with a cherry, orange slice or pineapple slice as desired and serve immediately.

Remember, it's best to drink responsibly even if the first rule of your book club is 'What happens at Book Club, stays at Book Club'. As the perfect host, why not serve some suitably kitsch 70s snacks? Here's a recipe to get you started.

CHEDDAR FONDUE

- 1 large garlic clove
- 12 ounces / 330g Emmental Cheese
- 12 ounces / 330g Medium Cheddar
- 1 cup dry white wine
- 1 tbsps corn flour
- 1 tbsp lemon juice
- Salt and Pepper
- Some nice fresh crusty bread

DIRECTIONS

- Cut the garlic in two and rub the inside of the pan with the cut edge of the garlic. Add the wine and heat slowly until warm.
- Cut the cheese into smaller pieces. Then add the cheese to the pan, bit by bit until it is all melted. Stir regularly to mix with the wine.
- Then add some salt and pepper to taste, the corn flour and the tablespoon of lemon

juice. Make sure the heat is adjusted so that
the cheese is slowly bubbling.

Emmental is a very mild, neutral cheese so good
substitutes would be Gruyere, French Comte, or
Jarlsberg. You may also try slightly aged Provolone,
Havarti, or mild Cheddar. But you can basically use
any cheese if you aren't very picky. So other options
include regular Cheddar, Gouda, Parmigiano-
Reggiano, or Brie.

Finally, if you do go ahead with your seventies-style
book club, I'd love it if you could send me some
photos.

www.ingramcontent.com/pod-product-compliance
Lightning Source LLC
Chambersburg PA
CBHW061011120726
47910CB00006B/1876